# The Secret Ingredient of Wishes

# The Secret Ingredient of Wishes

## SUSAN BISHOP CRISPELL

Thomas Dunne Books

ST. MARTIN'S PRESS ☙ NEW YORK

THOMAS DUNNE BOOKS.
An imprint of St. Martin's Press.

THE SECRET INGREDIENT OF WISHES.
Copyright © 2016 by Susan Bishop Crispell. All rights reserved.
Printed in the United States of America. For information, address St. Martin's Press, 175 Fifth Avenue, New York, N.Y. 10010.

www.thomasdunnebooks.com
www.stmartins.com

Designed by Anna Gorovoy

The Library of Congress Cataloging-in-Publication
Data is available upon request.

ISBN 978-1-250-08909-0 (hardcover)
ISBN 978-1-250-08910-6 (e-book)

Our books may be purchased in bulk for promotional, educational, or business use. Please contact your local bookseller or the Macmillan Corporate and Premium Sales Department at 1-800-221-7945, extension 5442, or by e-mail at MacmillanSpecialMarkets@macmillan.com.

First Edition: September 2016

10  9  8  7  6  5  4  3  2  1

FOR MARK

# *Acknowledgments*

To my agent, Patricia Nelson, you are a rock star. I am so lucky to have you on my side with all of your enthusiasm, exclamation points, and spot-on insight into revisions. My books could not be in better hands. And to #TheRevisionists, I am so happy to have found you all through Patricia.

A massive thank-you to my amazing editor, Kat Brzozowski. I will be forever grateful that you fell in love with this book so quickly and so completely. And thank you to the whole St. Martin's team for making this experience so wonderful.

There are not enough words to express my gratitude to Karma Brown. Thank you, thank you, thank you for all of the hours you put into helping me make this book shine. I would not be writing these words right now if it wasn't for you and your Pitch Wars mentor magic.

A lifetime of hugs to my brilliant/talented/fangirling/insert-kickass-adjective-here critique partners Rebekah Faubion, Jessica Fonseca, and Courtney Howell. I am so damn grateful for your friendship every day.

To my parents, Elwynn Schwartz and George and Susan Bishop, your never-ending love and support mean the world to me. So much love to my sister, Karen Johnson, for being one of my best friends after so many years of us both wishing the other would disappear. And to my in-laws, Gary and Pat Crispell, thank you for always treating me like one of your own.

So many hearts to JoAn and Stacy Shaw for being my stand-in parents and weekly coffee companions; Suzanne Junered, Sarah Collier, and Ashley Williams for being my oldest and dearest friends; Krysti Wetherill, Lindsay Smith, Erin Capps, and Thalia Floyd for demanding to read my books and being the most loyal friends a girl could have; Ashley Harp and Katherine Vernon for thinking I'm cool enough to hang out with you, and for being the names at the end of the sentence "When I grow up, I want to be . . ."

And the biggest thank-you to my husband, Mark (even though he might never read this), for sharing me with these characters and for never complaining when I got lost in my fictional world. ♥

# The
## Secret
## Ingredient
### of
## Wishes

*1*

Birthday parties made her nervous. Itchy. She didn't mind the screaming kids, puddles of melted ice cream, or even the clowns who twisted dogs out of skinny, colored balloons.

It was the birthday candles—and subsequent wishes—that did it.

Wishes had a funny way of coming true around Rachel Monroe. Whether she wanted them to or not.

Too bad that excuse didn't fly with four-year-olds. So there she sat, sideways in a plastic booth, next to a pile of discarded plates and crumpled, pizza-sauced napkins, flicking her gaze to anything in the cramped party room but the source of her discomfort.

"Ray!" the birthday girl, Violet, yelled, waving her twiggy arm in a circle to beckon Rachel over. "Cake! Cake! Cake!"

Rachel scooted out of the booth but stayed a safe distance from Violet and her unicorn-shaped cake with four candles protruding from its back. The ice cream cone horn was slathered in white icing and silver sprinkles. "I'm not hungry," she said and avoided looking at her best friend, Violet's mom Mary Beth Foster, who was no doubt rolling her eyes at Rachel's wariness.

Violet stared, mesmerized, as Mary Beth lit the candles and said, "Make a wish, baby." Then she scrunched up her face, squeezed her eyes tight, and blew as hard as she could.

Mary Beth gave her daughter a thumbs-up, then walked to where Rachel stood—still a good five feet away. She brushed her auburn bangs out of her eyes and gave Rachel's hand a squeeze, whispering, "Nothing bad is going to happen."

Rachel squeezed her hand back, grateful that Mary Beth had always believed her about wishes. *But*, she thought, *experiencing it first-hand made it hard not to believe*. "Reflex," she said. "Sorry."

Logically, she knew Mary Beth was right. But moments like that sent her right back to her teenage years when she couldn't tell what was real and what was all in her head. "When everyone tells you you're crazy for years, it kind of sticks, you know?"

"I know," Mary Beth said, rubbing Rachel's back. "But you can handle it."

"Really, Maeby? Because from where I'm standing, it feels like if I can't even make it through a four-year-old's birthday party, I'm pretty much screwed."

"Thinking like that is not going to help, Ray. You've got to focus on the good. A wish was made, and nothing happened."

Rachel took a ragged breath and focused on Mary Beth's husband, Geoff, as he sliced up the unicorn cake. A faint outline of the Blue Sun logo bled through the button-up shirt he wore over his favorite tee. "Well, yeah, there is that."

She shrugged, like it wasn't a big deal, but her nerves refused to settle down. Sometimes the wishes, which floated down on small, white slips of paper unnoticed by everyone but Rachel, went wrong. And there was nothing she could do to fix them. Still, the fact that Violet's birthday wish hadn't immediately materialized in front of them meant Rachel might have a better handle on things than she'd thought.

"There's also the fact that I refuse to let you backslide," Mary Beth said. "We didn't go through years of sharing our feelings with a bunch of other head-case teens just to relapse when things get hard. You're going to be okay. I promise."

"How are you always so sure?"

Mary Beth shook her arm gently, forcing Rachel to look at her. "Because you'll do anything to keep from letting down the people you love."

*I've done enough of that already.* Rachel shoved the guilt down and forced a smile. "All right, all right. Point made. I will stop obsessing and enjoy your kid's birthday."

Geoff, having broken free from the mass of cake-devouring kids, sandwiched himself between his wife and Rachel and draped his arms over their shoulders. "Don't tell me you ladies are skipping out on the cake."

Mary Beth wrapped her arm around his waist, pulling him closer. "Just letting things calm down first."

"I just gave massive amounts of sugar to a roomful of kids. A rush like that could last a week," he said.

"I guess we better go get some before they come back for seconds," Mary Beth said.

"I'll be there in a minute. I just need to . . ." Unable to decide on a suitable excuse, Rachel trailed off. She shrugged out from under Geoff's arm.

His thick eyebrows pulled down in confusion as he watched Rachel retreat. "Don't take too long. Presents are up next and Violet's got your gift on top of the pile."

Mary Beth gave Rachel a tentative smile and tugged her husband toward Violet and her mound of presents.

Rachel found the bathroom door hidden between the soda fountain and the token machine. She could just make out the melody of some teenybopper song over the clanging, whooping, and beeping of the games from the arcade on the other side of the door.

She hadn't seen a wish appear in years. And then a month ago, some unknown person somewhere else in Memphis had wished for their deepest desire and it found Rachel as she swept the front walk of the coffee shop where she worked. She left it unread—and ungranted—on the sidewalk, hoping that was the end of it. But another one turned up a few days later curled into the bottom of a mug with the dregs of someone's coffee. Then another appeared in the pocket of her favorite jeans when she pulled them from the dryer. Wishes had come almost daily after that, and she'd done a good job of pretending they didn't exist. But if anyone would have a wish strong enough to push through Rachel's defenses, it would be Violet, who'd been talking about her birthday wish in high-pitched squeals and a perma-smile for weeks.

Rachel twisted on the faucet and splashed water on her face. The shock of cold helped to dull the worst of her nerves. Even if the wish appeared, she didn't have to end her wishing boycott. Didn't have to read it and make it come true. She didn't have to make another wish come true ever again if she didn't want to.

Because if the ability refused to give back what it had taken from her, she was done with it. For good.

With a deep breath, she reentered the mayhem and hoped her resolve didn't crumble under the weight of Violet's pleading brown eyes.

"Ray, c'mon! Presents!" Violet called as soon as she saw Rachel. Her blond hair was a mass of stringy tangles. A cluster of pink icing was crusted at the tips as if she'd tried to make her hair match the flowing mane on the cake. Her lips and tongue were stained purple from the dye the baker had used on the vanilla cake to make the unicorn's inside match Violet's favorite color.

Before Mary Beth had even pulled the empty plate out of her way, Violet hugged the box wrapped in Sunday funnies and tore through the paper.

Nudging Geoff's shoulder, Rachel asked, "Does she have retractable claws?"

"She's our very own Wolverine," Geoff said, chuckling.

"Too bad I got her a kitten. She might accidentally stab it while trying to get it open." Geoff raised an eyebrow, and Rachel laughed. "Kidding."

With the wrapping paper floating to the ground beside her, Violet tugged on the lid of the box. It opened with a soft pop. The pink and orange plastic slug night-lights looked even cuter in person than they had online. Their crooked antennae-like eyes stared up at Rachel as Violet showed them off by dancing them back and forth through the air.

"Bunnies! I love them!"

"How can you love them? You don't even know what they are," Rachel teased. She took the slugs and placed them in the white fitted base. "They're not bunnies, they're slugs. And they're also night-lights. You can pick them up and carry them around at night and they'll make it so you can see in the dark."

Violet launched out of the booth and threw herself at Rachel. The force of it knocked her back a step. "I love you."

"I love you too," Rachel said. Leaning down, she didn't even attempt to avoid the icing on the girl's puckered lips as she smacked a kiss on her mouth.

"Wanna know what I wished for?" Violet asked before Rachel could pull away.

"If you tell me, it won't come true," Rachel said, hoping the threat would be enough to tamp down some of Violet's desire for whatever she wanted.

Violet shrugged, her eyes bright with wanting, and leaned in to Rachel's ear, whispering her secret with warm, vanilla-scented breath. She held a sticky finger to her lips for secrecy, then raced back to her parents.

Rachel's laugh bubbled out of her when, with a quick flash of white, a small piece of paper materialized in mid-air. Grabbing the wish, she read it and shook her head. *Leave it to Violet to wish that hard for something that doesn't exist. Poor kid's in for a hell of a letdown when this doesn't come true.*

# 2

Rachel dreamed about unicorns. Despite the absurdity of Violet's wish, it had rooted in Rachel's subconscious while she slept, and she awoke the next morning with a stress headache that felt like dozens of hooves bucking against her skull. Massaging the base of her neck, she closed her eyes against the dull grayish-blue light that slithered in between the slats of the metal window blinds and reminded herself this particular wish was not one she needed to worry about.

She hadn't always known she could make wishes come true. At first, they seemed like happy coincidences. Like when she was five and her favorite stuffed animal, a rabbit called Bit, appeared in her bed with both ears still attached—despite having been thrown in the garbage the week before, his fluffy brains spilling out of the hole in his head. When her mom asked her how she'd gotten him back, and fixed, she just smiled and said, "Magic!"

As she grew, she discovered that it wasn't just her wishes that came true. She didn't have to be in the presence of someone making a wish for it to appear, just in the same town, as she discovered one year at sleepaway camp. And most of the time, she had no idea who a wish belonged to. She just knew that when a wish was strong enough, it would pop into existence, written on a scrap of paper like the ones that came out of fortune cookies, and make its way to her. She'd find them floating in the air, and tumbling out of the cereal box when she poured her breakfast, and underneath her pillow at night.

No one else seemed to notice them appear, but once she'd touched them, igniting their power, anyone could see them clutched in her hand or stuffed into the pocket of her jeans. And anyone could read them if they managed to snatch them away from her. Anyone could discover what she could do if she wasn't careful, even if they were unlikely to believe it.

So she waited until no one was looking to pick up the wishes. Then she hid them all in a wooden box on her dresser, the papers stacked a few inches high in neat rows, and smiled to herself when she overheard kids at school excitedly whispering about how they'd gotten exactly what they wanted.

When her mom found the stash when Rachel was eight and asked why she was collecting these bits of paper with wishes written across them, Rachel confessed they weren't hers but that she had made them come true. Her mom nodded, like she believed her, and joked about all of the things she'd wish for. Then she told Rachel to be sure and add her wishes to the top of her pile so they would come true first.

But that was when her parents thought she just had a very active imagination, before anyone said there was something wrong with Rachel's brain.

Rolling out of bed, the headache reined in to a dull ache, she thought as she always did after a wish appeared about wishing things could go back to the way they used to be. Before Michael—the little brother she wished away one rainy, ordinary afternoon because he was irritating her. Before her parents watched her warily and spoke to her in soft, concerned voices, reminding her over and over that she never had a little brother. Before her dad walked out on them and her mom started to believe in Michael too, and, unable to live with the possibility she'd had a son and lost him without even remembering he existed, downed a handful of Rachel's antipsychotics and chased it with a five-dollar bottle of Cabernet a month after Rachel's eighteenth birthday.

But no amount of wishing could change the past. In the eight years since her mom's death, she'd tried countless times to set everything right.

And she'd failed.

She paused in the hallway on her way downstairs. She'd inherited her childhood home after her mom died and hadn't changed a thing. Discolored patches of wallpaper created a mosaic on the wall as if half a dozen frames had been removed from the collage of family photos and the wallpaper refused to blend back into one monotonous shade of green.

The wall had once held pictures of Michael next to the rest of her family. She could see his face as clearly as if he were standing in front of her. The curly brown hair and easy smile he'd inherited from their dad. The three-quarter-inch scar through his right eyebrow from when he'd fallen out of bed at age three and cut his head open on the nightstand.

But everyone else insisted Michael had never been real. They said he was just a delusion her mind had created. *The first symptom of her psychotic break.* That was the line the doctors gave her parents when she was ten to convince them to sign the papers and have her hospitalized for a month in the psychiatric ward.

Pinching her eyes shut, she counted to three. With each number, she inhaled long and deep before releasing it. *He's gone. And there's nothing I can do to bring him back.* She touched one of the discolored spots on the wall as if she could will a photograph to appear. Breathing in deep, she imagined what Michael would look like now. *Would his hair still be scruffy and tease the collar of his shirts? Would his baby face have slimmed down so his jaw and cheekbones are sharp and angular like our father's? Would he still smile at me in the way that said we were about to do something silly?*

But try as she might, the face remained stubbornly childlike. Something in her brain refused to let him age past four—the age he was when she wished him away.

When she was younger, Rachel told her parents and the doctors she no longer believed Michael had been real—it was less painful than meeting their faces, lined with worry and disappointment. But her memories of him were still very much alive. Especially here, in the house where she'd ended his existence.

She kept waiting for them to disappear like the doctors had promised, but some small part of her refused to let him go.

In the kitchen, she started a pot of coffee and set to work on the dishes that were piled in both sides of the sink. Violet's voice happily shouting "Ray!" broke her concentration. Startled, Rachel dropped a plate into the sink from her soapy hands, but thankfully it didn't break. Her phone's screen lit up on the windowsill when Violet's voice—the ringtone she'd set for Mary Beth—called out her name again. She bumped the faucet handle with her wrist and dried her hands on the towel hanging from the oven door.

"Did you do this?" Mary Beth asked when Rachel picked up.

"Do what?"

"A pony. On my front porch. With a sugar cone strapped on to its head with a piece of elastic." The words tumbled out in the thick Tennessee twang that always showed up when she was really agitated. "She said it's what she wished for and you made it come true."

*How the hell could Violet's wish come true? Unicorns* do not *exist. There's no way I did that.* Rachel tapped her nails against the ceramic mug in her hand. "Just wait. There has to be an explanation that doesn't involve me."

"Vi said she wished for a horse with a horn on its head and that's basically what I've got," Mary Beth said. "Are you sure you didn't do this? Not even accidentally?"

"You know I don't do that anymore." Rachel ignored the voice in her head telling her she still could do it even if she didn't want to. That she was solely responsible for the pony appearing at Mary Beth's house. That more wishes could start appearing again, and who knows what else she might accidentally cause? What she might do to Mary Beth or Geoff or their girls if she wasn't careful.

The pounding in her head roared back full force at the thought. She'd been so determined in the past few years to keep the wishes at bay. And with one careless action, she'd put everyone she loved at risk.

"I know you don't. I just thought that if you had you might know how to get rid of it. You know, poof it back to where it came from before Vi sees it and gets it into her head that she can wish for more things."

Hands shaking, Rachel set down her coffee mug. She couldn't blame Mary Beth for being nervous. Not when Rachel was stuck on the fact that wishing something into existence—even a low-rent unicorn—wasn't that far off from wishing something or someone out of it. And she could never let that happen again.

With her brother and parents gone, Mary Beth was the closest thing Rachel had to family. And they protected each other with a fierceness reserved for few others. Even though the thought of leaving her sent Rachel's heartbeat into warp speed, the only way to ensure she didn't accidentally bring any harm to Mary Beth or her family was to leave town. Put space between her and wishes she couldn't bear to have go wrong. Loneliness had to be easier to live with than being responsible for ruining more lives.

"I'm sorry, Mae. I'll fix it. I promise."

She had a little money saved. Not much, but it was enough to get her out of town and keep her from going hungry until she could figure out a permanent solution to her wish problem. From the hall closet, Rachel unearthed the spiral-bound map her parents had used to plan all of their vacations when she was little, and she carried it to her room. The pages were smooth and sturdy from lack of use. They made a low slapping sound when she pulled her thumb along the edges. Closing her eyes, Rachel fanned through it again. After a few seconds, she stopped and looked down at the page. Ohio.

"No," she said and tried again.

Delaware.

"Don't think so."

Missouri.

"Shit," she grumbled. She tossed the map onto the foot of the bed. A few pages fluttered from the impact and the blue of the Atlantic Ocean caught her attention. Grabbing the spiral, she pulled the map back into her lap and studied it. North Carolina. She traced her finger across Tennessee and farther along I-40 as it stretched the length of both states, ending at the coast. "A beach could be nice."

Half an hour later, Rachel had a duffel bag of clothes on her shoulder and a box of keepsakes, including her box of collected wishes, which she couldn't leave behind, tucked against her side. After one last check of her room to make sure she had everything she wanted, Rachel pulled the door shut behind her. She ran her hand along the smooth stretch of wall at the top of the stairs where her brother's door would have been—if she hadn't made him disappear. She stopped herself from whispering goodbye, and then she walked away.

# 3

Not long after Rachel passed the North Carolina border, her relief at finally making it out of Tennessee evaporated. A rockslide had taken out part of the interstate that wound through the mountains and forced her to detour onto a smaller highway that headed more south than east. Her map sat abandoned on the passenger seat as she focused on following the steep, curving mountain roads.

She must've missed the signs signaling the end of the detour after the road flattened out again because the other cars she'd been with since somewhere after Knoxville had disappeared. Most of the towns she drove through now were blink-and-you'll-miss-it small, and she cringed at the thought of living somewhere where everyone knew you. Rachel had grown used to the anonymity that came with living in a larger city, and even though she'd lived in Memphis her whole life, she kept to herself and no one besides Mary Beth noticed.

She was just thinking about the new places she would discover at the end of her drive when her car sputtered to a stop in the middle of one of these tiny towns. She glanced at the car's dashboard, where the needle on the gas gauge hung below E. She was sure the last time she'd checked, barely fifteen minutes ago, she'd had close to half a tank. "Shit." She slapped her palm on the steering wheel, heaving a frustrated sigh.

Rachel's right calf, stiff and sore from hours of driving, cramped as she got out of the car. Even lifting her feet as high as she could, her shoes still scraped the concrete as she walked. Branches from knobby oak trees hung across the narrow street, their leaves creating a dense canopy overhead. The houses tucked back behind wide lawns were old and elegant, even as their faded paint and lopsided porches begged to be restored.

She ran her fingers over the vines of honeysuckle clinging to the fence in front of one of them. The red, pink, and yellow flowers looked like flames licking along the wood fence. Their sweet perfume permeated the air.

"You lost?" a gravelly voice called.

A gray-haired woman wearing an oversized men's plaid shirt watched her from the front yard of an old Victorian-style house, leaning on a shovel handle. The spade sunk a few inches into the dark soil of a pepper patch.

"No gas," Rachel replied. She stopped in front of the white fence, its paint blistering and peeling. "But now that you mention it, where am I exactly?"

"Didn't you see the sign? You're in Nowhere, North Carolina. Home of the world's largest lost and found."

"Must've missed it. Is it really home of the largest lost and found?"

"Among other things." The woman walked toward her, limping slightly like she had a stitch in her side. "Catch Sisson," she said, extending her gloved hand.

The old woman's firm grip surprised her. "Rachel."

"Well, Rachel-with-No-Gas, c'mon in. I'll get someone over here to help you out."

"It's all right. I'll just walk to the gas station."

"Don't argue with me, girl. It's a good two miles to the station and you look about to drop. Also, I don't see a gas can in those hands of yours." Catch flipped up the latch on the gate and flung it open, forcing Rachel to sidestep to avoid getting hit. The gate groaned as if sick of letting strangers in. "And I don't want it on my head if you let yourself get hit by a car."

She followed Catch up the flagstone path. Moss sprouted between the stones and obscured the edges. It squished under her Toms.

Deep-orange day lilies flanked the back of the flower bed and small purple flowers pushed through them on spindly green stems. A tree dripped with fist-sized peaches in the middle of the yard, scenting the air with a sweetness that made her stomach grumble.

The house was three stories, with pale-teal clapboard and cedar shake siding and a turret that spiked up on the left. The white trim cracked and bubbled around the screen door.

"Sit down," Catch said. She pointed to the pair of wooden rockers. The paisley cushions, faded and squashed flat, invited her to sit like so many others obviously had before her. "I'm gonna make a call. Would you like some pie?"

Rachel shook her head, taking the chair closest to the stairs. When she leaned back, the chair smacked into the house with a sharp crack. She jumped up, reached a hand out to check for splintered wood.

She settled for leaning against the porch railing. Unlike the house, the porch looked like it had been rebuilt within the last few years. The paint shone slick and even. The floorboards were firm under her feet.

Catch's raspy voice carried through the screen as she said to whomever she had called, "I've got a girl stranded over here. If that's not enough incentive, I made a habanero peach pie this morning. I'd be willing to part with a slice or two in return."

The door slapped shut behind Catch a moment later when she came back out, rattling the thin windowpanes on either side of the door. The plate in her hand remained steady.

"Just shove the rock back in place," Catch said. She kicked the small stone back under the rocking chair runner and handed the slice of pie to Rachel with a smile that dared her to refuse it. "It'll keep the chair from hitting the house again. It's on Ashe's to-do list, but damn if that boy doesn't find a dozen other things to do when he's here."

Sitting again, Rachel leaned back slowly. The chair dipped a few degrees then stopped, the rock crunching under the weight but holding. She relaxed her grip on the plate and inhaled the sweet scent of the peach pie. She would've eaten it even if it hadn't smelled like heaven on a plate, but after the first bite, she was grateful Catch had ignored her initial refusal.

"So, tell me. What're you doing running out of gas in the middle of Nowhere?"

"Honestly, I'm not really sure. I thought I had enough to get back to I-40 after the detour, but then it was all of a sudden on empty."

Catch pressed her lips together and made a low *hmm* sound. She drew her gaze over Rachel as if she was looking for an answer to whatever question made the skin around her eyes wrinkle. "Well, you coulda landed in a lot worse places."

"I really appreciate you helping me out," Rachel said. She licked the syrupy juice off the fork as the spice from the habanero pepper mixed in with the peaches tickled the roof of her mouth.

"Where were you headed?" Catch asked.

"Whatever's at the end of I-40. A beach, a little quiet."

She stared down the street. A trio of kids played in the road, chasing each other and screeching in delight. Lightning bugs danced in the air, their flickering bulbs just visible in the shade of the draping oaks. But night hovered at the edges, waiting to douse the street in darkness. And then the bugs would be scooped into mason jars with holes poked in the lids and shown off with a quick shout and jumble of excited words to all passersby.

Taking a sip of what smelled to Rachel like scotch, Catch said, "One thing I've learned, you always end up right where you're meant to be, whether you agree with it or not. Just give it time. You might feel lost now, but you'll find what you're looking for."

Rachel shivered at Catch's words despite the summer heat. Part of her wanted to believe this woman even though she'd just met her and Catch was probably just giving her the standard everything-will-work-out speech she'd give to any lost soul who turned up on her porch. But for Rachel there was nothing—no one—to find. Years of disappointment had taught her that.

She stood up, the chair creaking back to its original position. "It's getting late. I should probably try to find a place to stay tonight while your friend is getting the gas. Is there a hotel nearby?"

"You're not going anywhere when I've got plenty of rooms right here. Got them all prettied up and then thought, 'What in the hell do I want to open a B&B for?' so I scrapped the whole damn idea and now have a bunch of rooms no one sees but me. You can have your pick. But I'd take the attic suite if I were you. Gives you the most space. And the best view."

"That's really nice of you, but I don't want to be any more of a bother."

"Nonsense. I know we don't know each other, but that's not a good reason to turn down a perfectly good offer."

Rachel eyed the old woman. Beneath the gruff, take-charge attitude that had etched hard lines at the corners of her mouth and eyes, something softer was hidden, something that looked a lot like loneliness. And that was something Rachel knew all too well. "You're really okay with someone you've just met staying in your house? For all you know I could be—"

"Crazy?" Catch said. "We're all a little crazy, Rachel, though I prefer 'eccentric.' It doesn't have to be a bad thing."

Rachel desperately wanted that to be true.

Catch patted Rachel's arm and looked toward the road, her eyes wrinkling even more at the edges as she squinted. "Sounds like that's your gas."

A black pickup truck rumbled to a stop in the gravel drive that ran up the side of the house. Rachel couldn't make out the driver's face in the fading light. He hauled a gas can from the back of the truck. Dirty-blond hair hung in his eyes as he walked toward them.

"Sorry it took me so long. Got waylaid by Dean." He held up the rusted can. The red had scratched off in places, revealing a dingy black beneath. "This must be the strandee." He wiped his gritty palm on the thigh of his jeans. It came away with more dirt. He shrugged and tried again on his white undershirt, then extended his hand to her.

Rachel took the can from him instead. The less interaction she had with people, the less likely a wish was to materialize. She had to hold the can with both hands and still leaned forward with the weight.

She tilted her head back, as much to regain her balance as to shift her gaze away from the shirt stretched tight across his chest at her eye level. His face, long and lean like the rest of him, ended in a square chin covered in a layer of stubble, and his full lips tugged to one side in a half smile. "Thanks for this. What do I owe you?"

Before he could respond, Catch cut in. "Set that down, Rachel, and let the boy do it."

She obeyed more because her hands were burning where the handle dug into her skin than because she wanted to. The can grated against dirt and particles on the stone. It sent a shiver up her spine.

"I'm Ashe," he said. "Catch's back-door neighbor."

"I've known him since he was old enough to toddle through the grass and help himself to my cherries. Ruined a perfectly good pie, this boy. Had to throw the damn pie crust out when I went out to pick 'em and saw he'd eaten his way through two thirds of the ripe ones."

Curiosity overruled her flight instinct, and Rachel asked, "So, now you do favors for pie?"

"Favors are less painful than getting caught thieving. After the cherry incident, Catch switched me so many times my legs were raw."

Catch smacked a hand on his chest. "I'd do it again."

"I know." Ashe smiled at her. Barely there dimples winked in his cheeks, and Rachel found herself wanting to smile too. Whatever loneliness she'd sensed in Catch was offset by Ashe's easy charm. "Is that your Pathfinder parked on the side of the road a few houses back?"

"Guilty."

He lifted the can, one-handed, and said, "If you give me your keys I'll go fill her up and drive her down here for you."

"I'll come with you," Rachel said without thinking. So much for keeping her distance. She dug her keys out of her pocket and cupped them in her palm. They were lighter without the work keys she'd handed back to her boss, along with her resignation, on her way out of town, their sound unrecognizable.

Catch winked at Ashe, not bothering to hide the gesture, and chuckled into her drink when Rachel raised an eyebrow at her.

The sidewalk narrowed, forcing him to fall in line behind her. At five four, she barely came up to his shoulder. The gate sighed when she pushed through it.

"Sorry you had to do this," she said when he matched his pace to hers.

"It's no problem. I had to come back this way anyway. I noticed the Tennessee plates. Where're you headed?" Ashe asked.

"Somewhere on the coast."

"You just got in and started driving?"

Rachel jangled her keys in her hand. "Pretty much." She pressed the key fob as they approached her car, and the locks clicked as they disengaged.

Ashe walked to the gas tank and waited for her to lean inside and pop the cap. He pulled a funnel from his back pocket and stuck it in the throat of the tank. His hair fell back in his face. He shook his head to move it and caught her watching him. His mouth quirked up in amusement.

He turned back to the gas can, and she settled in the driver's seat to wait.

"All set," he said a couple minutes later. He pounded on the side of the car like it was a flank of a horse to get it moving.

"One more favor and then I'll leave you alone," she said.

He rested one arm on the top of the door and the other on the roof, blocking her exit. He smelled like sweat and sawdust, and it was a pleasant combination. He looked down at her and the streetlight hit his face. His eyes were a deep ocean blue, and she didn't want to look away.

"Weird," he said. The smile returned, with just a hint of interest.

"What?"

"You don't see too many people with amber-colored eyes. But you're the second person I know with them. I used to tease my little brother about his and tell him he was an alien. Made him cry when he was real little. Now he likes to rub it in that chicks dig it."

Goose bumps rose on her arms at the mention of a little brother. She cranked the key in the ignition, trying to give herself a moment away from Ashe's gaze. Some country singer she couldn't name whined from the stereo. "Can you tell me how to get to the gas station so I can fill up and get on my way?"

"I could, but it wouldn't do you any good. Dean was closing up when I was there. Poker night."

"The only gas station in town closed so Dean could go play cards?"

Ashe rapped his hands on the roof of her car. "It's Tuesday. That's what he does." He smiled wide, and Rachel found herself smiling back. "I can take you to a hotel if you need. It's not the best, but it'll do for the night, I'm guessing."

With the dimples and broad shoulders and hands that were constantly touching things around him, she was pretty sure he could make anywhere do for a night. Or even a couple hours. The fact that she'd even thought about him like that after only knowing him a few minutes brought her guard back up. "Does that line work on the girls around here?" she asked.

"Not a line. Just an offer."

Rachel nodded slowly, careful not to look at his face in case he smiled again. There was something contagious about it. His smile.

"Catch knew Dean closed early today, didn't she?" she asked.

"Everyone does. Why?"

"She offered to let me stay with her tonight."

"Did she now?" His tone hardened, and Rachel started to ask if that was a problem but closed her mouth when he stepped back from the car and glared in the direction of Catch's house. "You'll wanna pull all the way down the drive." He started back toward the house without another word, and Rachel followed slowly in her car, wondering what she'd said wrong.

The inside of Catch's house smelled like fruit. Not any particular variety, just a melding of sweet and tart. The hardwood floors were so dark Rachel couldn't see the individual planks, though she could see faint imprints of Catch's dusty shoes. The foyer opened up all the way to the roof, and rooms jutted off in multiple directions through elaborate wooden archways. The walls of each room were different colors—lilac, peach, ice blue, budding-leaf green.

A round table sat in the middle of the room. Eight or nine pies covered the polished surface. Each had a unique design etched into the crust. Different colors bubbled out of the holes, hinting at what fruit was nestled inside.

Rachel's stomach growled despite having already eaten a piece of pie. She clamped her arms around her middle to dull the sound.

"We'll eat soon," Catch said to her. As Ashe started up the stairs, she called after him, "Will you be staying too?"

He didn't respond, the thudding of his work boots the only sound as he continued up with the straps of Rachel's duffel bag clutched in one fist.

"His loss," Catch said with a shrug. "I'm making his favorite. C'mon. I'll show you the room, let you get settled before dinner."

The walls were bare as the stairs curved up through the second floor. No family photos, no antique clocks or quirky paintings of fruit. Just a flat wall the color of the inside of an apple. All the doors were closed as they walked down the hall. A window at the end overlooked the side yard, a layer of dust collecting on the sill.

They took another set of stairs at the end of the hall that led directly into the room above with no visible door. The soft-gray walls made the room seem darker despite the table lamp Ashe had clicked on ahead of them. The muted light made it cozy, like the room existed for reading under the covers on rainy days. Her bag sat on the foot of the bed, which fit into a notch under the window on the far wall and filled the width of the room. The exposed rafters had been stained dark to match the floors. A ceiling fan whirled above, fluttering Rachel's hair.

Suddenly exhausted, Rachel wanted nothing more than to fall onto the fluffy white comforter and thick pillows and sleep for days.

"Obviously bed's there," Ashe said, pointing to it. He walked around the room as he showed it off. "The window tilts out, you've just gotta slide it up a few inches first. Closet's there behind that door, and you've got a pocket door here to close the room off from downstairs."

"No lock?" Rachel asked with a half smile.

"Nah, but I put a booby trap on one of the steps, so don't get any funny ideas," Ashe said, the frown from a few minutes before still firmly in place.

A hint of worry tinged the annoyance in his tone, shedding light on his mood change. He knew nothing about her, and she was staying with someone he cared about. To ease the tension, Rachel said, "So no ransacking the place once Catch falls asleep then? Damn. You're gonna ruin all my fun."

Ashe's lips twitched, but he didn't let the smile form. "Aren't we a smartass?"

"Bad habit," Rachel said, determined to if not win him over, at least ease his mind where she was concerned.

"Oh, Ashe, leave the girl alone." Catch shoved his shoulder to get him moving toward the door. He stopped on the top step and rolled back the door. "Let's both give her some space. She looks dead on her feet. Rachel, got anything else you need right now?"

"A bathroom?"

"One floor down, third door on the right," Ashe said.

"I'll set out some clean towels. Make yourself at home," Catch said.

"Thanks."

She waited until their voices, still bickering, faded down the hall below before pulling the door closed. She leaned back against it and felt the tension leaving her body. Staying in a stranger's attic had never even crossed her mind as a possibility when she'd set out that morning, but she had to admit the room, with its comfy-looking bed and constant scent of baked fruit, was much better than a crummy hotel.

Her legs still ached when she walked to the bed, tiny tendrils of pain shooting up her calves that almost made her knees buckle. A flutter of white outside the window caught her eye. Bracing a hand on the back of the chair near the bed, she forced herself to take a closer look and was relieved to see it was just Ashe and his white T-shirt, not a slip of paper floating by. He paused halfway across the yard, at the edge of a cluster of trees that rustled their leaves in the warm night air. He looked up, caught her staring. The smile from earlier, the charming one that made Rachel's brain turn off, came back to his face. He started walking again, his stride a little more confident, a little more purposeful.

Rachel would've snatched the curtains closed if there had been any. Instead, she eased her tired body onto the bed and curled up on top of the comforter.

She woke disoriented. The clouds had dispersed and the silvery moonlight drifted in the window. She stared across the room as her eyes adjusted to the dim light. The velvety armchair solidified first with thick, squishy blobs for throw pillows, followed by the carved wood desk. The built-in bookshelves were cavernous black holes.

A bird sang a mournful melody from one of the dozens of trees creating a miniforest in the backyard. A light cut through the yard, giving vague shapes to the trees. It took a minute to realize it crept up from downstairs. Glancing at her watch, she saw it was not quite 3:00 A.M. Her stomach protested her lack of dinner in a loud series of gurgles and grumbles.

Without a light in the stairwell, she made her way down slowly, fingers gripping the railing and feet testing each step before putting her full weight on it. She followed the scents of brown sugar and bacon down the second set of stairs, through the foyer and dining room, and into the kitchen. She squinted at the brightness.

"Couldn't sleep?" Catch asked. Her short gray hair stuck up on one side like she hadn't brushed it after getting out of bed.

"Guess not," Rachel said.

"There're drinks in the fridge." Catch nudged a bowl of chopped peaches toward Rachel and then went back to whisking a frothy yellow batter.

Rachel slid onto a stool at the island. Elbows propped on the counter, she leaned closer to where Catch worked on the other side. "What kind of pie is that?"

"Breakfast pie. Eggs, bacon, sausage, sweet and hot peppers." She poured the chunky filling into the pie dish. "Most folks call it a quiche."

"Do you do this every day?"

"Most days. Depending on the requests." Catch licked a splash of the egg mixture from her thumb. Her lips curved into a wide smile, showing a silver cap in the back of her mouth. "But since I plan on asking Ashe for another favor, I figured I better pull out all the stops."

"I think he'd do it without the pie," Rachel said, popping a slice of peach in her mouth. Even in the little amount of time she'd spent with Ashe, his loyalty to Catch was obvious.

"Oh, I know. But I feel bad using the boy without some sort of payment. He's been awfully good to me through the years. Least I can do is take care of him right back."

Jealousy stretched its legs in the corner of Rachel's mind. It didn't matter how old she got, she would always miss her parents and the relationships they could have had if she hadn't messed everything up. Seeing how easily other people could have a family, even with people they weren't related to, hurt more than she'd expected. She locked the feeling away with the memories of her mom's death and her dad's departure that she tried to ignore. "It's nice that you have that," she said.

The oven beeped as Catch keyed in the baking time and punched Start. "So, what's keeping you awake?" she asked.

Rachel let out a long sigh in place of all of the guilt she kept inside. "Everything. What to do next, if where I'm headed is the right place. If I just shouldn't go back home."

"Who says you have to leave? Nowhere's a great place to get lost for a little while. Maybe being here will do you some good, and I might not mind the company."

Something in Catch's voice gave weight to the statement. Like she could uncover all of Rachel's secrets in no time at all. Having to explain to Catch she'd been in therapy for most of her teenage years was one thing. But having to admit what she could do with wishes and what she'd done to her brother and, as a result, to her parents would ensure Catch would send her packing. And then where would she go?

"Why do you want me to stay?" Her voice came out harder than she meant, but Catch didn't even look up.

"I have a tendency to take in strays. A lot of people come to me for help, but it's the ones that don't think they need it that I can't resist."

Rachel ate a few more pieces of the peaches, the juice dribbling down her fingers. Catch handed her a napkin. "What do you do for them, these so-called strays?" Rachel asked.

"I bake them pies," Catch said, laughing, as though it were the most obvious thing.

A smile threatened the edges of Rachel's lips despite herself. "Do you think you'll make me one?"

"When you're ready. Until then, we'll just get to know each other. How's that sound?"

"I think I can handle that."

They lapsed into silence as the oven ticked and hummed. Catch scrubbed the dishes she'd used and Rachel settled in beside her to dry them. A frog the size of a peach pit crawled up the window above the sink. The light, the color of distressed jeans, drifted in around it. His raspy song penetrated the silence. Catch rapped on the window to get him to move along.

Heat pulsed from the oven, wafting over the counter in a steady current. Rachel wiped at her sweaty hair that clung to her forehead.

"Can I ask you something?" she asked.

"Shoot," Catch said.

"What you said about how being lost was a good thing. What did you mean by that?"

"We're all looking for something in life. For some, it's money, others it's family, companionship, acceptance. Sometimes people get so caught up in the looking that they miss out on what's right in front of them." Catch handed her a plate, suds still clinging to its edges, and Rachel dried it before setting it on top of the others. "And more often than not, that's even better than what they thought they wanted in the first place."

If the answer to all of her problems was staring her in the face, Rachel still couldn't see it. But, God, did she want to. Maybe she owed it to herself to see if Catch could help. "Is that what you think I'm doing?"

Catch peered into the oven window, squinting through the layer of grease staining the glass a pale brown. When she turned back to Rachel, her eyes were bright. "I don't know you well enough to say that. I just want to make sure you're paying attention, that's all."

# 5

After finishing up her middle-of-the-night baking session with Catch, Rachel had gone back to bed. Sometime later, and still half-asleep, she swatted the air to stop the buzzing that had invaded her dreams. It did no good.

The light from the window burned an unforgiving orange when she opened her eyes. Her phone hopped along the shelf above the bed as it vibrated again and toppled onto the pillow next to her. She couldn't remember turning the phone to silent as Mary Beth's name flashed on the screen.

Rachel jerked up, her legs tangling in the sheets, which were plastered to her skin with sweat. She'd known it wouldn't take Mary Beth long to realize she was gone, but faced with having to fess up before she even had a plan in place made her mouth go dry, all explanations for not saying goodbye evading her. She answered anyway.

"What's going on?" Mary Beth said in place of a greeting. "I stopped for coffee and Erik said you'd quit. No notice. No nothing."

"I didn't have two weeks to give him," Rachel said.

"Why not?"

"Because if I gave myself time to think about it, I might've stayed."

"Wait, what do you mean 'stayed'? Where are you?"

Kicking off the sheets, Rachel held her breath until the burning in her lungs drowned out the prickling of nerves in her stomach.

"I told you I would fix things. I got far enough away that even if Violet wishes for something else, I can't accidentally make it come true."

"Where are you?" Mary Beth repeated.

"Nowhere, North Carolina."

"I'm sorry, did you say North Carolina? As in you're no longer even in the state? And you didn't think to tell me you were leaving? Not even a courtesy call?"

"Yes," Rachel said, her cheeks flaming with guilt.

Mary Beth cut her off before she could say more. "First, I can't believe you up and left town without even telling me. That's seriously shitty, Ray."

"I know," Rachel said. "I'm sorry. But I couldn't stay."

"Uh-huh," Mary Beth said, ignoring her apology. "And second, you couldn't find someplace better than a Podunk town?"

Rachel laughed despite the annoyance in her best friend's voice. "No. The town's really called Nowhere. But it is aptly named. The gas station closes before dark, for a poker game apparently, hence me still being here."

"So where did you stay? Please don't tell me your car."

"Of course I didn't sleep in my car." Not that she wouldn't have if it had come to that. Beggars couldn't be choosers. "I was going to find a hotel, but then this woman, Catch, took me in for the night."

"That was nice of her. And also kinda strange."

Rachel sat up, twisting to see out the window above the bed. "I know. Nowhere really is like one of those small towns you see in sitcoms that you never think actually exist but kind of wish did. I mean, I've only met Catch and her neighbor who brought me gas, but if I had to base the town solely on them, I'd say it's got some definite positives."

"A gas-gifting neighbor, huh?" Mary Beth's voice softened, and Rachel imagined her raising her eyebrows with a wicked grin on her face. "Is he cute?"

"Even with a whole damn state in between us, you're still trying to set me up? That's dedication, Mae."

"You're the one who put a whole state between us. Without telling me. So your argument is invalid. And anyway, with everything that's been going on lately, you could use a good distraction. So, is he?"

"Yes," she admitted, realizing she knew the exact shade of his eyes without even concentrating. Rachel scooted to the window and cracked it. The breeze was gentle and sticky, rustling the leaves of the dozens of trees in the yard, and the air smelled of warm fruit. She rested her forehead against the window and took a deep breath. "But I'm not interested in a fling. Not really my thing."

"C'mon, Rachel. Even after a year with Jason you wouldn't open up to him about therapy or your mom. The way I see it, you have two options. One, find a guy you can trust to like you for you—difficult past and all. Or two, a no-strings-attached relationship where you get all of the sexy-time perks without any of the emotional pressure."

Could she trust someone other than Mary Beth enough to confess all of her secrets? Refusing to let the idea take hold, Rachel said, "Falling into bed with some random guy isn't going to fix any of my problems. Right now, I just want a place where I can figure some things out."

"All right. I'll let it go for now," Mary Beth said. "As long as you promise to try and let go of all the guilt you've been holding on to as long as I've known you."

The first soothing tendrils of relief worked their way through Rachel's chest at her friend's support. Not that she expected anything less from Mary Beth, who had been estranged from her parents and sister for almost as long as Rachel had known her. They'd become each other's family and swore to make each other's happiness a priority in their friendship.

"Believe me, I wish I could," Rachel said.

"Well, yeah, when all you do is halfheartedly wave your hand and kind of mumble 'shoo' at it, you can't actually expect it to go anywhere. You have to mean it, Ray."

"I'm pretty sure I told it to 'get.' But you're right, the hand motions could've been a little more emphatic."

"Seriously, try to let it go, okay? For me," Mary Beth said. Without waiting for Rachel's assent, she said, "So, back to this town. Think you'll stay longer than a night?"

Rachel hugged the spare pillow to her chest. She had no real reason not to stay. And Catch's theory that being lost in Nowhere could do her some good had apparently taken root while Rachel slept and didn't seem as far-fetched as it had the night before. "I might. I mean, I'll have to find a job because I don't have a lot of money saved, but I'll be okay for a few weeks."

"Whoa. I didn't mean for good."

"Who's to say I'll find someplace better? I could end up driving all over the country looking for the perfect town. And that would take money, which I'd need a job to get. And I can't get a job if I'm skipping town every few days."

"I know. But you don't have to settle for the first place you find either."

Rachel tossed the pillow aside and dropped back into the rumpled sheets that smelled of lavender. "I know I don't have to. But I have to do something, Maeby." And Nowhere seemed as good a place as any. If she was lucky, the wishes hadn't followed her to Nowhere and everything she'd run from would stay firmly in her past.

"Just promise me if you're not happy, you'll try someplace else."

"Someplace else meaning home?"

"Obviously that would be my preference. But I understand how starting over somewhere without all of the bad memories and constant reminders of things you can't change could make you happy. If it's what you need, I'll be okay with it. And I'll eventually forgive you for not saying bye."

Rachel laughed. Mary Beth could hold a grudge, but thankfully never against her. They were all each other had for a few heartbreaking years in their teens and neither of them ever forgot it. Rachel would sooner hurt herself than Mary Beth. Which was precisely why Rachel couldn't be anywhere near her friend if she couldn't control her ability.

———

The voices in the kitchen grew louder the closer she got to them. Rachel kept her steps light, only a slight hitch in her breath at eavesdropping on Catch and Ashe.

"This is just crazy," Ashe said. "One night I can understand, but living here? You can't take in some strange girl just because she needs—"

"Yes, I can," Catch cut in. "Where would you or your brother be if I'd left you to fend for yourselves while your parents were too busy spitting at each other to notice y'all?"

"That's different, Catch. You'd known us our whole lives. And we were kids. She's a grown woman, fully capable of taking care of herself."

Rachel pressed against the doorframe between the foyer and the dining room. She could slip back upstairs, pack her bag, and be out the front door before either of them realized she was gone. And she might have given in to the urge if she'd had anyplace else to go.

"Just because she should be able to doesn't mean she is. That girl needs my help whether either of you realizes it. Now, I don't want to hear another word about it. Got me?" Catch's raspy voice was firm, determined.

Ashe's loud sigh carried to Rachel. "Yes, ma'am."

"And when she comes down here, I want you to be nice to her. No arguing."

"Yes, ma'am," he said again.

Someone set a plate or something on the counter. The ceramic scraped along the granite with a shrill scratching. Rachel crept back up the stairs to the landing. She'd been right the evening before when she'd guessed Ashe thought it was a bad idea she was staying in the house with Catch. Well, she'd just have to prove him wrong. As she started back down the stairs, she let her flip-flops slap each step so they wouldn't think she'd overheard them when she walked in.

Ashe sat at the island, digging in to a plate of breakfast pie. He glanced up, nodded.

She took the seat next to him and said, "Not even a good-morning pat down to make sure I don't have my ax hidden in my shirt? I must not be giving off my menacing vibe today."

He cracked a smile, then buried it in his coffee cup.

She added a check mark to the Rachel column of her mental scorecard for the small victory. "How's the bribe working?" she asked Catch.

"I hadn't gotten to that yet, Little-Miss-Big-Mouth. Shoulda shoved this plate in front of you the second you sat down." Catch dumped a plate with a triangle of pie and a few slices of pear in front of Rachel. Silverware clattered down a second later.

Rachel stuffed a forkful of hot egg pie in her mouth, and Ashe turned to her, eyebrows raised in curiosity.

"I thought something tasted funny about this pie," he said. He cut off another hunk and inspected it on the end of his fork. "Yep, there it is. Artificial guilt flavoring."

"Oh, shut up, you," Catch said.

"Whaddya need?"

Catch smacked at his arm with a damp dish towel, then did the same to Rachel, who couldn't help but laugh. "Since you're here, I was thinking it would be nice if you showed Rachel around town."

"You didn't tell me I was part of this bribe," Rachel objected.

"You'll learn," Ashe said to her. He polished off the last bite of his breakfast, eyed her barely touched piece, and said, "That's worth at least two servings, I think."

He leaned across Rachel to reach the pie dish. His arm grazed hers as he sat back and carved out a piece almost twice the size of his original one. He shrugged at her when she continued to stare at him.

"I'm in if she is," he said.

"Oh, she's in," Catch said.


Twenty minutes later, Rachel followed Ashe through the backyard to his house. It was barely past eight, but the air was already thick with humidity. A bird jabbered at them from one of the trees before taking flight. The cherry tree shook, its plush leaves stirring up a tart, ripe scent that tickled the back of her throat. Another tree, thick with bright pink and yellow peaches in varying stages of ripeness, rubbed against her arm as she passed, almost as if it had reached out to pet her.

"So, Catch got you to stay, huh?" he asked. He flipped his sunglasses down to block the early-morning glare.

"For now," Rachel said, squinting without the sunglasses she'd left at Catch's. "Mostly because I don't know where else to go."

He was a step ahead and turned to look at her when he asked, "Were things bad in Tennessee? I mean, did you leave a bad situation?"

"No." Even if she'd wanted to explain what she could do with the wishes, she would have no idea how to. So she just said, "But they weren't really good either. They just were."

"Sorry, I shouldn't have asked. Catch is always telling me to mind my own damn business."

"It's okay."

They walked in silence the rest of the way. A few steps out of the trees and they were at the back deck of the gorgeous house she had glimpsed from the attic room at Catch's. Windows ran along the back of the house from floor to ceiling. The glare from the sun made it impossible to see inside. The tiered roofs created subtle overhangs for the levels below and she could imagine leaving the window open even when it rained. On the second floor, a minuscule balcony jutted off the back of the house with enough room for one chair to fit between the wall and the railing.

Ashe stopped at the base of the deck stairs, as if deciding whether or not to invite her inside.

She shielded her eyes from the sun with a cupped hand and looked at him. Thanks to the reflectiveness of his sunglasses, she couldn't tell if he was looking back, but if she had to guess, she'd say he was. And that he had no intention of making the next move.

So it was up to her.

All she had to do was talk to him. And if she was steering the conversation, she could keep topics off of ones that would lead to questions she couldn't answer.

"How'd you end up living in the family home?" she asked. When he quirked an eyebrow at her, she added, "Catch told me you grew up here and I assume you don't still live with your parents."

"I've always loved this house." He ran a hand over the porch rail. "My mom was always trying to change things. Take out a wall here, add a bathroom there, rip out the eighty-year-old mahogany floors to put in Travertine. I needed to get it away from her before there was nothing of the original architecture left. So, for their twentieth anniversary, I designed a new house for them with all the details she wanted and none of the ones she didn't."

He inched the back door open, keeping an eye on something across the room as the hinges sighed, and held the door for Rachel.

"How old were you then?"

Ashe gave her that smile again. The one that said, *Yep, I'm as good as you think.* She hated that she believed it so easily. She was a master at keeping people out, or so her ex-boyfriend attested. How Ashe could get through her defenses with a damn smile both baffled and unnerved her. Turning away, Rachel focused on the curved wood railing that led to the second floor. The rungs were dusty, but the banister itself gleamed.

"Twenty-three," he said. "I was pretty young when Dad and Carol Ann got married, but since my real mom took off when she found out about my dad and Carol Ann, Carol Ann's the only mom I've got. I've just got to grab something real quick." He ducked into a room to his left and came out a moment later stuffing a handful of papers into a legal-size envelope.

Rachel followed him back across the room. A folded blanket and pillow sat on the pool table that separated the kitchen from the living room. "I guess since you're in this one, she liked it. The new house."

"She loved it at first," he said, tucking the envelope under his arm. He held the back door open for her and followed her outside. "Until she went out there one day to check on the progress and found my dad screwing another woman on the granite countertop she'd picked out."

Rachel cringed and said, "Sorry," but Ashe waved it away. "You know, I've heard that's the only way to really test out granite to make sure it's installed properly." The words were out before she considered how he'd take them.

"That was not at all the reaction I was expecting."

Her face burned when she realized he thought she was making a suggestion instead of a joke.

Before she could set him straight, he added, "Well, if it's what you've heard I might have to try it out next time." She dropped her gaze to the ground to avoid eye contact, and he chuckled. Whether at her reaction or because he was joking too, she didn't know. "Anyways," he said, "after that she didn't really want the house anymore. She moved about an hour away, so my brother, Scott, has to split his time off from college between there and here."

The sun soaked through her shirt and heated her skin as they followed the stone path to the driveway. She rubbed at a dribble of sweat on her neck with sticky fingers. "Do you think he'll come back when he graduates?" Rachel asked.

"He's got a few more years, then vet school, but yeah. This is home."

Ashe reached the door handle of his pickup before she did. She stepped back from the passenger door and waited.

"You gonna get in?" he asked.

"Sorry. I thought you needed to get something out," Rachel said.

"Nope. Just gettin' the door for you."

Rachel told herself it was just because he was a gentleman and not because he thought she'd been flirting with him. But she couldn't deny the sweetness of the action.

She stepped onto the running board and pushed off the door to maneuver into the bed of the truck. Even with the added half foot of height, she was still barely eye level with him. When she wobbled, Ashe steadied her with a hand on her lower back. His fingers brushed a swath of skin as her shirt rode up an inch.

"So, where are we headed?" she asked, trying to ignore the jolt of heat that traveled up her back from where his fingers had been.

"Downtown. I've gotta drop this off at my dad's, but then we can walk around a bit. Show you enough that Catch knows we upheld our end of the bargain."

She cut her eyes to him without turning her head. "Is there going to be a quiz at the end? Because I didn't bring anything to take notes."

Ashe closed the door, cutting off his laugh.

She watched out the window as they passed old house after old house with doors propped open in welcome and rockers waiting patiently on front porches for friends to stop by for a long chat, deciding she might be able to imagine why someone would want to make this place home.

# 6

The converted warehouse that housed Ashe's dad's law practice had been sectioned into office and retail space. With its gritty brick exterior, small square windows, and metal doors, it stood out from the quaint wood buildings that occupied most of downtown.

Ashe tapped the envelope against his palm. He tried to smile, but his look carried a chill despite the warmth of the sun beating down. "Okay, so I need to run in here for just a minute. And I know this is shitty of me to do, but I was wondering if you minded waiting out here? This isn't something I want an audience for."

*Things must be pretty strained with his dad.* "Yeah, of course. And I won't even tell Catch you left me to fend for myself . . ." Her voice trailed off as a young man walked out of a building a few blocks up. He reminded her so much of Michael—the same heart-shaped face, same mop of shaggy brown hair falling over his eyes, same crooked smile. But a grown-up version.

She blinked and he was gone.

In his place were shoppers fanning themselves with to-go menus and tourist brochures, cars idling as pedestrians claimed right-of-way, and a murder of crows dotting the town square, waiting for someone to drop a bite of bagel.

She took a few tentative steps toward where the young man had been, a strangled sound coming out of her throat before she could stop it.

"Rachel?" Ashe said. When she didn't respond, he placed a gentle hand on her shoulder. "Hey, you okay?"

She blinked at the sidewalk as if that would make him reappear. "Yeah. Sorry. I thought I saw—" she said. Her heart rammed against her ribs, threatening to crack those closest to it. After a few seconds, she turned back to Ashe. "Never mind. Must be the heat."

He frowned, his hair falling across his eyes as he leaned closer to her. "Maybe you should come inside after all. Sit down for a minute?"

Cold air rushed out when he opened the door. With his hand still on her shoulder, her skin erupted in goose bumps.

Rachel glanced up the street again. "I'm fine. Really. You go on in and do what you need to do."

"You sure?" he asked.

"Yeah. I'll be okay in a minute."

Ashe still looked unconvinced. "If you pass out on me, Catch will have my hide."

She pulled her hair up and gathered it into a ponytail, the breeze caressing the back of her neck. She took in a deep breath. "I won't."

Ashe hesitated, his eyes narrowing as he studied her face. She stared back and smiled until he seemed satisfied she was okay and went inside.

*Breathe*, Rachel told herself.

Her lungs burned from holding her breath. Exhaling, she looked to see that Ashe wasn't still watching her. Then she took off down the sidewalk. Her heart thundered in her ears. Sweat and goose bumps battled on her skin. She wiped her palms on her thighs and forced air into her lungs. In and out. In and out.

*It wasn't Michael.*

Even as she thought it, she looked left and right, trying to find the young man again. No one looked familiar. She passed building after building, storefronts and offices half-concealed by blinds. The windows reflected the morning light so everything inside was hazy, indistinguishable. She strained to find the navy plaid shirt and dark hair she'd seen a few minutes before.

She kept walking. And searching.

The sun blinded her when it shot through a gap between two buildings. She stared at the pitted concrete in front of her until the sun spots dispersed. Light-headed, Rachel caught a flash of blue disappearing around the corner a few blocks up. Her shoes slapped the sidewalk and she hurried to close the distance. She passed street signs without reading them.

By the time she reached the next street, it was empty. Here, at least, the buildings blocked the sun. She searched shops as she passed, seeing flashes of clothing—bright colors like cherry and lemon, avocado and melon. But no young guy wearing blue.

But she had seen him. Hadn't she?

"Damn it, Rachel," she whispered. She stopped in the middle of the sidewalk, forcing a mother pushing a double stroller to swerve around her. "Pull it together. There's no one here. He is not coming back."

Though it had gotten easier to say over the years, something ballooned in her chest, making her choke on the words. As if just by saying them she was wishing him away again.

On the day he disappeared, she hadn't seen her brother in hours. Not since he'd bulldozed her Lego castle with a swift kick, scattering the pink and purple and white pieces she'd spent days snapping into place, and she'd shouted that she wished he'd get lost so he'd stop ruining all her stuff. She'd read the wish she found buried in the rubble of her castle but figured Michael's version of "lost" would be sulking in one of his hiding spots she had yet to discover. He was six years younger than her, and at age four, he was still small enough to fit in under-the-sink cabinets and way in the backs of closets where no one could see him.

He wasn't in his room when she went to apologize, so she set a plate of thumbprint cookies on the floor in front of his door where he couldn't miss them when he came out of hiding. She'd only given him the blue, green, and yellow ones—the pink ones he always said were only for girls. Snagging a yellow one off the stack, she popped it in her mouth, the sprinkles baked into the edges crunching with the first few chews.

She had tucked the wish safely in her pocket, where her mom wouldn't be able to find it and yell at her for being mean to her brother.

She tried to concentrate on rebuilding the front wall of the castle, but every creak and thump in the house had her jumping up from the floor and rushing to the door to tell Michael she wasn't mad at him anymore. But it was never him.

After an hour, the ground floor, including the throne room, the ballroom, and the kitchen, were back in place in the castle. Her fingers ached from pressing the plastic pieces onto one another. When her mom knocked on her door, she shook her hands back and forth, half-waving and half-trying to get the blood flowing again.

"Why are there cookies in the hallway?" her mom asked.

"They're an apology. I think I hurt Michael's feelings," Rachel said.

"What?"

Rachel knew her mom would be mad about how she'd treated her brother, so she focused her eyes on the Lego princess as she placed her next to the prince so they could dance. "He ruined my castle," she said, pouting. "I can't help it if Michael's a baby about getting in trouble."

Her mom's eyebrows drew together so they looked like one furry caterpillar on her forehead. "Who is Michael and why would he ruin your castle?" Her mom gripped the door handle and eyed her carefully.

Rachel's hand hit the newly rebuilt chandelier, knocking it from the castle's ballroom ceiling when she jerked around to roll her eyes at her mom. "My little brother Michael. I left the cookies in front of his room so he'd see them and know I was sorry for yelling at him, even if he did knock down my castle."

"Rachel, I don't think imaginary brothers need real cookies. Think you can go put them back in the kitchen before they get stepped on?"

"Michael isn't imaginary." Rachel gaped at her mom, the chandelier gripped tightly in her hand. She felt funny, like she did when she had a high fever or went to bed too late.

"Oh, right. Of course he isn't," her mom said in that overly sweet voice she used when she and Rachel were playing pretend. "I'm serious about putting the cookies away, though. If they're still there the next time I come upstairs, I'll throw them out. Got it?"

"Yes, ma'am," Rachel said, confused but happy that at least her mom didn't seem mad.

She waited until she heard her mom talking to her dad downstairs before moving the cookies. The plate was where she'd left it, but instead of her brother's bedroom door, a painting of a Snow White–type cottage set in a thicket of woods hung on an otherwise blank wall. *Where's Michael's room?* She ground her knuckles into her eyes and counted to five before looking at the wall again. Moving closer, she stepped on the plate. It broke into three large, jagged pieces. A few of the cookies crumbled under her bare foot, and she jumped to the side so she didn't get cut by the sharp edges of the plate. The wall was solid when she ran both hands along its smooth surface.

The door was gone. Like it had never been there at all.

Standing on the unfamiliar street in Nowhere, Rachel could still see the blankness of that wall, still feel the numbness that filled her with dread at what her parents would do when they realized she'd made Michael disappear with her stupid wish.

Back when she thought they might actually believe her.

She reached a shaky hand to a parking meter to steady herself. Closing her eyes, she counted to five like she had back then, inhaling on the odd numbers and telling herself everything would be okay on the evens. But now she knew no amount of wishing could bring back someone who no longer existed. Just as she knew the person she'd been following through the streets was most definitely not Michael but just a familiar-looking stranger, no matter what her insides were telling her.

Something about the air was suddenly fresh and earthy. It smelled like cucumbers and lilac and almond milk, soothing her like the deep breaths hadn't. And the breeze blew a few degrees cooler, as if this stretch of street was encased in a bubble of calm. Eyes now open, Rachel looked around to see if anyone else had noticed the change in atmosphere, or if that was all in her head too.

The park across the street was full of oblivious people. Children screeched and shrieked as they chased each other around the fountain. Arcs of water shot up from the ground at varying intervals to catch them off guard, and they screamed again. A chocolate lab lapped at one of the streams of water. It continued licking the air after the water disappeared and then turned in a circle trying to find where it had gone.

She scanned the way she'd come but didn't recognize the street or the buildings. Was it one block or two to get back to the one she'd followed when she left Ashe? *Shit.*

Rachel looked up to find someone watching her from inside one of the shops. Lettering on the window identified the shop as LUX, an organic skin-care boutique. She could just make out the staring woman's short, curly brown hair and milky skin behind the shop window's pale pink letters.

The woman popped her head out of the doorway. "Are you okay, hon?"

Straightening, Rachel tried to return the smile. "I think so. Just a little dizzy. And lost," she admitted.

"Well, where are you trying to go?"

"I'm not sure. We stopped at an office so Ashe could drop something off, but—"

"Ashe Riley?" the woman asked.

She tried to remember when he'd introduced himself the day before and came up blank. "Um, maybe. Does he build houses?"

"Designs them. And does contractor work when forced. I'm Everley Hayes, by the way. Come on in outta the heat." She pushed the door wide. Her capri yoga pants and tank top hugged her toned body.

A gush of cool air caressed Rachel's skin. "I'm Rachel."

"Can I get you something to drink? I've got coconut water or sparkling water with orange slices in it," Everley said.

"Regular water is fine, thanks, if you have it."

"Good call. Plain's probably the way to go if you're not feeling too hot." Everley walked to a glass-front cooler and pulled a bottle out. The plastic was thin and crackled when she handed it to Rachel.

Rachel wanted to rub it on her neck, but she settled for uncapping it and taking a long swig. Her head unfogged enough to chase some of the dizziness away, though her hands continued to shake. She took another sip. "Thanks."

"So, what did Ashe say to tick you off?"

"Sorry?" Rachel asked.

"I figure he must've done or said something to make you walk off and get yourself lost."

"I was just—" *Following a ghost*, she finished silently. "I thought I saw someone I recognized. But it wasn't him."

It would never be him.

"Then if you're not mad at Ashe, want me to give him a call and tell him where you are?"

Her pulse had slowed to an almost normal pace and she let out a steadying breath. "If you don't mind. I don't want him to have to tell Catch I got lost on his watch."

"You definitely don't want to piss off Miss Sisson. Gimme just a minute," Everley said.

As Everley pulled out her cell phone, Rachel turned to check out the store. White built-ins lined the blush-colored walls. Milk bottles and mason jars and round metal tins with screw-on lids glinted in the sun. Their milky contents were offset with labels and tags with the shop's logo printed in charcoal and pink. Baskets on a table in the front window overflowed with slabs of soap that were swirled and lined with a fusion of sultry colors. Rachel touched one. One side was rough with crushed almond shells and bit at her fingers through the plastic.

A slip of paper was tucked into the weave of one of the baskets. Before realizing what it was, she smoothed it out with a finger and read it. *I wish I could tell her no.*

With a sharp breath, she let the wish curl back on itself. But it was too late. She'd granted the wish without meaning to. And whoever had made the wish in the first place would have to live with the consequences. All because Rachel had hoped the wishes wouldn't follow her here and she had let her guard down.

Everley's husky laugh pulled her attention back. She hung up and said, "Good thing I called. He was fixing to deploy a search party for you."

"Oh, God." Heat rushed to Rachel's cheeks, and she turned to look for him out the window.

"I'm kidding. He just noticed you were gone. He'll be here in a few minutes."

Rachel glanced down at the curled paper in the basket and then quickly turned back to Everley. "Thanks."

"So, how do you know Ashe?" Everley's eyebrow cocked in interest.

"'Know' is a strong word. We just met yesterday when I ran out of gas and Catch let me crash at her house. He's showing me around as a favor to her."

"Ah, that explains it. I thought I was going to have to give him hell for seeing someone and not telling me."

"So the two of you are friends?" Rachel asked. She bumped the water bottle against her thigh and drops of cool condensation dribbled down the skin below her shorts.

"Since we were kids," Everley said. "My boyfriend, Jamie, is his best friend, so we're sorta like family."

The door opened a few minutes later, letting in a wave of hot air and Ashe a step behind. His eyes swept over Rachel and settled on Everley. "Thanks for calling, Ev," he said.

Everley winked. "No problem, cutie."

"You okay?" he asked Rachel.

"Yeah, I'm fine. Sorry I walked away," Rachel said, hoping the flush was gone from her cheeks. "Just wanted to do a little sightseeing."

"C'mon, Ashe, what do you think's gonna happen to her here? Nowhere's like the safest town ever."

"Have you looked at her?" Ashe gestured to Rachel. He didn't look happy. "She looks like she's seen a ghost."

*There's no way he knows.* Rachel pinched the crook of her arm. *Snap out of it.* She looked up, his icy-blue eyes narrowing on her. She forced a smile.

"It's just the heat. I gave her some water. She'll be fine," Everley said.

"Yeah, 'cause your water's about as refreshing as drinking a salad."

"I gave her *bottled* water, smartass."

Ashe grinned at her and turned to Rachel. "You ready?"

She nodded. "Thanks for your help, Everley. It was really nice to meet you."

"Sure thing. Come back and see me sometime, okay?" Everley said.

Ashe cupped Rachel's elbow and ushered her out into the steamy air. Whether he was trying to steady her or keep her from wandering off again, Rachel couldn't tell.

"Please don't tell Catch about this," she said. "I don't want her to worry."

"Wasn't planning to. But are you gonna tell me what happened?"

"It's not important."

"Sure it's not," he said. His voice was a mix of annoyance and amusement. But he didn't push. He turned a corner and gently pulled her with him.

"Do you think we can just go—" Rachel stopped herself. Nowhere wasn't home. It was just a town she was temporarily living in. "Back to Catch's?" she said.

"Whatever you want to do."

The thought of lying to Catch about why she'd left Ashe made her dizzy. She concentrated on the steadying hand on her arm. His palms were calloused, his fingers rough. She stared at the spot of sweat that blossomed on the front of his shirt instead of watching where they were going.

They reached his truck within minutes. She'd walked up and down the street and still had no clue where she'd gone or how she'd gotten there. She swiveled to look at the ancient buildings and wooden street signs behind her, but it was like seeing them all for the first time. No flash of navy or mop of brown hair in sight.

# 7

Rachel would've told him not to walk her in, but she somehow knew he wouldn't listen. Her legs held steady as she slid from the truck into the gravel driveway, all shakiness from her brief hallucination gone. Ashe walked beside her with his hand resting on her lower back. The air smelled like rain. Damp, sweet, and electric. She heard the first rumble of thunder as they walked in the back door.

The kitchen was empty. Without Catch, the room seemed sterile, like a demonstration kitchen that was all for show. The stand mixer was tucked under one of the cabinets, gleaming, and bowls of whole fruit were lined up on the island looking almost too perfect to be real.

"You gonna be all right?" Ashe asked.

"Yes," Rachel said. "I'm fine, okay?"

"Want me to wait around until Catch gets back? She usually goes out delivering pies in the mornings. Depending on how many she made, she could be a while."

"Thanks, but like I said, I'm good. I think I just need to go lie down for a bit."

"Okay, well, my cell number is in there." He pointed to the top drawer on the end. "There's a whole list of numbers. You can't miss it. I can be here in ten minutes if you need me."

*Southern gentleman to the core.* It made her smile.

"Go," she said. "And thanks."

The smile he gave her made her legs go weak again. She held on to the counter until he'd jogged down the steps and she heard his truck growl to life.

Sitting on a stool at the island, she lifted a corner of the tinfoil covering one of Catch's pies and sniffed. It was buttery and nutty with a hint of something dark. *Comfort in pie form.* She sighed and peeled off the rest of the foil. The surface of the pie was jagged with pieces of pecans that jutted out at all angles. One slice was already gone.

After opening a drawer and finding whisks and spatulas and measuring spoons, she tried another. She located the knives and forks in the third one she opened, then cut a sliver of pie, not even enough to be called a slice. The filling oozed as she scooped it onto her fork, dribbling melted chocolate and pecan chunks in gooey brown sauce onto the plate. She wiped the blade of the table knife with her finger and thumb. Then she licked them clean.

The bitterness of the semisweet chocolate lingered on her tongue.

Rachel took a full bite of the pie and reached for the stack of recipe cards held together by a rubber band. Curiosity got the better of her manners, and she slipped the band from the cards. Pale dust settled on the counter along with pieces of brittle rubber when it broke.

The recipes were in shorthand, only a third of which she understood. She'd always thought baking was about precision, and Catch's methods were anything but. The measurements consisted of a *handful* of this, *two scoops* of that. One called for a *half bucket* of what she thought said key limes. She skimmed half the pile before shuffling them back into one stack. She tossed the rubber band in the trash, rinsed her plate, and loaded it and the utensils into the dishwasher.

A clock chimed from one of the other rooms. She followed the deep tolling through the dim dining room, its thick tan curtains flanking the shuttered windows into the foyer. The front door was propped open with a crumbling brick. The screen door was latched, as if one hook and eye would keep anyone out. Not even the sunlight had to force its way in.

She hesitated at the foot of the stairs as the spines of dozens of books in the room to the left of the door caught her attention. The wood creaked beneath her feet. Before she could talk herself out of it, she moved into the room. It was small, cozy, with wall-to-wall bookshelves and two faded wingback chairs. A fireplace was set into the middle of one bookcase. The hearth was swept clean. Fresh logs sat in the dormant cavity.

Like the rest of the house, the library was stuffed with cookbooks with titles like *Whip It: 25 Quiches in 25 Minutes*, *The Secrets of Vegan Baking*, and *Soufflés and Cakes That Won't Fall Flat*. There were books on hot peppers and fruit-producing trees, and cheeses of the world, and harvesting your own honey. Some were still shiny and stiff. Others were the muted yellow of the inside of a lemon peel. Rachel left finger smudges on their glossy covers when she pulled them from the shelf at random.

Nestled in among the books was a frame made of twigs. Bubbles of dried hot glue held the crumbling sticks in place. Bark shavings flecked off when she picked it up. They scattered to the floor when she blew on them. She studied the boy in the picture. Ashe's face was rounder and his smile unrestrained, but she could see how the boy had grown into the man.

"Making yourself at home?" Catch asked from behind her.

The frame made a cracking sound when Rachel dropped it back onto the shelf.

"I'm sorry. I didn't mean to snoop," she said, heart pounding. She hoped she hadn't broken the frame.

"If you went through my underwear drawer, it would be snooping. Otherwise, it's just getting familiar with your surroundings. Now, how about keeping me company while I make a few more pies? I picked some peaches on my way in."

"Sure," Rachel said, even though Catch hadn't waited for a response before heading back to the kitchen. She glanced at the photo again and then followed.

"So, I hear you went and got yourself lost again," Catch said.

Rachel stared at her, mouth dropping open. "Ashe said he wouldn't tell you."

"He didn't. But things have a way of coming out around here. Some people take precautionary measures to keep their secrets, well, secret. Others just let things happen as they will. And there are a few that simply ain't worth helping."

"Where do I fit?" Rachel asked.

"Jury's still out." Catch plucked a peach from the cloth sack on the counter and held it out to Rachel. "Now, how are you at peeling peaches?"

She took it and rubbed her thumb over its velvety pink skin. It was still warm from hanging in the sun a few minutes before. It smelled sweet and hopeful. "I'm sure I'm not near as good at it as you, but I'm happy to help."

Catch placed a paring knife on the counter before setting a pot of water on to boil. "You gotta blanch 'em first, and then the skin peels right off."

"How long have you been baking?" Rachel asked.

"Too damn long."

"Do you still enjoy it?"

"Some days yes, some days no. But it's what I do, so I can't turn my back on it."

They worked side by side, dropping a few peaches at a time into the boiling water for thirty seconds, and then transferring them to a bowl of ice water to stop the heat from cooking them.

Rachel fished them out of the ice bath and lined them up by the cutting board. When she slid the blade into the first one, red juice dribbled down her fingers. She made a second incision and pried out the wedge. Her fingertips sank in, leaving subtle indentations. Setting it on the counter, she worked on the next slice, piling them up until there was nothing left but a knobby pit, which she dropped in the sink with a metallic thud.

The skin was soft, pliable. She picked at the edge with the tip of the knife and peeled it from the yellow meat of the peach. It came off in one long, flimsy strip, curling around her thumb. She flicked it onto the counter.

"Not exactly the way I woulda done it. But it's effective. I'll give you that," Catch said.

"It's how my mom always did it." *Because Michael loved peaches, but didn't like the fuzz.* Even when her mom didn't remember him anymore, she still skinned the peaches. It was one of the ways Rachel tried to convince her mom that he had existed. It was one of the things that helped push her mom over the edge.

Catch eyed her as if she could tell that Rachel had held something back. Rachel focused on the peaches and almost wanted to tell Catch everything. Almost.

They were back in the kitchen after dinner, Catch with her nightly scotch and Rachel with a glass of white wine. The knock on the back door was so light at first Rachel thought it was a branch brushing the side of the house. It sounded again a little louder, a little more urgent. She jolted when the pale face appeared in the window.

Catch let the girl in with a shake of her head.

The girl wiped at her cheeks with the backs of her hands and stared at the floor. Her doughy face turned a blotchy pink and her wrinkled dress drooped at the neckline. She pressed her lips together as if trying to keep words from escaping.

"Well, c'mon now. Out with it," Catch said.

The girl glanced at Rachel, her long dark lashes fluttering as her eyes widened.

Catch pushed back from the counter. "Oh, don't worry about her. She's not telling nobody what happens here."

"O-okay. Um, I need your help, Miss Sisson."

"I kinda figured that since you're here. Just tell me what you need. I can have the pie over to you in the morning before your head stops spinning."

The girl's head bobbed up and down as she blurted, "I had . . . I was with Duke Davis tonight. Like, *with him*. I don't know why I did it. I didn't mean to. It just sorta happened. I know what everyone already thinks about me. Please don't let them find out about it. Please."

Catch put a hand on the girl's shoulder to keep her still, focused. "How many am I baking for? Just him this time?"

The girl didn't seem fazed by the insinuation, though she couldn't have been older than late teens. Rachel shifted on the stool and looked away.

"Just him. And me. Can it make me forget it happened in the first place too?"

"You know it doesn't work like that, child. But no one else will know, you can be sure of that," Catch said. "I'll take care of it. Though I hope you were smart about it, because you know I can't do anything about all that." The girl nodded, and it seemed to Rachel this wasn't the first time the two had had this conversation.

"You just go on home now and get some sleep. I'll bring it to you first thing in the morning." Catch ushered the girl to the door. She turned the lock once the girl had vanished into the dark and pulled down the white vinyl shade. "Looks like I've got a pie to make. You interested in helping?" she asked.

Curious as to how a pie had anything to do with the girl and a boy she clearly regretted sleeping with, Rachel agreed. She scooted the stool closer to the counter and waited.

Catch worked the dough into a loose ball the size of an orange with nimble hands. Sprinkling more flour on the counter and rubbing it around with one hand, she pressed and pulled the dough five times before slapping it down in the center of the white circle.

"Hand me that rolling pin," she said.

Rachel lifted it from its nest on a towel and passed it over. She studied Catch's face for some sign that the old woman was messing with her, implying the pies had magical properties. When Catch raised an eyebrow at her, Rachel caved and said, "Okay, so I have to ask. How can a pie make sure no one finds out?"

"My pies are well known around these parts for their silencing powers. If someone's got a secret they let slip, and they want to make sure it doesn't get blabbed all over tarnation, they come to me and I help them out."

*Catch can make secrets disappear.* Excitement and disbelief buzzed along Rachel's skin at the thought, making her shiver. If Catch could do that with secrets, maybe she could make the wishes disappear too. Leaning over the counter for a closer look, she tried to appear nonchalant as she asked, "How does it work?"

Catch pushed the rolling pin across the dough, a hasty back and forth in the shape of a *V*. The edges of the circle were scraggly, uneven. "Why? You got a secret to tell?" She eyed Rachel over the table and chuckled.

"Just curious," Rachel said, trying to keep the desperation out of her voice. "So you make magic pies and people think it's completely normal?"

"Oh, they'll swear it's not real right up until the day they need my help."

Of course people pretended Catch's magic wasn't real. It was safer to deny something that couldn't be defined by the laws of nature than to be branded as crazy. Rachel was living proof of that. But they believed Catch when it mattered. And maybe that made all the difference in whether or not Catch's magic worked on them.

Rachel had convinced herself long ago that even having someone believe her about Michael when he first went missing wouldn't have made a difference. But now she couldn't help but wonder how differently things might have turned out if just one person had.

"Why do people still eat your pies? I mean, they have to know the person feeding it to them is trying to keep them from telling anyone what they know."

"It's a give-and-take kind of thing. If they keep someone's secret, that person will keep theirs when the time comes. My pies are just the insurance."

Catch pressed the dough into a tin pan and used a rubber brush to paint words on the bottom in butter. She closed her eyes, her lips moving but no sound escaping, and then wiped her hands on her navy polka-dot apron. Handing Rachel the bowl of peaches, she motioned for her to dump them into the pie crust.

Whatever Catch had written to bind the girl's secret had spread out into a thin layer of butter, hiding all traces of the letters. Rachel tipped the bowl down. The slices of fruit marinating in sugar and their own juice tumbled out and mounded in the dish. She took the wooden spoon Catch waved at her.

She still couldn't quite wrap her brain around the fact that Catch's pies were a normal part of life in Nowhere. Would people have accepted her ability as easily if she'd grown up here instead of Memphis?

Spreading the fruit into an almost even layer, she said, "So, no one thinks you've lost your mind?"

"Just because it sounds strange doesn't mean it's not true. I've baked a pie for nearly everyone in Nowhere at some point in their lives. Some, like the girl we're making this one for, come to me pretty regular. Ann Louise, bless her heart, couldn't hold her liquor if she were a cup. And she can't seem to turn the boys away when she's a couple drinks in. So I'm thinking maybe it's not such a bad thing that what I can do helps keep everybody out of her business."

"Maybe she should just stop drinking," Rachel said, guilt over her mom's heavy drinking making her voice go sharp.

Catch's head whipped around, ready to put Rachel in her place, but whatever she saw on Rachel's face caused her own to soften. "That's not for us to say."

Hands shaking, Rachel mumbled, "Somebody should. Before it's too late."

"That may be. But she came to me for pie, not a lecture, so that's what I'm gonna give her," Catch said. She slid the pie into the oven, the glass dish scraping over the metal rack in a high-pitched squeal, and set the timer. "If and when she gets to the point where she's ready for help, she'll stop coming to me and go to someone who can give her what she needs."

Rachel couldn't look at any of Catch's pies the same way. Though most of them were just plain old pies. No magic required. The fact that they could be something more sent a current of anticipation through her body.

And she thought for the hundredth time since the night before, *Maybe Catch can make all the wishes disappear.*

She hadn't worked up the nerve to ask Catch yet—really it was more telling Catch about her past than asking for a favor that stopped her—but the end result was the same.

Then while eating breakfast Catch offered her a different kind of favor. "I talked to Everley, whose froufrou soap shop you stumbled into," she said. "And if you're interested, she said she's looking for some part-time help."

Whether Rachel was interested or not hadn't really mattered. In addition to giving her a place to stay, Catch had now found her a job. That kind of looking-after wasn't something she could turn down.

So she took Catch's directions—scribbled in a tight scrawl just barely large enough to read—and somehow she found her way back to Everley's shop.

The space next door to LUX had the same wide front window, but instead of lotions and soaps and other skin-care products, it had a SORRY FOR THE GOD-AWFUL MESS sign taped to the inside of the glass. She looked in as she passed. Ashe stood next to a petite brunette, scowling. His hands, spread wide against one wall, held in place a large sheet of paper that curled at the edges.

Rachel moved away from the window before Ashe could see her. She'd only known him for a couple of days but she already knew it was best to stay out of his way when he had that look on his face. As she opened the door to LUX, the same calming feeling she'd had the day before washed over her. The scents of chamomile, lavender, aloe, and mint were subtle, yet distinct, despite swirling in the air together.

"I've been hoping all morning that you'd come back," Everley said. She snipped another piece of ribbon from a spool before setting the scissors down and coming out from behind the counter. A few pieces from the pile she'd been building spilled to the floor in a flutter of pale pink.

Rachel picked them up and handed them back. "Thanks again for helping me out yesterday."

"You are so welcome. I'm sorry you were having such a crap day, but you look tons better today, no offense."

"Today is much better." She looked to where the wish had been the day before, but it was gone. *Fool me once*, she thought, and vowed not to read anything that had the potential to be a wish to keep from accidentally granting any more. "So, Catch mentioned you were looking for some help."

"I am. Have you worked retail before?"

"Bookstores mostly. And a decent stint at a coffeehouse. All in all, I think it's about six years of retail and/or customer service."

Everley twisted the ribbons around her fingers and let them go as she thought. "Great. The coffee shop wasn't an organic one by any chance, was it?"

"No. Just your we-burn-all-our-beans-on-purpose type."

"Ooh, Janelle down at Elixir, our local coffee shop, would love that description. Do you happen to know anything about holistic medicine or organic soaps and lotions?" Everley asked.

"I know what they are. But that's as far as it goes," Rachel said.

"That I can teach you. If you're interested."

"That would be—"

A groan emanated from behind a plastic tarp blocking a doorway in the wall, cutting her off.

"Ev!" a voice called from the other side of the building. The woman Rachel had seen fighting with Ashe pushed through the plastic sheeting separating the rooms. In a pencil skirt, sleeveless plum-colored shirt, and kitten heels, she looked grateful to be out of the construction zone. "I'm going to kill him."

Ashe was a few steps behind her, his shoulders pulled back so he looked even broader, taller than usual. "Hey, Rachel," he said, smiling before it dropped off his face, his scowl deepening when he looked to the woman again.

"Hey," Rachel said.

"Jordan, this is Rachel," Everley said, placing a hand on Rachel's arm. "She just got to town and is staying with Miss Sisson."

Jordan put her anger on hold long enough to give Rachel a smile and say, "Nice to meet you."

"You too," Rachel said.

"I'm expanding into the space next door. Ashe designed what it will look like. And Jordan's going to make it all look fabulous." Everley gave them both pointed looks as if to say *don't screw it up.*

"It would be easier if Ashe and his immovable walls weren't getting in my way." Jordan shoved him lightly and scrunched up her face in annoyance when he didn't budge. She was almost as short as Rachel, her dark hair twisted into a sleek bun to match the classic lines of her outfit. Rachel itched to brush off the streak of white powder on Jordan's skirt.

"No, things would be easier if *someone* quit trying to redesign the space every other day," Ashe said. He shifted away from Everley when her hand twitched toward him as if she smacked him regularly.

"I swear to God, if y'all don't start getting along I'm going with Jamie's fight-to-the-death idea," Everley said. "Winner has to do whatever the hell I want over there."

"How is that winning?" he asked.

Without thinking, Rachel said, "Well, you get to live." Ashe turned to her, his blue eyes narrowed as he tried to figure her out, and she smiled to let him know she was teasing. She wasn't sure if her ease around him was due to the calming effect the shop—and its owner—seemed to have on her or if she just wanted to determine if they could be friends.

Ashe dropped his head so a hunk of hair fell across his eyes. "Funny." His jaw was tight, whether from annoyance or trying not to laugh, Rachel couldn't tell.

"Ooh, I knew I liked you," Everley said, pointing a finger at Rachel, who felt the sincerity of the words all the way to her toes.

"Getting along with her is not as easy as you'd think," Ashe said. "Now, if you'll excuse me, I've gotta go figure out how in the hell to make this whole thing work." He scowled at the room at large, then shoved back through the plastic into the work zone.

"So no fight to the death?" Jordan asked.

"Maybe next time," Everley said, chuckling. Then she turned to Rachel and said, "So we're all good, right? You'll be back later this week to start work?"

"Sounds good."

And just like that, Rachel had a job. If only everything in her life could fall into place that easily.


Instead of going inside when she got back to Catch's, she followed the path into the backyard, tempted by the sweet scent that carried to her from the grove of trees she had seen from her attic room. The trees were only a few feet taller than she was, but when Rachel wandered between them, letting the soft leaves slip through her fingers, the rest of the world faded away. She stopped just before the trees ended near Ashe's yard. She wrinkled her nose and almost choked on the scent of rotting fruit that emanated from the last tree, its leaves half-dead and crackling in the breeze.

Turning away from the trees, she found Catch watching her from the kitchen window, but from the distance Rachel couldn't make out her expression. She headed toward the house, the scent of rotting fruit dissipating with each step. By the time she reached the back porch, she wondered if she'd even smelled it at all.

Inside, the air was almost as hot as it was in the yard, without the benefit of the slight breeze. She lifted her hair off her neck and fanned herself with her free hand.

"Everything all right out there?" Catch asked.

"Just checking out your fruit trees. They must produce a lot of fruit for you to bake as much as you do."

"They do when they want to." Catch peeled plastic wrap from a thick disc of dough, and a cloud of flour puffed into the air when she slapped the dough onto the counter. "You wanna roll that out for me? An eighth-inch thick."

Taking the rolling pin, Rachel moved across the counter from Catch and started working the dough. "Is this pie just a pie, or are you making it for someone?"

"And how is that any of your business, Miss-Likes-to-Change-the-Subject?"

"I'm sorry. I didn't mean it like that," Rachel said, her cheeks heating up. "I'm just curious. Not about the secrets. I don't want to know those. But how did you know you could do what you do with the pies? That doesn't seem like something you just stumble into."

Though that's exactly what Rachel had done. She'd never met anyone else who could do anything strange, magical. But she'd always hoped she would. Not just so she'd have someone to confide in who wouldn't call her crazy, but maybe they would've understood her ability in a way she never had. Maybe together they would've made things better.

Maybe she and Catch still could.

"Someone always has to be the first to fumble their way through learning the rules to something they don't understand. If you're lucky, it's not you and someone else can teach you when your time comes." Catch added sugar, salt, orange juice, and vanilla into a bowl of halved strawberries and mixed them together with her hands. "My great-gran was the first in our family. She was widowed young and had kids to feed, so she used what she knew of herbs and the fruit trees that grew on her land to make pies. And she wasn't one for talking, which made her really good at listening. Her friends and neighbors would sit in the kitchen while she baked, telling her things they couldn't keep to themselves, knowing she wouldn't tell a soul. After a while, she noticed that whatever secrets were told while she was baking couldn't be shared by anyone who ate the pie."

*Spoken words were enough for wishes but not for secrets?* "So it only works if they eat the pie?"

Catch nodded. "Just a bite'll do it. But most people eat the whole thing anyway just because it's pie."

Satisfied with the size and thickness, Rachel set the rolling pin aside. "I'm still surprised more people aren't suspicious of all the pies being eaten in this town. Wouldn't they want to know if someone's keeping a secret from them?"

Laughing, Catch rinsed her hands and wiped them dry on her apron, leaving watery red smudges on the fabric. "Oh, I'm sure they do. But that's between them and the one who ordered the pie. Once the pie is made, I stay out of it."

"Does it ever go wrong?" She didn't look at Catch when she asked. Couldn't. Not with the guilt of wishes she'd screwed up burning across her face.

"Wrong how?"

"I don't know," she said. *Wrong like erasing a person.* "Do some secrets get out anyway?"

"Not unless the owner of the secret lets it slip. Then it's fair game for anyone to talk about," Catch said. She worked her fingers under the dough and lifted it onto the waiting dish.

Rachel leaned against the counter, another question tumbling out in her desire to know as much as she could about Catch and her pies. To see if there was a way for Catch to bind her ability along with all the secrets she was keeping. To see if there was anything good that could come from granting wishes. "Do you ever turn people away?"

"Of course I do. Not everyone deserves my help. And besides, some secrets can make things better when they're shared."

"How do you know what secrets shouldn't be kept?"

"I don't know until I hear it. And then it's just a gut feeling. But I'm big on trusting my gut."

Rachel nodded. But she had no idea if her gut could be trusted. At least not when it came to making wishes come true.

# 9

Rachel started her new job the following week, after Everley rescheduled twice due to a design change in the new workspace that was taking all of her attention. Not that Rachel minded an extra few days spent baking with Catch and napping on the front porch. But she was grateful to get back to the routine that came with having a job. The busier she was, the less time she had to obsess over wishes and binding secrets, and whether the latter could cure her of the former.

"You do all this yourself?" she asked, scanning the dozens of different product types spread around the shop in even more jars and bars and tins and bags. All were stickered or tagged with LUX's logo and a pink or gray ribbon tied on for decoration.

"I do," Everley said, looking around the shop with a proud smile. "I started with just soaps, but the more I learned, the more I wanted to do a whole line of face creams and lotions and scrubs. People come from all over the state to buy from me. I even have one woman in Texas who has me ship stuff to her."

"That's cool. So, what's this?" Rachel asked, holding up a small vial of milky liquid. The cork stopper had been sealed onto the glass tube with dark red wax.

"That's chamomile and lavender bath scent. A couple drops in the bath water will make the whole room smell fantastic." Everley waved an arm through the air. "Feel free to open things up and take a look. Smell stuff. Try to get a feel for the types of things we have and where they're displayed. I've got an inventory sheet in a binder behind the counter if you want to see what's on hand."

Rachel hunted in the cabinet and found the binder buried under a stack of gift bags. She found the most recent inventory stats about halfway through the book and then flipped to the next page to start filling out a new form. The first item on the list: almond-and-honey salt scrub. For a girl whose beauty products consisted of black eyeliner, a tube of mascara, and one shade of lipstick, this should be interesting.

She wandered to the left front corner and started reading labels. As she worked her way down the list, she sniffed and rubbed lotions on her forearm that caused a slight tingling sensation as her skin cooled a few degrees and dabbed on a thin sheen of honey-flavored lip balm. She straightened as she went, aligning bottles and stacking bars of soap so their edges were straight.

The door let in a gush of hot air as an elderly man walked in, his shoes shuffling on the floor. The skin around his eyes wrinkled behind his glasses as he surveyed the shelves of products.

Rachel wrote down the number of honeysuckle candles she'd just counted and greeted him. Instead of moving to help him, Everley just smiled at Rachel, then tilted her head toward the man, encouraging her to assist him.

Setting the binder down, she caught his eye and asked, "Can I help you find something?"

"I hope so. I've never been in here before, but Martha at the drug-store sent me over. She said if anyone had something that might work, it'd be y'all."

"Well, I hope so too. It's my first day here but I'll see what I can do."

"I didn't think I recognized you," the man said. He smiled at her, the papery skin of his cheeks sagging around the set-in laugh lines flanking his mouth. "I've lived in Nowhere all my life and delivered most of the babies born here for more than fifty years. Good to know I didn't forget someone." He patted her arm, chuckling.

Rachel laughed with him. "Wow, strangers must really stick out to you, huh?"

"Yes, but I'm always happy to see a new face around here. Now that that's settled, I'm looking for some lotion for my wife. Back when we first got married she used this nice-smelling lotion, like roses. They don't make that kind anymore, but I thought maybe you'd have something that would come close. I know it would make her happy."

"Let's see what we can find." With his hand still on her arm, Rachel led him to the shelves of lotions. "I came across a wildflower lotion that reminded me of my grandmother. She used to wear tea rose perfume. Just let me figure out which one it is."

She trailed her fingers along the embossed labels on the mason jars as she read their names.

"Far right, bottom shelf, rose-colored rubber band around the lid," Everley called from across the room.

"Thanks," Rachel said, locating the sample jar and holding it up for the man to test the scent.

He shook his head and said, "Do you mind putting it on? I don't want to go around smelling like I've been with some other gal when I go visit my Anne this afternoon."

"Sure." Rachel pumped a small drop onto her hand and rubbed it in. It was roses and dewy leaves and a hint of spice. "Does this smell like what you remember her wearing?"

He wrapped his cool fingers around her wrist and lifted her hand to his nose. Closing his eyes, he inhaled and swayed slightly. "Now that brings back some good memories. It's different, but familiar. I might just have to get a bottle for me too. Not to wear, of course, but just to keep at the house to open and smell when I need a reminder of how things used to be."

"Is your wife not at home with you?" Rachel asked.

"She has Alzheimer's," he said, lowering his eyes. "She stays where she has people who can look after her and keep her calm when she doesn't remember where she is."

"Oh, I'm sorry."

"I know she's not going to get better, but I wish for just one more good day with her. Just one day where she remembers me and knows how much I love her." He picked up one of the bottles and rolled it in his hands. "Since smells are supposed to help with memories, I'm hoping this lotion can bring back a little spark for her."

A piece of paper no longer than her index finger fluttered around her feet, tickling her ankles. Her first instinct was to ignore it, like she had so many other wishes over the years. But this old man seemed so selfless, so sincere in his love for his wife, that letting his wish go unanswered almost seemed cruel.

For the first time in years, she contemplated purposely granting a wish.

Maybe in another life she could be like Catch, embracing her ability and helping those who were desperate enough to ask. But in this life, she had no control over how a wish turned out. And what if instead of restoring sweet, perfect memories, the wish only brought back painful ones?

Rachel waited until the door shut behind him and then bent to snatch it up. She hesitated a moment, her trembling fingers obscuring the black words. Then she wadded it up without reading. That was the only guarantee nothing would go wrong.

She worked on the inventory for the rest of the morning, her eyes darting to the crumpled wish buried in the trash can. She tested so many products, she joked with Everley that the scents might never come off. She ate a protein bar for lunch because it was the first thing she saw in the Village Market a few doors down. Everley tried to convince her to take a break, but Rachel did better when her hands and mind were occupied.

She was three quarters of the way through wiping down the shelves with a damp cloth when a brunette in a blush-colored shift dress walked in. Everley kissed the woman on the cheek when they embraced. The keyhole slit in the back of her dress ran from the neckline halfway down the spine and was just wide enough to show off a strip of smooth, tan skin.

Rachel pushed up from the floor and rubbed her palms on the

apron Everley had given her. The woman swept her gaze right over Rachel and watched the doorway that led into the expansion.

"Don't you dare start any trouble, Lola," Everley said.

"What? I'm just here to get some night cream. I can't seem to get rid of these circles." She rubbed under her eyes at the flawless skin.

Something about her was familiar. It pecked at Rachel's brain, trying to make the familiarity known. She shook her head and looked away.

"Funny how you've been making special trips in here to get things I know you don't need since Ashe started working next door."

"That's not why I'm here." Lola unscrewed the lid of a mason jar and sniffed. "Did you change the scent on this one?"

"Nope. Still white tea and aloe. Why?"

"It doesn't smell the same. Are you sure nothing's changed?"

Everley took the jar from her, smelled it, then recapped it. "Positive. Now, quit stalling. Even if he does see you over here, he's not going to come talk to you."

"Oh, thanks, Ev. Do you enjoy reminding me that my husband hates my guts?" Lola spoke slowly, adding extra emphasis to the vowels and the hurt in her voice.

*Husband?* Neither Ashe nor Catch had mentioned him being married. But from the sound of it, Rachel guessed they had good reason not to. She kept her eyes trained on the inventory sheet as if she wasn't listening to every word.

"I meant that he won't be the way you want him to. He's not there yet. Maybe you should give him a little—"

"If you tell me to give him space, Everley, so help me, God, I will strangle you."

"Then who would you go crying to?" Everley asked.

Lola shifted her attention to Rachel as if noticing her for the first time. "To her. She can be my new best friend," she said. Turning back to Everley, she added, "Who is she?"

"This is Rachel. She's the one staying with Miss Sisson. Rachel, this is my best friend Lola."

"Lola *Riley*," she clarified, with a possessive curve to her smile.

"I thought you were dropping it," Everley said.

"As long as we're married, I'm a Riley," she said to Everley before turning to Rachel. "And it's so good to meet you, Rachel. I hope you're liking it in Nowhere so far." Her voice was slightly higher pitched, like she was talking to a child or an animal, someone not worth her time.

Rachel bristled at being sized up. She was used to people treating her like that once they knew she'd been hospitalized for exhibiting delusional behavior. She'd hoped she was done with all that now that she was someplace no one knew her. She walked to them and set the rag on the table. Despite the three- or four-inch height difference, she met Lola's appraising stare. The crisp scents from the lotions seemed to sour for a second. Rachel glanced at Everley and forced a smile.

"Everyone's been nice so far," she said.

"I hear Ashe has been showing you around town for Miss Sisson. He's over at her place a lot, but if he's bothering you, don't feel bad about telling him to come back home." Lola's laugh came out light and easy, but Rachel sensed there was a lot more behind it.

"He's not," Rachel said. "He's been really great, actually."

"Well, I'm glad to hear that," Lola said, though she looked anything but.

Everley put a warm hand on Rachel's shoulder. "Lola," she said. The one word forced her friend to take a step back and smile almost like she meant it.

"Sorry," Lola said. "I just wish he'd forgive me already and let me come home. Dragging it out is just ridiculous."

A soft rustling of paper pulled Rachel's attention. She shifted slightly, trying to act like she was still paying attention to whatever Lola said, and looked up. A scrap of paper fluttered from an empty spot of air near the ceiling. She froze, unable to tear her eyes from it. It landed behind the counter with a soft swish of paper on wood.

Her fingers itched to hide the wish. To destroy it so there was zero chance of it coming true. Rachel forced herself to look away.

Ashe hovered just on the other side of the doorway separating the two rooms. He scowled at Lola as she continued complaining about how Catch poisoned Ashe against her. He fisted his hands at his sides and said, "Stop it, Lola."

Lola had the good sense to look contrite. "Ashe, I'm—"

"Don't. I don't want to hear it." He stormed back into the other side.

When Lola started after him, heels stabbing the floor with each hurried step, Rachel ducked behind the counter. She wanted nothing to do with the drama between Lola and Ashe. She had enough to worry about in her own messed-up life.

Something crunched under her foot. She extracted the slip of paper, careful to keep the words facedown so she couldn't accidentally read it, and ripped the wish Lola had made into half a dozen strips.

"No," she whispered. "You don't get to come true. Not if this isn't something he wants."

Rachel found another five slips of paper before she left work around eight that night. They popped up behind bottles of creamy lotion and were twined into the sides of the baskets. One balanced on the edge of the fan blade as it whirled softly above until Everley walked in the back to make another batch of cucumber water. Only then did the paper tip over the edge and drift down to rest on Rachel's outstretched hand. She'd stuffed them all, unread, into her pockets where they refused to crumple.

She blamed Violet's birthday wish. Accidentally granting it had changed things. Opened some sort of crack in her resolve, allowing wishes to slip through despite her refusal to do anything about them. If she didn't find a way to shut it again, the wishes might never stop.

The kitchen at Catch's house was empty, and Rachel was grateful for the solitude. The light over the stove burned a dim light that shone on enough of the tile floor that she could make her way around the island and into the even darker foyer.

Hurrying up the stairs, she tried to ignore the papers in her pockets but they seemed to be getting heavier by the minute. Her shoes scuffed on the carpet runner that ran the length of the second-story hallway. Her pockets felt weighed down, like they'd been filled with wet sand instead of two-inch strips of paper. She stumbled on the carpet's edge but somehow managed to keep herself upright.

Rachel rounded the corner and took the steps to her room two at a time. She trailed one hand on the wall as she ascended. With the door open, a stream of moonlight from the window illuminated the top half of the stairs. She tugged the door closed behind her. It slid along the track with a dull rumbling, and it banged the side wall, then rolled back a few inches. She looked over her shoulder, half-expecting to see someone there. Finding no one, she dug the wishes out of her pockets. The paper pressed crisp and cool against her sweaty fingers. Hands shaking, she stuffed them into the wish box she'd brought from her parents' house and set it on the desk at the top of the stairs.

She forced herself to walk calmly across the room. The hairs on the back of her neck stood up and her arms erupted in goose bumps. Dropping to the bed, she glanced at the box. If she didn't know better, she would have sworn the wishes had multiplied.

She crawled across the bed and shoved open the window. The air, hot and heavy with humidity, rushed in, bringing the scent of apples and something sweet she couldn't place. She turned as the air whispered her name. Leaning on the windowsill, she scanned the yard.

Ashe stood in the yard, so still it looked like he had grown up from the ground. He was far enough away that she couldn't be sure if he'd called out to her or if she'd imagined it. Rachel started to pull back inside when he looked up. She could just make out his half smile through the dark.

"Going to bed already?" he called up.

"Is there some thriving nightlife in Nowhere I've managed to miss?"

"We don't let just anyone in on the debauchery that goes down in this place. You've only been here a week. Jury's still out on whether or not you can handle it."

"What makes you think I want to join in?"

"What? Hanging out with me and a plate of Catch's pie isn't your idea of a good time?" Ashe held a plate in the air as if to prove his point. A sliver of moonlight peeking through the clouds caught it, making the ceramic gleam white.

"The pie, maybe," Rachel said with a laugh. But the thought of sitting close enough to him to eat off his plate made her skin warm. She tried to shove the thought away.

"Then I expect to see you down here in a minute." He walked back toward Catch's house and out of sight.

Rachel watched out the window for a moment, then headed down to meet him. She stopped in the kitchen long enough to get her own piece of blackberry pie, careful not to make too much noise and disturb Catch, who had already gone to bed.

"You had like thirty more seconds and then I was giving up on you," Ashe said from the darkness of the back porch. "Anyone who can resist Catch's pie is not someone I can be friends with."

"Guess it's a good thing her pies are growing on me, huh?"

"Guess so."

She dropped into the chair next to him, hiding her smile behind a forkful of pie. "Do you do this a lot? Come over and sneak pie after Catch is asleep?"

"It's not sneaking. But yeah, this is a pretty regular thing."

"Why don't you just take a pie back to your place instead of having to come over every night?"

He slumped down farther into the chair and kicked his feet up on the railing. His elbow bumped into hers, jostling her plate. "For one, I like coming over here. The company's usually pretty good," he said and slid his eyes to hers as if to say she was letting him down in that department. A smile tugged at the corner of his mouth. "And two, it's easier to justify eating as much pie as I do if I have to walk a little ways to get it."

She laughed. "Completely justifiable."

"Catch told me you've been helping her out some with the baking. You must've really won her over in the past week."

"What makes you say that?"

"Most people only get to touch her pies when they eat them. And by most people, I mean everyone. She's very territorial when it comes to her kitchen," he said.

Rachel's hand paused with the fork halfway to her mouth. "Are you serious? She barely even gives me a choice before she hands me something to do." She'd just assumed Catch was that way with everyone. The fact that she wasn't sent a flush of gratitude through Rachel's chest.

Ashe set his empty plate on the deck, the fork clattering against the plate. "Consider yourself lucky, then. She doesn't open up to a lot of people. Even ones who were in her life and her kitchen every day for years."

She wondered if he was referring to Lola. But she kept the question to herself. Just thinking about Ashe's wife reminded her of the wish she'd ignored earlier. And the ones she'd hidden upstairs. She laid her head back against the chair and looked at the blackening sky instead of at him.

"Wishing on shooting stars?" he asked.

"I don't need stars for that," Rachel said.

# 10

When Rachel woke, the sound of rain beating against the house drowned out the fluttering of paper. She listened, eyes closed tight, grateful for the reprieve. For a few seconds, she thought she'd imagined the wishes fluttering against each other in the box, as if trying to get her attention. It wasn't until a drop of cool water hit her forehead and dribbled into her eye that she jerked fully awake. She lurched forward as the rain pelted her. Still disoriented from sleep, she almost toppled off the side of the bed. She groped for the light on the windowsill. The wet chain pull slipped through her fingers.

She tugged on the window. It didn't budge. She crouched, pressing down on the lip and putting all of her weight into it. She grunted. It still didn't move. Not even an inch. The rain soaked through her tank top within seconds, and the tips of her hair clung to her collarbone.

"Damn it," she said.

She sank back onto the bed as the rain continued to pour in.

Grabbing her pillow and the comforter, Rachel dragged them off the bed, more water dribbling down her arms, and yanked off the sheet next. She balled it up and stuffed it into the window opening to buy a little time. She reached for her phone and realized she didn't have Ashe's number. Leaving it on the desk far from the window, she jogged down the stairs on the balls of her feet.

The dark kitchen confirmed her instinct to call Ashe. If Catch wasn't already up and baking, Rachel didn't want to wake her. She found the list of names and numbers where Ashe had told her it would be and dialed his number on the old house phone attached to the wall between the kitchen and the laundry room.

He picked up on the second ring and instead of saying hello, he asked, "What's wrong?" His voice was tense, hard with worry.

"It's Rachel. My window is stuck open and the rain is soaking everything. I can't get it to close, and I don't want it to ruin any of Catch's things. I didn't know what else to do," she said in a rush.

"But Catch is okay?"

"Yes, I think so. I didn't want to wake her up."

"So, you thought you'd wake me up instead?"

Rachel startled as lightning flashed across the sky. Thunder followed a few seconds later. "If I'd gone to her, she would've called you, so you'd be woken up anyway. Can you please just come help me?"

"I'll be there in a minute."

By the time she got back upstairs to wait by the window, he was already racing through the backyard, rain soaking him. She didn't hear the back door slam shut and could just make out the footfalls of his shoes on the stairs.

When he stepped into the room, she momentarily forgot why he was there. His T-shirt slicked across his chest and molded to the tight muscles underneath. He dragged his wet hair back off his face and caught her staring at him. His smile was quick and sent a jolt of heat through her.

She looked away. "No umbrella?"

"I don't mind being a little wet." He walked across the room, water and grass transferring from his shoes to the floor with each step. "So, let's see this window." He walked over to the bed, toed off his shoes.

"What're you doing?"

"Unless you can make me levitate, I'm going to have to get on the bed to see what's going on with the window."

"Right. Sorry," Rachel said.

Kneeling on the bed, he yanked on the window. It didn't budge for him either. He tried to push it open a little farther, the muscles in his arms tightening and flexing beneath the sleeves of his tee. He slipped a mallet from a belt loop on his jeans and tapped the rubber end along the top edge of the window frame. It shifted an inch or so. He stood, braced his butt against the side wall, and shimmied the window back and forth. With another nudge of the mallet, it dropped with a sharp *thwack*.

Rachel jumped and steadied herself with a hand on the back of the chair. Her fingernails dug into the soft velvety fabric.

Ashe slid the window up and down a few more times to make sure it wasn't a fluke. "Should be okay now. If it starts acting up again, just give a holler," he said.

He started to move off the bed, but paused in front of Rachel's family photo on the shelf. Squatting, he lifted the thin gold frame. He narrowed his eyes at the empty space between Rachel and her parents, where Michael had been.

Holding the picture so it faced her, he asked, "Why are you standing so far away from your parents? Did you have an imaginary friend or something you wanted in the picture with you?" He flashed her a teasing smile.

Rachel grabbed it from him and hugged it to her chest. "That's just the way the photographer positioned us," she said to keep him from asking any more questions. To keep the truth of her brother from coming out. She carried the picture to the other end of the room and set it facedown on the desk. She leaned against the closet door, watching him. "Thanks for fixing the window."

Ashe climbed off the bed and then sat on it to retie his laces. He looked up at her from under thick, dark lashes. His smile was crooked, like he knew she was hiding something. "Anytime," he said.

Instead of going back downstairs, he stopped in front of one of the bookcases. She told herself that he was just checking to make sure she hadn't nicked the shelves. But she knew better. Even before he ran his index finger along the edge of the wish box—which sat open on the desk though she didn't remember opening it—she knew she should have thrown them away or burned them. Keeping them all out in the open was just the type of thing that would pique Ashe's interest. Though she hadn't expected to have him in her bedroom to ever see the box and wonder what it was.

Curiosity lit up his eyes when he looked at her. "What's this?"

Rachel stood and shifted so her body was angled away from the wishes like her world didn't revolve around them. "Nothing." She sucked in a breath when he dipped his hand inside to tease the paper.

"Hexes on former boyfriends?" Ashe removed a few pieces of paper. Even from the distance, Rachel could see ink, still dark and solid, refusing to fade despite her ignoring them. He fingered one with his thumb, but kept his eyes on hers instead of reading it. "Super-secret spy hit list?"

"Put them back," she said. It came out as a half command, half plea. She balled her shaking hands at her sides and waited. After another few seconds, she said, "I mean it, Ashe."

He dropped the pieces back into the box one at a time. One caught on the lip of the box and hung there until he flicked it back inside. Holding his empty hands up in surrender, he said, "So, you do have secrets."

"And you don't have any respect for other people's privacy. Now get out."

"Oh, c'mon, Rachel. You can't be mad at me for being curious."

Rachel gave him a little shove to get him moving. He believed in what Catch could do, so he might believe in her too. But that wasn't a risk she was willing to take. Not yet anyway.

She was still getting used to the idea that her job was more hanging out with a friend for six hours a day than actual work. Rachel tried to keep busy, earn her keep. But Everley was making it increasingly difficult.

"You did that yesterday," Everley said as Rachel Windexed the front window.

Not bothering to turn around, she replied, "Doesn't mean it doesn't need it again."

"I don't pay you enough for you to work twice as hard as me. Please come sit down. Oh, and here comes a very good excuse."

The man walking through the construction doorway was well over six feet tall, with skin the color of the bark on the black cherry tree in Catch's yard and a bright smile. Even in the heat, he wore a full suit with a fuchsia tie knotted tight at his neck. He shifted a take-out bag to one hand and gave Ashe a combination hand-shake hug.

"That one's taken," Everley said, catching her staring.

"Lucky girl," Rachel said. "He's gorgeous."

"Yes, I am. And oh, yes he is. You should see him without his clothes."

"That might be a little awkward, seeing as how he's *your* boy-friend and you're *my* boss," Rachel said.

Everley grinned at her. "Spoilsport."

"Hello, ladies," the man said when he came in. "I thought you might like some lunch." He tangled his hands in Everley's hair and molded his mouth to hers. Everley slid her hands inside his suit jacket and pulled him closer until there was not even air between them as their greeting continued.

Rachel tried to blend into the background.

"Cut it out," Ashe yelled from the other side. "Some of us are trying to eat."

"And some of us are giving our girl a proper hello," he called back. But he released Everley, and, smiling at Rachel, he introduced him-self. He was even better looking up close. His head was shaved close and he had a thin goatee of black stubble. Rectangular reading glasses framed thick, long eyelashes and golden eyes. "How're you liking Nowhere so far?" Jamie asked her.

"It's nice. A little slower paced than Memphis, but I'm enjoying that actually."

"You should try coming here after law school in D.C. That's a hell of an adjustment." He set the paper bag on the counter and emptied it. "One apple walnut salad, one strawberry pecan, and two grilled cheeses. You two can fight over who gets what."

"You're not staying?" Everley asked. She stuck out her bottom lip and pouted.

"Can't. I've got to take a deposition at one. See you for dinner?"

Everley grabbed him by the lapels and pulled him back to her for another kiss. "You're on." She smacked his ass when he turned around.

"Be good, ladies," he called as the door closed behind him.

Holding the salads behind her back, Everley said, "Pick a hand."

Rachel played along, pointing and saying, "Left."

"Ooh, good choice. Strawberry pecan." She handed the clamshell container to Rachel along with a small container of pink dressing with poppy seeds floating in it.

Rachel shook it and watched the oil bubble back to the top. She pried off the top and poured half on her salad in three concentric circles, making sure she coated each section evenly.

"You might as well just dump the rest on there. It's that good." Everley upended her container onto the middle of her salad. She used her fork to toss it all around. "You coming over to eat with us, Ashe?" she yelled.

Rachel stiffened at the idea of being close to him again. She tried not to think about how good he'd looked soaking wet and smiling at her like he knew exactly what it was doing to her.

Ashe's voice was bright, playful when he called back, "I don't think my burger is allowed over there in vegan-hippie land."

"Damn right it's not," Everley said, laughing.

"So how long have you and Jamie been together?" Rachel asked.

"Four or five years, I guess. We broke up for about six months once, but we don't really count that. I mean, my grandparents took a twenty-some-odd-year break, married other people, and then got back together."

"Wow."

"They celebrated their fiftieth anniversary a few years back. If they don't count a quarter of a century apart, I don't think six months is even a blip on the radar."

"Well, I guess that's one way to reach the milestone anniversaries."

Everley waved her fork through the air, dribbling dressing onto the floor, as she said, "They're a little weird. But who am I to buck family tradition?" She grinned at Rachel. "So, is there somebody waiting on you back home?"

"I'm not good with relationships," Rachel confessed. She folded her napkin in half and tucked it under the salad container. "I'm not sure if it's that I don't like them or they don't like me. Either way, I don't seem to stay in them very long." She imagined Mary Beth chiding her that her relationships might have worked out if she'd trusted any of the guys enough to be honest with them about her past.

"I was like that before Jamie. I tried on boys like most girls tried on shoes. Lola always lectured me about how great it was when you found the right one and kept pushing me to settle down. But I figure if it's meant to be, it'll work itself out with or without me."

Rachel glanced at the wall that separated Ashe from them. She wondered what had happened to make Lola change her outlook on love, what had happened to make Ashe so willing to end their marriage.

That's not something she wanted to be in the middle of. With the way the wishes had been acting, she might be tricked into hurting Ashe with one of Lola's wishes if she got too involved. She needed to leave it alone. Leave him alone.

# 11

The wishes in the box had been multiplying for days, but somehow they never spilled out over the rim. She found them under her plate at breakfast, in the pockets of her bathrobe, and beneath the sheet of glass on her family photo, filling the empty space. A few even popped into existence in the air above the box to save her the trouble of picking them up and adding them to the mass of white that was accumulating.

When another piece of paper appeared as she headed downstairs, she flicked it off the door handle and continued down without a backward glance.

"What are you baking today?" Rachel asked when she got to the kitchen.

Catch raised her eyebrows at her. "Why? You have something specific you need me to make?"

Rachel thought of the piles of wishes, and the empty space in the family photo that looked like someone had been rubbed out. "No."

"Suit yourself. As for your question, I'm making some tarts and a whole mess of pies for the farmers' market tomorrow. C'mon. I could use an extra pair of hands," Catch said. She handed Rachel a thick braided basket and shoved through the screen door.

The basket was heavier than it looked. Carrying it in one hand, it scraped against Rachel's calves when she followed Catch into the yard.

"What kind are they?" she asked, pointing to the trees.

The branches reached three times as wide, but the trunks weren't much thicker around than the fruit they produced. The leaves varied in size and shade of green, throwing that section of the yard into contrasts of bright and dark, shadow and light.

"A mixture. I've got dwarf golden queen peaches there and some Moonglow dwarf pear next to 'em. There's a cherry over there at the end and a few semidwarf Fuji, Honeycrisp, and Lodi apples in the back."

Rachel could only tell the difference between them by the types of fruit. The varieties of each were lost on her.

"What's the shriveled one?"

"A pain in my ass. Damn plum tree just won't die."

"You don't like plums?"

"Not those. But I can't seem to kill it." Catch stopped in front of the dwarf pear. She stroked its trunk like a cat. She rubbed the leaves between her fingers and they gave off a sweet, fragrant scent.

Rachel leaned close to the leaves. They tickled her cheeks. Closing her eyes, she inhaled and could already smell the tart they'd yet to start making. "I didn't know trees did that. I thought it was only herbs that were aromatic."

"My trees are special. They don't always act like normal trees. And their fruit don't taste like normal fruit. That's why they make the best pies."

Rachel stepped back and noticed black patches crawling along the underside of a couple leaves. Lifting the tip of one, she turned it over. In the light it was pale green and velvety. She turned the next one looking for the spots that had been there a moment before.

"What is it?" Catch asked.

"Oh, I just thought I saw something. Dark marks or spots or something. Must've been a trick of the light."

Catch studied the tree, eyes narrowed in interest. Then she threw a hateful look in the direction of the decaying plum tree. "Stop it," she said. Her voice was firm, like scolding a disobedient child.

"Was it an animal or something?"

"Just forget about it. But if it comes back, you let me know."

"Yeah, sure," Rachel said. She blinked against the bright green of the trees in front of them. Whatever had happened—imagined or not—Catch seemed to know exactly what it was. Though she apparently wasn't keen on sharing it with Rachel. She set the basket on the ground between them. "It was probably just me seeing things."

"Well, let's get these picked. You want to look for ones that are about as wide around as your fist." She held her knobby, clenched hand out to demonstrate. Her knuckles were swollen and red, probably from all the dough kneading and work she did around the gardens. "Well, maybe not your scrawny fist," she added when Rachel held hers out too.

"I think I get the point," Rachel said.

"Good. Now before you start picking 'em, make sure they're ripe. But don't squeeze too hard or you'll bruise 'em."

Rachel reached for one. The skin was grainy, but slick. Her fingers sank into the pear's flesh with minimal pressure and brown juice oozed out. It trickled down her fingers, stinging and turning her skin a blistering red as it went. Jerking her hand away she said, "I don't think your tree likes me." She shook her hand, and the juice dripped off.

"Good Lord," Catch said. She threw out her arm to block Rachel from the tree. "Just stay back a minute." She took a small spray bottle from her apron pocket and began misting the tree with a milky white liquid that clung to the leaves. Within seconds it evaporated in the heat.

"What's going on?"

"I told you the trees sometimes have a mind of their own. And one of them is trying to spread its poison to the rest. This'll stop it for now and we can move on about our day. Give me your hands. We need to get that cleaned off."

Catch sprayed the liquid onto Rachel's hands. Some of the mist landed on her shirt, leaving dark specks on the cotton. Despite the oppressive heat, the liquid was chilly. It tingled as it ate through the juice on her hands. It smelled like licorice and lemon. She held her hands out, fingers splayed, as the mixture turned runny and dripped off.

"Don't worry. I'll rinse you off with the hose before we go in," Catch said.

"I'm more worried that my skin is going to melt off."

"I ain't gonna put something corrosive on you or my trees. Now just keep holding 'em like that until I'm done." She squeezed and plucked, squeezed and plucked until the basket was laden. She hefted it with both hands so it rested against her thighs, as if she could move it along with the sheer force of her body.

"Come hose me down and I'll carry it," Rachel said.

"And how are you gonna do that? This basket probably weighs as much as you."

*You're one to talk.* "Then I'll take one side and you take the other. I can't just stand around while you break your back carrying that."

Rachel followed her around the side of the house where the hose was curled up, sleeping in the sun. She scrubbed her hands in the warm water. They felt like the underside of a rabbit pelt and were the pink of fresh skin after a scab falls off. She rubbed them back and forth trying to decide if she still had feeling in them.

"Oh, you'll be fine," Catch said.

Dropping them to her sides, Rachel went back to fetch the basket. They carried it together. Their steps were jerky, lopsided, the basket bobbing between them.

"I think I'm going to have a bruise," Rachel said after hoisting the fruit onto the counter.

"I've got something for that too, if it comes to that."

"Did you make it?"

"God, no. Your boss and I have an arrangement. I give her fruit. She makes me ointment, lotion, salve, what have you."

"Did she make whatever it was you sprayed on me?"

"That one's a personal concoction. I had to come up with something to keep the plum tree at bay. This isn't perfect, but it's the best I've been able to come up with so far." Catch pulled the spray bottle from her apron pocket and stashed it under the sink next to a bottle of dark liquid.

Rachel picked a pear from the top of the pile. It was firm and lumpy. When Catch handed her a peeler, she started to slice small strips of skin from it. Without something to put them in, they littered the counter like wood shavings.

"Who the hell taught you to peel something like that?" Catch scolded.

She took the pear from Rachel and set it on the counter. Selecting another one from the basket, she took a second peeler and, holding it sideways, wound around the pear so that the skin came off in one long trail. She set the naked fruit in a colander on the counter.

"Are you going to kick me out of the kitchen if I butcher it?"

"Maybe," Catch said, cackling. Her laugh echoed around the room. She thumped Rachel on the back. "Go on, then. We don't have all day."

Rachel's first attempt resulted in six strips of skin. Her second, seven. She scraped a knuckle on her right hand raw and had to stick it in her mouth to staunch the bleeding before Catch could see.

She peeled one for every three of Catch's. When she started on the last one, she'd managed to get down to two or three longish strips.

Catch shrugged, unimpressed. She uncovered a tart pan with six scallop-edged wells already pressed with dough.

Rachel took the paring knife from the block and started slicing the pears lengthwise in thin strips. As the pieces started to pile up, she asked, "How many tarts are we making?"

"So, it's 'we' now, is it?"

"Well, you are letting me live in your house free of charge. I figured the least I can do is help you bake so you don't look like you could keel over at any minute."

"Look that bad, do I, Miss-Pretty-Young-Thing?" Catch asked. Her raspy laugh rolled into a deep, hacking cough. With one hand pressed to her stomach, she extended the other to keep Rachel back. "Oh, don't look at me like that. I'm fine."

Rachel wanted to press her for an explanation, but the tight set of Catch's mouth, which caused the wrinkles around her lips to straighten out, said she had no right to whatever secrets Catch was keeping. Like with whatever was going on with the trees. It would only become her business if Catch decided to tell her.

# 12

The sky was still hazy and purplish pink when Catch backed the car up to one of the booths at the farmers' market the next morning. For once, Rachel understood why someone would have a car that more closely resembled a boat. She couldn't see the fabric or carpeting of the backseat, floorboards, or trunk through the stacks of cardboard boxes and baskets filled with sweets they had stuffed inside.

Ashe looked up from underneath a half-erected tent. His hand slipped on the rope and the white vinyl sagged on one side.

"Quit gawking before you bring the whole damn thing down on our heads," Catch said. She nudged Rachel in the back with her knobby elbow to get her to move out of the way.

He tightened his grip and flashed a smile at Rachel.

Rachel unloaded boxes of tarts, pies, and fried pocket pies while Ashe secured the tent ropes to paint buckets he'd hauled over from Everley's shop. Rachel had helped Catch wrap the individual-sized pies in plastic wrap the night before. The tips of her fingers were bruised from scraping over the tiny metal spikes on the lip of the box as she tore off sheet after sheet of plastic. They covered the table with as many as they could fit and then lined up the remaining supply behind the canvas chairs they'd brought.

Ashe set the cooler between them, toed it with the end of his boot. "It's gonna be hot today. Make sure you drink a lot," he said.

"Doubt we'll be here that long," Catch told him.

Rachel scanned the square. There were two dozen or so tents set up along the perimeter. Some had signs promoting their wares. Others, like Catch's, relied on the goods themselves to snag the attention of passersby. There were baskets of fruits and vegetables, bouquets of pink and yellow and purple flowers, loaves of bread, rows of herbs and other small potted plants, paintings and woodwork, organic soaps and lotions from Everley's store, jars of honey ranging from pale gold to almost black, and one tent that had jugs of moonshine stacked on the ground half-hidden by a table hocking flavored sweet tea.

Before Catch had retrieved the cash box from the car, a line had formed in front of their booth.

"What do I do?" Rachel asked.

"Tell 'em what we have and sell until we're out," Catch said. She helped the first person in line, shooing them away as soon as they'd swapped money for pie. "And if they're looking for something special, remind them my back door's always open."

"Got it."

Ashe lingered by the tent, eyes focused on Rachel. Heat crept into her cheeks. Her shirt stuck to her shoulder blades, exposing a strip of her skin above the band of her shorts each time she reached over the table to hand someone back their change. She felt his eyes still on her and tugged it back down. When she looked at him over her shoulder, ready to stare him into retreat, he sent her a lazy smile that sent a rush of heat across her skin. Her lips betrayed her by smiling back. She forced herself to turn around, to ignore the thrill of electricity that coursed along her skin. She focused on the twenty-something who couldn't make up her mind between the pear tart and a slice of the bourbon pecan pie. With a conspiratorial whisper of "If it were me, I'd have to get both. Calories be damned," Rachel convinced her to do just that.

For the next hour, she and Catch shifted around each other, handing off pies and making change with barely a word. It was easy. Comfortable. Like it was exactly what Rachel was supposed to be doing on a summer Saturday morning. They had depleted their stock on the table and were most of the way though the remaining inventory in boxes behind them before the crowd let up enough to breathe. Most customers just wanted pie, not what Catch could do for their secrets. But here and there someone would whisper in Catch's ear something Rachel couldn't hear, and her heart would kick up speed for a few beats as she scanned the air for a wish. But the morning remained blissfully wish-free.

A thick layer of clouds helped keep the heat to a bearable level. The breeze, however, stopped at the edge of the tent, blocked by the wall of people. Rachel wiped a layer of sweat from her brow with the back of her wrist.

"You need water," Ashe said as he waded back under the tent. When neither woman stopped long enough to get a bottle from the cooler, he did it for them. Uncapping the water, he shoved a bottle into each of their hands and didn't move until they had taken a few sips. "I can't stand here all day making sure you don't dehydrate, so please promise me you'll keep drinking. Both of you."

"Whatever you say, Mr. Gets-to-Work-in-Air-Conditioning," Catch said. But she took another drink to appease him.

Rachel tipped her bottle back as well, but something about the smile on one of the men's faces a few stalls over caught her attention, and she lowered it without drinking. It was familiar, but she couldn't figure out why or from where. He looked up, caught her staring, and ran a hand through his thick, salt-and-pepper hair.

"I'd steer clear of him if I were you," Ashe said.

"What?" she asked, dropping her gaze to the few remaining pies on the table.

"If you give him even the slightest hint that you'll talk to him, he'll come over here and then you won't be able to shake him until you've agreed to go to dinner with him."

"The town ladies' man?"

"Something like that," Catch said. Her lips tugged down in annoyance, then she took a long swig of water as if trying to drown whatever else she wanted to say about him.

"His ability to charm people is a little more super than natural," Ashe said. "Like Catch, but with decidedly less morals. And he uses it to his advantage whenever possible. Business, pleasure, just because he can. So just watch yourself."

"If people know he's like that, why do they put up with it?" Rachel asked, keeping her eyes off the man, though part of her yearned to get a better look. She wondered how many more people were like her and Catch.

"It's not like he can force anyone to do something they don't want to. He just makes ideas seem so damn good people find themselves going along with him without even thinking. And nobody blames him when he moves on to the next person in line, leaving a mess of broken hearts and bad decisions in his wake."

"Nobody but you?"

"He's my dad." Ashe raked a hand through his hair and said, "I got to learn the hard way."

Rachel nodded, knowing all too well how it felt to have a father who turned lives upside down, though hers had done it by disappearing.

"You've got a bad habit of doing that," Catch said to him. She stared over his shoulder, her frown melting into a grimace. "She could at least have the decency to not flaunt her cheating ass in public."

Ashe's face hardened, his mouth curling down. Rachel didn't have to look to know she was talking about Lola. But she followed Catch's glare so she didn't have to see the pain on Ashe's face.

Lola sidestepped Ashe's dad, turning her attention to a guy who was all cheekbones and thick wavy hair. Despite the noise of the crowd, she was well within hearing distance. Her dark hair danced around her face as she tilted her head back, laughing. She tucked it behind her ear and rested her hand on the arm of the guy she was talking to. There was something familiar about her underneath all of the polish and forced Southern charm. It pricked at the edges of Rachel's mind like a childhood memory long forgotten.

She cut her eyes to Ashe, whose grip on one of the tent's support poles turned his knuckles white. "Are you okay?" she asked.

"Of course he's okay," Catch answered for him. She clucked her tongue and shoved a pocket pie at the next customer in line. "What that girl does now is of no consequence to him. Or to the rest of us. Now both of you look away before she sees you and has the satisfaction of knowing she can still get under your skin."

But it was too late. Lola locked eyes with Ashe, letting her hand slip from the other guy's arm. The confusion clouding the guy's eyes evaporated when he noticed Ashe, and he nodded hastily to Lola before walking away.

Anger pulsed off Ashe in hot waves. Rachel retreated farther into the tent to keep her own anger at how Lola openly flirted with another man not twenty feet from her husband from fueling his more.

Not having the same qualms about keeping Ashe's anger in check, Catch mumbled, "Damn boy never listens to me when it comes to her."

Eyes still on Lola, his shoulders stiffened, but that was the only acknowledgment that he'd heard her. When Lola walked toward him, he met her halfway. He cupped a hand around her elbow when she tried to reach for him.

"Is that him?" he asked, nodding to the guy as he disappeared down the street. His voice traveled over the short distance, loud enough for everyone in the vicinity to hear. The hard edge in his tone said he didn't care.

"Who?" Lola asked.

"You know who."

"God, Ashe." She shook him loose. Arms crossed over her chest, the engagement ring she still wore sparkling in the sun. "Just because I talk to a guy doesn't mean I've slept with him."

"Coulda fooled me," he snarled.

"I know I screwed up, but that does not give you the right to talk to me like this."

When she whirled around, the skirt of her dress twirling around like an umbrella, he followed her. Rachel, along with half the crowd, watched them. The others pretended to be interested in whatever tent they were closest to. He waited until they were on the sidewalk before he stepped in front of her, forcing her to slam against his chest. She shoved at him before looking over her shoulder to see how many people were watching. She narrowed her eyes at Rachel and Catch like the confrontation was their fault.

"Just tell me who it was, Lola. I'm not going to do anything to him. I just want to know."

"We've been over this," she said. Her voice was low but Rachel could just make out the words. "I'm not telling you."

"He ruined our marriage. Why are you protecting him?" Ashe ran a hand through his hair, not looking at her.

"I'm not."

"Then just tell me his name," he insisted.

"Let it go, Ashe."

He turned away from her and caught Rachel's eye. She looked down at the tart in her hand, embarrassment from watching his anger and heartache play out in front of everyone staining her cheeks pink. She understood the need for answers—she'd been there more than once with her parents and therapists where the wishes and Michael were concerned—but sometimes trying to force an issue just made it that much harder to prove. She'd never figured out why no one else remembered her brother when she still did, and she doubted Ashe would ever get a name out of Lola.

When Rachel found Ashe an hour later in the construction half of Everley's shop, he was scribbling something on the checklist he kept taped to the far wall.

"You okay?" Rachel asked. She stepped into the room but stopped before she got too close to him.

"I will be. It's not like arguing with Lola about who she slept with is anything new." The truth of it hung on him, dragging down his shoulders and making his blue eyes dull. He sat on a large paint bucket in the center of the room.

"Still sucks, though," Rachel said. She'd never allowed herself to love a guy enough to be hurt that way by him, but she could imagine how it could haunt a person. How it could drive them mad and steal their grip on reality, even if only temporarily. She shifted her weight back toward the door. "If you want to be alone, I can go."

He tapped a second bucket of paint with his boot for her to join him. "Nah. It's cool. I'm not getting much done anyway. As it is, I might accidentally shoot someone with a nail gun," he said.

She walked farther into the room, extending a pie dish toward him. "Catch thought you could use this," she said, handing it to him. "There weren't any forks."

"Thanks. You gonna help me eat this?"

"I should—"

"No, what you should do is stay. I don't need to eat this whole thing, but I will if you're not here to stop me." Ashe walked to a tackle box on a shelf and pulled out a plastic fork and spoon. He sat back on his bucket and handed her the fork when she sat on the other one.

"I'm not sure how I can say no to that," Rachel said, twisting the fork in her hands. "Especially if I don't want Catch to kick me out for allowing you to wallow in self-pity."

"I do not wallow."

"Could've fooled me."

He dug into the pie, cutting a slice with the edge of the spoon. Strawberry glaze clung to the plastic. He paused with the spoon halfway to his mouth. "After I lick this, I'm going to put it back in the pie. Just thought you should know before I did it."

"But the fact that I plan on eating some isn't going to stop you?" Rachel asked. The intimacy of the situation made her pulse race. She stared at his lips for a fraction of a second before forcing herself to look away.

"It is *my* pie." He smiled at her before sticking the spoon in his mouth.

"Not this piece." She stuck her fork into the crust and carved out her own slice. The sun-warmed strawberry filling tasted like it had just come out of the oven. For the first time in weeks, she was thankful it was so damn hot outside.

They lapsed into a comfortable silence as they took turns digging out bites. The bells on Everley's door chimed as customers came and went. Every so often, a fresh scent of cucumber or coconut or freesia would drift in to mix with the sawdust and paint fumes.

Ashe stared across the room at nothing, as if the scent had muddled his mind. Shaking his head, he asked, "Are you sick of pie yet?"

"I think I've eaten more pie in the past few weeks than I have in my entire life," she said.

He pulled the pan away from her.

"Not that I'm complaining," Rachel said, leaning over him for another forkful. Her elbow brushed his stomach and she braced a hand on his knee to keep from falling off the bucket. The heat from his leg seeped through his jeans and warmed her hand. She took a deep breath and pulled away. When she held her fork in the air, triumphant, a glob of strawberry glaze dripped to the dusty floor. "Damn it."

Ashe suppressed a smile. "You do realize the punishment for wasting perfectly good pie is death, don't you?" he asked, in as serious a voice as he could muster. He looked down at the floor again, shaking his head. With no napkin to clean up the mess, he left it there to seep into the concrete.

"At least I'll die with a happy stomach."

"Since it's your first offense, I guess I can let it slide." He held the dish out to her. They'd already eaten more than half of it.

"I should really stop eating." She reached for another bite, hesitated, and then dropped her fork into the pan. "I'm done. The rest is yours."

"If you think I won't eat it all, you are sadly mistaken. I've got to prepare for the pie-eating contest in a couple weeks. This is my year. I can feel it."

His crooked smile removed all traces of his earlier heartache and frustration. Rachel couldn't help but laugh at his enthusiasm. When he smiled at her like that, something inside her wanted to make it last as long as possible. "Is there really a pie-eating contest?" she asked.

"At the barbecue festival. Catch's grandmother started it, then her mom took over, then Catch. She never had any kids, though, so I'm not sure who her successor will be. A few other ladies have their eye on it, but it just won't be the same if the pies aren't made with Sisson recipes. And Catch isn't about to give those up."

"I'm sure she'd give them to you."

"Only as a last resort. Even then I'd have to promise never to use them, which would defeat the purpose altogether." His smile turned sheepish when she raised a questioning eyebrow at him. "I kinda blew up a mud pie in her oven when I was a kid. Don't think she's completely forgiven me yet. So, she'd be better off giving them to you," he said.

*Yeah, maybe after I've been here twenty years.* The idea that she could put down roots in Nowhere was too overwhelming—too permanent—to even consider yet. "So not very likely, then, huh? And anyway, her trees don't seem to like me much." Rachel shook her head, then regretted bringing it up. How could she explain that Catch's trees tried to poison her? It sounded crazy, which was something she tried hard to avoid. But Ashe seemed to bring that out in her—an inability to keep her guard up around him.

He didn't seem fazed. "They're finicky. The trees. But once you get to know them, you'll figure out what they want."

She swallowed hard. "What do you mean?" She leaned closer to him, her nerves buzzing along her skin.

"Well, the peach trees like to caress people as they walk by; the pear can be stingy with its fruit if the other trees get picked more often than it does; and the plum produces sweet, tart, bland, or sour fruit to match its mood." He grinned and took another bite of pie. "But since I planted the plum tree after accidentally running over its predecessor with my bike, it's only fitting that it's imbued with some of my personality to balance out the other trees."

Rachel searched his face for any sign that he was mocking her. All she found was the familiar confidence that made his eyes sparkle. "You're serious? You actually think they have personalities, like people?"

Ashe nodded. "And whatever is going on with the plum tree seems to be affecting the others. Catch'll find a way to fix them, though. Most of them have been around for generations, so she won't let them go without a fight."

"I get the sense she usually gets her way," Rachel said.

"She got you to stay."

She was surprised to find that made her happy. And a little nervous. With the number of wishes following her around, it was only a matter of time before someone discovered what she could do. And even in a place that accepted Catch's ability so easily, there was no guarantee that they would accept her. "I should go."

Ashe stood when she did. He set the flimsy metal dish on the seat she'd vacated. His fingers wrapped lightly around her forearm, holding her in place. "What are you doing later?" he asked.

She paused at the door. "Besides trying to fight off a sugar coma? Probably just being antisocial as usual."

"Maybe I'll see you at dinner, then."

"Maybe," she said. "Thanks for sharing your pie."

She pushed through the sheet of plastic covering the doorway without looking back. The more attached she became to people in Nowhere, the harder it would be for her to leave them if the wishes continued to plague her. But the way her heart hammered at even the thought of going anywhere else told her she was already in trouble.

# 13

Rachel spent her day off playing phone tag with Mary Beth and thumbing through recipe books. She'd scoured the library for a novel but concluded that Catch didn't know what fiction was. Nothing she tried took her mind off her conversation with Ashe for very long.

By mid-afternoon, she had almost convinced herself to ask Catch if it was possible to bind her ability. But that would require admitting to Catch what she could do. Rachel wasn't sure she was ready for that. When she walked into the kitchen and found Catch dozing over a cookbook, she tried to sneak back out. The back door was open, the screen door unlatched. It screeched as the wind caught it and threw it open wide.

Catch's head jerked up, the knife slipping from her grasp to clatter against the floor. Dried chocolate pie filling flaked off the blade. Rachel was across the room before Catch seemed to register what had happened. Her eyes were glazed, distant, when they followed Rachel to the door.

After pulling both doors closed, Rachel retrieved the knife and set it on the counter out of Catch's reach. She mentally traced the deep lines in the woman's face and the almost-purple hollows of her cheeks. She and Catch came out of their respective dazes at the same time. "You okay?" Rachel asked.

"Fine. I'm fine," Catch said, her voice betraying her irritation at the question.

Rachel held up her hands in surrender. "It was just a question. No need to bite my head off."

Catch muttered something that almost sounded like "Sorry" and took a long drink of water, the glass shaking in her hand. Her face regained a bit of color. Rachel wondered if she should let Ashe know Catch seemed sick, knowing Catch would never admit it even if she were unwell.

They both turned at the light rapping on the door. Whoever was on the other side was standing far enough to the side that Rachel couldn't see more than a shoulder. It was bare except for the purse strap the woman clutched with manicured nails.

"Get on outta here, now," Catch said, turning to Rachel and shooing her away with a wave of her wrinkly hand. "This one doesn't concern you."

Lola shifted into view, biting her lip and looking through the yard toward Ashe's house. Her hair was pinned up in loose curls.

"You know what she wants?" Rachel asked. She stood, but didn't head out of the kitchen.

"I've got a pretty good idea. And since I don't plan on helping her, I can't have you around to hear what she has to say." She flapped a dish towel at Rachel, smacking her thighs three times in rapid succession.

Rachel rubbed at the red streaks blooming on her skin. "Make her beg a little first."

"You are bad."

"Yeah. But I'm not the one that broke Ashe's heart."

"You've got a point there. Now get," Catch said.

Rachel slipped out of the kitchen and tiptoed up the stairs. She made it halfway up before curiosity got the better of her. Sitting quietly on the step, she hugged the rail post and listened.

Lola's heels tapped across the kitchen tile. "Good afternoon, Miss Sisson. Do you have a minute?"

"You came to the side door, so I know this ain't a social call. Just say what you've gotta say, Lola."

"All right. I didn't want to have to come to you about this, but I honestly don't know what else to do."

"Confession," Catch grunted. "Pie won't do you much good, but God might."

"I'm not trying to put the cat back in the bag, I just—"

"Good thing. It can't be done. The best you can hope for is to keep things from getting any worse."

"So, you'll help?" Lola asked.

Rachel held her breath. *If she says yes, I'm going down there and tossing Lola out myself.* She scooted down one step, then another to hear better.

"I didn't say that," Catch said. Her tone was sharp, biting. "You got yourself into this mess. I'm sure you can find a way out of it that doesn't involve me."

"Everyone already knows what I did. But I don't want Ashe finding out who it was. That would kill him."

"You're the one that's done it to him, not me. So don't stand there and pretend like you care about him. That's my job now. And I ain't lying to the boy. He deserves better than that."

"I know you don't like me, Miss Sisson. You never did. But if you don't help me, Ashe is the one who's gonna get hurt even more."

"Too late for that, girlie. Now, get outta my kitchen," Catch said, her tone even but firm.

The door slammed a few seconds later. The windows in the dining room rattled with the force of it. Rachel slipped off her shoes and tiptoed up the stairs. She made it less than five steps when Catch yelled to her.

"I know you're hovering out there." The sharpness of her gravelly voice cut through the silence.

Rachel contemplated continuing up without responding. She paused in mid-step, foot frozen in indecision.

"You may as well come back in here so we can have ourselves a little chat about what you overheard," Catch called.

Shoes in hand, Rachel slunk back to the kitchen. "I'm sorry, Catch." She kept her eyes trained on the floor.

"Well, she didn't say anything you didn't already know." Catch thrust the side door's lock into position as if that would keep all the town's depraved secrets out. "Ooh, that girl really burns my butt. She's got some nerve coming here asking me to cover up something like that. What's worse, she thought I'd actually do it. What kinda woman would that make me? I'd tell Ashe everything just to spite her if it wouldn't wreck him."

"You know who she slept with?" Rachel asked.

"I had the misfortune of catching them at it. Right in my own damn backyard too."

Rachel looked out the back window. She could see why someone would think it might be a good place for a tryst. The trees at the back of the small orchard were shapeless blobs. Bodies could be swallowed whole in their shadows. Specks of light from Ashe's house filtered through the indistinguishable leaves, making the yard look alive.

"What did you do?"

"Threw the biggest rock I could find. Caught him just above his right ear. I was aiming for her, but when I saw him the next day with a lump the size of Alabama on his head and realized he'd been the one with her, I was damn glad I'd missed her. Good thing Little-Miss-Cheater-Pants was smart enough not to come over to my house and ask for my help then. I might've beaten her senseless with my rolling pin." She rapped the flour-dusted rolling pin against her other hand with a few loud smacks.

"If Lola could do that to someone like Ashe, she didn't have any sense to begin with," Rachel said. "And I don't think anyone would've held it against you for mangling her pretty face once they found out what she'd done."

A smile tugged at Catch's lips. "And to add insult to injury, every plum growing on the tree closest to where they'd been with each other rotted on the branch the next day. Not even the birds would touch 'em."

Rachel paused, considered Catch might not like the next question, then asked anyway. "Don't you think Ashe deserves to know?"

Catch turned on the sink faucet and took a sponge to the rolling pin in quick, jerky movements. "He's still got a better heart than most, despite having it trampled on by a harpy. Knowing the truth would only hurt him more. And I'm not going to be the one to do it. I just wish he—"

Rachel grabbed Catch's arm, her fingers pressing harder than she intended into the soft flesh. "Don't."

"What? I'm not allowed to want him to move on, to be happy?" Catch demanded, yanking her arm free and fisting her hand on the counter. She dropped the rolling pin into the sink with a heavy thud and pinned Rachel to her seat with a watery stare.

"No, you are. Of course you are," Rachel said. Her face burned with embarrassment. "I want that for him too."

"Then what's the problem?"

"I just don't want you wishing for things that might not make him happy."

Catch stared at her, one gray eyebrow stretching toward her hairline, and asked, "And after a month you think you know what makes him happy?"

"No. But I do know that no good's ever come from wishing," Rachel said.

"Well, Little-Miss-Doom-and-Gloom, too damn bad for you, 'cause I'm gonna do it anyway. And you're gonna sit there with your mouth shut until I do."

She could sit there. Just hearing the wish wouldn't make it come true. But she couldn't let it happen without one last caution. "Just don't wish for anything you might regret. Please."

Catch hesitated, as if she understood how much power her words held and needed to get the phrasing exactly right. "I wish Ashe would find someone to love him like he deserves to be loved and who makes him laugh, 'cause that boy has a good laugh, and the world would be a better place if it happened more often."

It was a good wish.

A wish that might work out the way it was supposed to.

If Rachel let it.

Her eyes flicked up, immediately scanning for the wish to appear before she'd even decided what she wanted to do about it. And she waited. The seconds ticked by with no paper disturbing the air.

Relieved that Ashe's happiness wasn't pinned on her, she dropped her gaze and found the wish resting faceup on the counter a few inches from the tips of her fingers. She slid it toward her, tucking it under her palm, not ready to face it.

Mary Beth called back ten minutes after Catch ushered Rachel out of the kitchen claiming she needed a little peace and quiet. Violet's voice cut through the still air of her bedroom, making Rachel laugh despite the disgust that had settled in the house like a fine dust since Lola left.

"Hey, stranger," Mary Beth said.

Rachel took a deep breath and expelled the remnants of her bad mood. "I'm sorry, who is this? You sound familiar, but I can't quite place the voice. How do we know each other again?"

"We shared our darkest secrets in a roomful of people. You're the godmother of my kids, I think. But maybe that becomes null and void when said godmother moves away."

"If I remember correctly, you're the one who said this might be a good thing."

"That was before I knew leaving meant falling off the face of the Earth. Is it too late to take it back?" Mary Beth asked.

Rachel curled her legs to her chest and leaned against the sill below the window. The air from the ceiling fan was cool on her skin. "I miss you."

"I miss you back."

"You sound good. I take it living in some old lady's attic is working for you?" Mary Beth asked.

"Strangely, yeah. Things are a little odd here, but it feels right, like this is the way life is supposed to be and everyone else has got it wrong." Rachel looked out at the trees and her heart gave a little pang of worry for Ashe and what he would do if he discovered what was killing the plum tree. Turning her gaze away, she said, "Okay, enough about me. How are the girls and Geoff?"

"They're great. They miss you almost as much as I do. Violet keeps asking me when you're coming home. And every time I tell her it'll be soon 'cause I can't bear to tell her I have no clue when you're coming back." Her voice was quiet, like saying it any louder would somehow make it true.

The idea that she was in no hurry to go back to Memphis didn't give Rachel the immediate knot in her stomach she'd expected. "I'll send her a postcard so she knows I haven't forgotten her. And once I know what I'm doing, I'll come back and visit or y'all can come here."

"I'd feel better about you being there if I could meet Catch and the sexy neighbor."

Rachel laid her head on her arm, imagining having Mary Beth here. In Catch's kitchen, eating pie. Sunlight poured through the window, hugging her skin so a soft heat buzzed up her arms. Her eyes drifted back to the brown leaves of the plum tree. The bark was a dark ashy color, and it tilted toward Ashe's house like it wanted to spill its secrets to him.

"Hey, Mae?" she asked.

"Yeah?"

"Whatever happened with the pony from Vi's birthday?"

"Animal control came out and removed it. Said they'd had no reports of missing ponies but they took it with a promise to Vi to find it a really good home. Then she made them agree to send her the address so she could go visit it."

"Of course she did."

"Yeah, well, wishes for magical unicorn-ponies don't come true every day."

*No, they don't. But other wishes do.*

After she hung up with Mary Beth, she slid the wish about Ashe out from under her pillow where she'd stashed it and read the inky words. She pressed the small white strip of paper to her chest as she thought, *Please let Ashe be happy.*

# 14

Rachel already regretted agreeing to go to the barbecue festival with Everley. Going to an event that promised to put her in the same vicinity as Lola had her stomach in knots. When she'd granted Catch's wish about Ashe, she hadn't considered how Lola would react to Ashe moving on. But then she remembered how possessive Lola had seemed over Ashe the first day they'd met, and with most of the town present, there was a high probability of it blowing up in Rachel's face.

She stopped twice on the flagstone path that led to Everley's door, debating what Everley would do if she didn't show up.

The house, like Everley's shop, was chic and modern. The creamy honeysuckle paint was trimmed in a shocking white. The muted aqua front door added a dash of whimsy. Two rocking chairs, a small table, and an orange tabby curled in a ball on one of the cushions took up three quarters of the small front porch. The never-ending glass windows and doors reflected the well-manicured lawn.

The six-foot hydrangea at the corner of the porch burst with dozens of clusters of pink and green flowers. The humming of a distant lawn mower mixed with the bees buzzing around the flowers in wooden planters that lined the porch steps, giving the early-afternoon air an electric feel.

She hurried up the walk and rang the doorbell before she changed her mind.

"You are not going to Brews N Cue in shorts," Everley scolded when she opened the door and saw Rachel's outfit—a pair of khaki shorts that hit mid-thigh and a faded blue T-shirt.

"What? It's like a hundred degrees out here," Rachel said.

"God, you're such a guy. Follow me."

The rooms in Everley's house whizzed by in flashes of lavender and moss and corn silk as Rachel tried to match Everley's long strides. They ended in a coral-painted bedroom. Even with the lights off, the room glowed.

Everley disappeared into a walk-in closet the size of Rachel's attic room. She emerged a minute later with a pear-colored slip of fabric dangling from a wooden hanger. "You, my fashion-challenged friend, are going to wear a dress. This dress, actually."

"That is way too nice for me to wear," Rachel said, letting the dress float to the floor when Everley tossed it to her. It gathered in a cool heap on her feet, the fabric spilling like grass clippings across the almost-black hardwoods. "I'll be eating barbecue. With messy sauce. I don't want to get anything on it."

"Oh, but letting it lay in a wrinkled heap on the floor is okay?" Everley asked.

"As long as I don't have to wear it, yes."

"You don't understand. The festival is an event. All the ladies get dressed up and the guys are on their best behavior. We have a pie-eating contest, and judges pick the best barbecue, and we have a Miss Cue contest where one girl is crowned the barbecue queen for the year. It's a big deal. You cannot go looking like that. I'm sorry. You just can't."

"Why are you wearing shorts, then?" she asked.

" 'Cause I'm not dressed yet. I bought this adorable little dark periwinkle strapless dress just for today. So, pick that one up and put it on before I'm forced to do it for you." Everley winked at her as she whirled out of the room.

With the threat hanging in the air, Rachel did as she was told.

There was no way to wear a bra with it, she realized, after twisting and converting her straps into every position she could think of. At least the dress's halter straps and empire waist made it so a bra

wasn't a necessity. She heaved the top up so another centimeter of
skin was covered.

Everley came back ten minutes later in a flowy purple dress that
hit a few inches below her knee. "How does this dress fit you?"
Rachel asked, tugging at the band of material covering her chest.
"I'm only a B cup and I'm not sure I'm going to stay in this thing."

"It's not mine. Catch *may* have mentioned that there were exactly
zero dresses in your closet," Everley said. "So I remedied that problem."

"Wait, you bought this for me?"

"And shoes too. A dress like that begs for new shoes."

Rachel took the box Everley handed her and slipped off the lid to
reveal a pair of off-white heels with peep-toes. "Thank you, Everley.
Seriously. This is beyond sweet of you. But—"

"No, don't you dare try and tell me you can't accept them. Because
you're going to wear the hell out of that outfit and remind a certain
someone there are other fish in the sea."

"What if said fish doesn't want to be noticed?" Rachel asked. But
she couldn't stop the hitch in her breath at the thought of Ashe checking her out. This was just the type of dress Mary Beth would have
forced on her too. All girlie and sexy and nothing Rachel would even
look at twice. "And what if said boy finds out he's being manipulated?"

"He'd be smart enough to thank me."


The riverfront park was swarming with people and barbecue smoke.
Wisps of white furled up from large black cookers, saturating the
muggy air with the scent of charcoal and tangy spices. Blankets,
chairs, and bodies covered so much of the grass that the small bits of
green that poked through looked like a trick of the light.

Rachel hung around the periphery while Everley trudged into the
masses, hugging every other person she passed. Rachel recognized a
few faces as customers from the shop. She waved to Miss Lavender-
Buttermilk-Hand-Cream. Exchanged hellos with Mrs. Peppermint-
Salt-Scrub. Then she pretended to be engrossed in the handwritten

menus nailed to posts at each booth. She read a few just in case anyone asked her about them: *Pulled pork sandwich. Pork plate. Pork shoulder. Pork butt. Pork ribs.*

"Don't y'all have some beef brisket anywhere?" Rachel asked when Everley emerged from the crowd.

"Blasphemy!" Everley said, laughing. "Old Eddie always enters a Texas style. He comes in dead last every year."

"Is his barbecue that bad?"

"I don't know. I've never tried it."

Holding her hand out, Rachel kept Everley from walking away before she could explain. "But don't you vote for the best? How can you do that if you didn't even try one?" Rachel asked.

Everley gave Rachel a pitying look and chuckled. "No self-respecting North Carolinian wants beef. Or tomato-based sauce. But he's down at the end, there. The only one without a line. I'm sure he'd enjoy the company."

"I'm sure I would too," Rachel said. She took two steps in his direction and stopped. Ashe was a few yards away talking to Jamie and a cluster of guys she recognized from the crew working on the addition to Everley's store. The low rumbling of their voices as they talked about some game they wanted to watch that night carried back to her.

"What's up with you and Ashe?" Everley asked. "Did you have a fight or something?"

"We're fine," Rachel replied, too fast.

"Liar," Everley said.

Rachel glanced at Ashe again. He looked happy, but she didn't know if that was due to Catch's wish or because it hadn't taken effect yet. She grabbed Everley's arms, backing them both up a few steps, and figured she could give Everley some part of the truth. "Fine. I think, like you, Catch is trying to set us up. Or at least put the notion in his head that maybe he should be interested in me."

Everley cocked her head and looked at Rachel curiously. "Why do you say that like it's a bad thing?"

"I don't want him to like me because you or Catch wishes he would." She wasn't sure she wanted him to like her in that way at all.

"I don't think it works like that. Plus, boy's got the googly eyes over you in that dress." Everley nodded to where Ashe and Jamie stood in the middle of the crowd watching them. "Can't say I blame him. You look fantastic. Just like I knew you would."

"Thanks," Rachel said, resisting the urge to tug the low neckline up again.

"In case you're curious, he looks damn good under those clothes."

"I'm not." Once Everley's admission sank in, Rachel whipped her head around to stare at her friend. "Wait, how do you know that?"

"He used to spend the night when Lola and I lived together in college. I walked in on him in the shower a few times. The first time was an accident."

"You're bad," Rachel said, laughing. "And the others?"

"Like I said, he looks good naked." Grinning at Rachel, Everley gave her a gentle nudge. "Go get him, girlie. I'm betting he'd have you out of that dress in five minutes if given half the chance."

Rachel thought of Catch's wish and felt guilty for wanting it to come true. For wanting what Everley pushed her to do. "This damn thing is suctioned on. I don't think anyone's gonna get me out of it without a good pair of pliers."

When Everley burst out laughing and sagged into her side, Rachel gripped her hand to keep her from toppling over. Her heels sank into the soft ground from the weight.

"Oh. My. God," Everley managed between breaths. "I just had the best image of the two of you trying out a whole set of his tools." She fanned herself with her free hand.

"Ladies," Ashe said as he and Jamie walked over to them. His smile was quick, charming. The sleeves of his linen shirt were rolled up, exposing pale hairs on his forearms that stood out on his tanned skin.

Rachel looked away, suddenly longing for her shorts and tee.

*Why the hell am I nervous?* It was just Ashe. Just Ashe looking at her in a dress she had no business wearing. Back home she did everything she could to blend in—jeans and T-shirts, hair pulled into a simple ponytail, thin application of black eyeliner and mascara. Even

Mary Beth had a hard time getting her in anything else. But a month around Everley and she was walking around in a dress and heels.

Everley wrapped her arm around Jamie and playfully kissed his neck. "Hi, cutie," she said, wiping the smear of lipstick from Jamie's dark skin.

"Sounds like I missed something good," Ashe said. He stood close enough to touch Rachel, and the memory of Catch's wish had her stomach twisting in knots when his eyes slid over her dress.

"Oh, you did. Believe me," Everley said.

"And you're not gonna share?"

"And risk it not happening? Not on your life." She winked at Rachel.

Rachel's eyes flicked to Ashe's lips quirked up in amusement. "No," Rachel managed, shaking her head. "Just no."

"Suit yourself." Everley curled her fingers around Ashe's forearm and pulled him a step closer. "Our girl Rachel here wants to go sample Old Eddie's barbecue," she said in a conspiratorial whisper.

Ashe groaned and hung his head. "Of course she does," he said.

"Didn't you tell her no one eats that?" Jamie asked.

"She won't listen. Mind taking her over there? I've got a reputation to uphold."

"I can take myself," Rachel protested.

"Uh-uh," Ashe said, "you're not going anywhere in that dress alone. Half the male population's already talking about asking you to marry them. You're safer with me."

She scanned the crowd and found more than a few men smiling at her. Ashe's dad inclined his head in her direction and lifted a plastic cup in greeting. She gave him a hesitant smile in return, then turned back to Ashe. "Am I?" she asked.

Ashe raised his hands in the air, palms facing her. "I promise to keep my hands to myself."

Rachel heard Everley mumble something that sounded a lot like *please don't*.

She wrenched her heels from the dirt and motioned toward the food.

The searing sunshine and the oppressive heat from the grills made her feel light-headed. The wooziness intensified until her vision grayed at the edges. "May I?" she asked, pointing at Ashe's cup.

He handed it to her, letting his fingers trail down her wrist when he let go. She shivered.

The sweet tea was cool and had a hint of orange. She sucked on a piece of ice and passed the cup back. "Thanks."

"Pick your hair up," he said.

"What?"

"Your hair. Lift it up."

When she didn't move fast enough, Ashe gathered her hair in one hand and twisted it off her neck. He rolled the side of the cup along the back of her neck, letting the condensation dribble down the plastic to collect in large beads on her skin. He laughed when she sucked in a breath.

Rachel jerked away from the cold and wound up pressed against his chest. The momentary relief the ice provided evaporated as his arm snaked around her waist and kept her from backing up again.

"No need to get all worked up. I'm just trying to keep you from passing out. Now hold still."

Ashe moved his hand back to her neck but didn't put any more distance between their bodies. Rachel held her breath. It did nothing to calm her racing pulse. She concentrated on the cold seeping into her skin and let her head drop to his chest as the dizziness receded.

"I'm okay," she said after a minute. Stepping back, she coaxed his hand away from her hair and let it fall back around her shoulders in a wavy cascade.

He tucked a strand behind her ear, trailing his fingers along her jaw. "You look like you'll live. Though if you're still thinking about getting barbecue from Eddie I'm not sure how long that'll last."

"It's a risk I'm willing to take," Rachel said.

He kept his hand on her back as they walked toward the last food tent. Smoke saturated the air so every breath tasted like hickory and greasy meat and charred corn husks. He stiffened next to her, his hand slipping from her back. Lola stopped a few feet away, eyes narrowing for a second before she hid the expression behind a wide smile. The cap sleeves of her pale yellow dress fed into a sweetheart neckline that made her look like a 1950s starlet.

"Well, hey, y'all," Lola said. "Don't you two look cozy. Rachel, I just had the strangest sense of déjà vu. I swear you're the spitting image of this girl I saw years ago, except she had hair so black you'd think the devil himself had painted it."

Rachel ran a shaky hand through her hair. Strands, slick with sweat, clung to her neck. She'd only had dark hair for a week when she was seventeen before her mom threatened to shave her head if she didn't turn it back. That was a few months before her mom had died. And Rachel's guilt for driving her mother mad with stories of Michael still colored everything she did.

If Lola knew about her hair, then she probably knew about her mom and Michael and what she could do with wishes.

She met Lola's stare, wondering how in the hell Lola knew, and saw recognition flash in her brown eyes. She racked her brain, wondering if she had met Lola somewhere before she came to Nowhere.

"What do you want, Lola?" Ashe asked.

"I'm just trying to be civil. That's what *you* want, right?"

"That's not what you're doing and you know it." He turned to Rachel, touching a hand to her shoulder. "You ready to eat?" he asked her.

"Sure," she said, her heart still racing, though she wasn't sure exactly why.

Ashe guided them around the throngs of hungry people brandishing cobs of corn with a good two inches of stalk still attached that they used as handles, and plates piled high with pulled hunks of meat smothered in runny clear sauce that was nothing like the sauce she was used to.

Rachel tugged at the straps of her dress again, suddenly feeling so out of place.

There was no line at Eddie's booth. He was propped up on an upside-down pickle bucket, legs stretched out in front of him. Eyes closed, he didn't notice them come up. Ashe kicked his foot. Eddie jolted awake, catching himself before he fell off the bucket, and said, "Ready to try the festival's only real barbecue?"

"Looks like you've got a taker," Ashe said to him when he straightened. "Our girl here isn't a fan of North Carolina style."

Eddie's smile was quick and crooked. He was missing his left incisor. Clapping his hands together, he said, "Best news I've heard all day. What can I do you for, darlin'?"

"Brisket on a plate. No bun. Lots of sauce. The hotter the better."

"Girl after my own heart," he said. He patted a hand on his chest. "And what about you, Ashe? Dare to try the best barbecue this side of the Mississippi?"

"Now that's a bold statement, Eddie. But I'll try it. See what you're always going on about. I want mine in sandwich form, if you don't mind."

"Coming right up."

When Ashe turned to look at her, she crossed her arms over her chest. He wasn't leering, but the way his eyes roamed over her bare shoulders and down her legs made her fidgety.

"I don't see it," he said after a minute.

"What?" she asked.

"The black hair. I mean, the blond fits you. I could maybe even see you as a light brunette, but definitely not that dark."

Rachel cocked her head and asked, "You don't think so?"

"No." He took their plates when Eddie was finished loading them down with fixings—beans with hunks of bacon, coleslaw, and a thick slab of grilled toast for Rachel's plate.

She took her plate from Ashe and inhaled. It smelled like home— rich, tangy, and sweet. She would've started eating it as they walked if Ashe hadn't stashed the plasticware and napkins in his pocket. She made her way to a table set up underneath the canopy of branches of an ancient oak tree. The leaves rustled in the breeze, the light soft and green as it filtered through the branches. And cool. For the first time in an hour, her breaths came easily.

She set her plate on the table and sat sideways on the picnic bench.

She tugged off her shoes. A blister was bubbling up on the back of her right heel. The red, loose skin stung when she ran her finger over it. She set her shoes on the scarred wood next to her, blocking anyone from sitting next to her.

Ashe followed with two bottles of water he'd picked up somewhere along the way. "That'll teach you to let Ev pick out your shoes. But anytime she wants to put you in a dress like that, you are not allowed to say no."

Her breath caught in her throat when she looked at him. The sincerity in his eyes made her blush. She hoped the light was dim enough that he wouldn't notice.

He moved her shoes to the ground and sat next to her. He left a few inches, but he was close enough to knock elbows with her when he dislodged something from his pocket. "Wet-Nap?" He ripped open the end and squeezed the edges to give her better access.

"Thanks. I didn't expect to get quite so dirty before eating." She took the wet towel from the pouch without looking at him. She scrubbed her hands, then fanned them in the air to dry.

"So, let's find out what's so special about this brisket, what do you say?"

"I'd already be done with it if you'd given me a fork." Rachel laughed when he pulled it from his pocket and tossed it to her.

"No way you're gonna eat all that."

"Watch me."

She poked the fork through its plastic bag, freed the napkin, and dug in. The sauce was thick and the heat of it burned her tongue. She couldn't help the satisfied moan that escaped her.

Ashe raised his eyebrows at her. "That good, huh? Should I leave you alone with that brisket?"

"What's gotten into you today?" she asked, laughing. He was happy, just like Catch had wanted. But his good mood, his easy laughter, felt too natural to be because of a wish. Like he'd managed to shake off some of the anger and hurt that had been weighing him down.

"I don't know. I was talking to my brother last night and he said I should lighten up and have some fun. So I'm trying. No brooding, no fighting with Lola. Just hanging out with a pretty girl eating barbecue and enjoying the heat. I figure life can't get much better than that."

She smiled at him. "I guess we'll see."

When he smiled back, it sent tingles all the way to her toes. She curled them into the grass, but it didn't stop the sensation. As much as she wanted to get lost in the moment, she couldn't let herself. Lola knew something—maybe everything—about Rachel's past, and she seemed angry enough to do something about it.

# 15

The hotter it got, the tighter Rachel's dress got. The soft fabric clung to her skin, and no matter how many times she pried it away, it slapped back to her as if magnetized. She was still tugging on it when she finally made it through the thick mass of people to Catch's tent.

"I might have to turn this into a kissing booth with the way the men are looking at you," Catch said. Her explosive laugh carried across the park. Everyone close to the tent turned to stare at them. Catch waved them off with a quick flick of her wrist.

"Blame Everley," Rachel said.

"You're just cranky 'cause Ashe finally clued in to the fact that you're a girl, and you like it. Which makes me right. Now cut that man some pie while I get these moving." Catch unloaded more boxes of pies on the folding table. She turned to the people still in line and hollered, "We're closed until after the contest. Come back then."

Rachel jabbed the knife into the gooey flesh of the triple berry pie and passed it to the man at the front of the line. "That's not the part I mind," she said to Catch when the crowd dispersed. "It's the fact that I don't know why he likes me. Which I was prepared to ignore for the day and just be happy for a change, but then you had to go and remind me that it matters."

"Why do you have to make it so complicated?"

"Because it is."

Catch rolled her eyes as she whipped the tinfoil off another pie. "How so?"

"He's still married, for one," Rachel said, spouting out the easiest excuse. She jumped into the assembly line and kept her eyes on the pies to keep Catch from seeing all of the things she'd left unsaid.

"Not for much longer. What else you got?"

*I made your wish for him to be happy come true and he's probably only interested in me because of it. Just like the other wishes that didn't go right.* "I don't know how long I'm staying."

"You and I both know you're not going anywhere anytime soon," Catch said.

Just because she didn't want to leave didn't mean she wouldn't. If Lola told everyone what she knew, and the town believed her, Rachel might not have a choice.

Catch passed the tray loaded with pies off to one of the contest runners. Rachel moved to her side and pulled foil covers off pie after pie as Catch lined them up. The air holes in the top of the crusts revealed peach, cherry, plum, pear, strawberry rhubarb, and apple insides. Others—lemon, coconut crème, key lime, and chocolate crème—were topless and needed to be squirted with whipped cream before they could be sent off to the contest stage.

"What if something happens and I can't stay?" Rachel asked after a minute.

"Then we'll deal with it. But don't let some stupid *what if* get in the way of enjoying a little slice of happiness. Lord knows it's hard enough finding it in the first place."

They emptied the last box and followed the runner to the main stage. They'd missed the first four heats while getting the pies ready, but Catch had timed it so they'd be there to see Ashe compete. He was already seated behind the folding table onstage. He was in the middle, with two guys on either side, and Jamie on the far end. They seemed to be throwing friendly taunts back and forth, but Rachel was too far away to hear exactly what they said.

The runner doled out pies as the emcee announced the flavors each contestant would be attempting to eat faster than the others.

A digital timer above the contestants was set to two minutes. If anyone could eat the whole pie in that short amount of time, Rachel was sure it would be Ashe. He ate more pie than anyone she knew.

With hundreds of bodies packed in front of the stage, there was little room for a breeze. What air did make it through carried a charred meat smell that made it hard to breathe. The announcer's voice crackled through the crowd as he warned the contestants to get ready. They straightened their backs in unison. A bullhorn cut through the hum of chatter. All five contestants plunged into the pies face-first as if they'd all fallen asleep at the same time.

Rachel shielded her eyes from the sun with her hand. Their heads bobbed up and down, side to side as they ate. "They're not allowed to use their hands?" she asked.

Catch fanned herself with a piece of cardboard she ripped from one of the pie boxes. "It's not called the Ultimate Pie Face-Off for nothing."

They watched, the clock counting silently down as the crowd began chanting names and encouragement. She and Catch joined in, urging Ashe on. She yelled louder when Everley squeezed in beside her and started screaming Jamie's name. Rachel's cheeks hurt from smiling.

With ten seconds left, the noise from the crowd ratcheted up a few more decibels, as if the added volume could give the contestants a final burst of speed.

With five seconds left, the words melded into an unintelligible rhythm that pulsed urgent and hot through the air.

With three seconds left, Ashe pushed back from the table, grinning as purple sauce dripped off his chin.

With one second left, Rachel had the overwhelming urge to kiss him.


She hadn't been able to shake the feeling twenty minutes later and was thankful Ashe was too busy waiting on the final scores and getting cleaned up to come find her. She couldn't pinpoint when the attraction had taken hold. Until a few days before he'd just been a good-looking, charming guy she flirted with, knowing it probably wouldn't go anywhere. But then Catch had made her wish. Now she couldn't stop herself from wondering what it would be like to kiss him.

She told herself it wasn't real. The universe wouldn't let her be the person who would make Ashe happy. Not after everything she'd done.

"Stupid, stupid, stupid," she repeated under her breath, willing herself to just forget about Ashe and how she felt when she looked at him. But her feelings for him had already started to take root, and it had nothing to do with a wish. She couldn't help but think what he felt for her was real too.

She focused on helping Catch dish out slice after slice to the line of customers that snaked around the park. There was no end in sight and that was fine with her. If she was dealing with people and pie, she wasn't thinking about Ashe.

It took more than two hours for the line to dwindle down enough that Rachel could see a definite end. Every time she thought they were about to run out of pie, Catch dragged another box from the trailer.

"No wonder you've looked so run-down lately. Do you ever sleep?" she asked.

"I look just fine, Miss I-Got-All-Dolled-Up-and-Now-Everyone-Else-Looks-Like-Crap," Catch snapped.

"I didn't mean—"

"I know what you meant. Old ladies just don't like to hear that they're getting old." She lowered herself into a canvas chair and propped her feet on an overturned bucket. "We're winding down, so I'm gonna head home soon. You should go find some people your own age. Get some use out of that dress."

She thought of Ashe, then of how exhausted Catch looked. How she'd found Catch asleep in the kitchen more than once, cheeks hollowed out and her skin so pale she looked half-dead. She hoped it was just normal signs of aging like Catch said. The alternative wasn't something she even wanted to consider. "I don't mind sticking around here for a little longer."

Catch backhanded her on the thigh. "Don't make me tell you twice."

Rachel rubbed a hand over her stinging skin. She slipped on her shoes and left before Catch could smack her again.

The band had changed several times during the afternoon from bluegrass to country and back again. The barbecue tents transitioned from food to beer. The people, however, were still everywhere. She maneuvered around them, slipping through small pockets of space between groups.

"Oh, Rachel," Lola called out in a singsong voice. She darted around the person she'd been talking with and latched on to Rachel's arm, pulling her to a stop. "Do you have a minute?"

Rachel freed her arm with a sharp tug. "I was just on my way to—"

"I'm sure no one'll mind if you're a teensy bit late. This'll just take a minute."

Rachel contemplated walking away, but she knew Lola would follow her until she'd said her piece. Staring at Lola, she waited.

"As crazy as it might seem, you and I have something in common."

"A strong dislike for each other?" Rachel said.

"No, we both have things we don't want everybody and their mother to know. I'd like to think we could help each other out. I know who you are. And that some people might say you're bat-shit crazy." Lola scanned the crowd, then continued in a voice so low Rachel had to strain to hear, "I know about the hospital. All those years of therapy must have been hard." Lola looked at Rachel the way a mother might look at a disappointed child, knowing full well they weren't going to get what they wanted.

Rachel took a step back, her mind racing for some explanation for how Lola could know about what she'd been through. She wanted to lie, to say Lola was wrong, but she could only manage a stunned, "How?"

"I probably wouldn't have made the connection, but I was thinking about the things from my past I wish I could change and had this flash of a memory about my sister. She was in that hospital too. I went with my parents to visit her once, when they thought she might've been getting better and wanted to bring her home. But Mary Beth didn't want to leave, and they wouldn't let me go back."

*Mary Beth.* Rachel's heart pounded so hard she wondered how Lola didn't hear it over the music from the band and the babble of voices roaring around them.

She should have been able to see it, though, the resemblance. Lola was more done up, but underneath the makeup and better-than-everyone attitude, the similarities were there. The deep brown eyes flecked with gold and heart-shaped faces offset with auburn hair.

Rachel assumed their smiles would be the same if Lola ever smiled and meant it.

"I know you know her. Mary Beth Beaumont?"

"I don't think so," Rachel said. If she could just make Lola believe her, this could all blow over without anyone else getting pulled into it. "I think you've got me mixed up with someone else." She took one step before Lola's clawlike fingers gripped her arm again.

Lola's smile was sharp when she held Rachel in place. "Now, you and I both know that you know her. Before she shut me out, she told me about you. How you wished away her nightmares and y'all became BFFs. I'd just hate for the whole town to know what you can do, because it might complicate the nice, quiet life you're trying to build here. But if you make a wish to get Ashe to forgive me, I'll make sure to keep that to myself."

Rachel let Lola continue to hold her in place, let Lola think she was considering the blackmail though there was no way she could give Lola what she wanted. Wishing for Ashe to be happy was one thing, but doing what Lola was asking? That wouldn't be fair. She had to find a way to make this all go away. Quickly.

"Just so we're clear, you expect me to make him forget you cheated on him, that you threw away your marriage like it meant nothing? And in return you won't tell anyone that you think I'm some fairy godmother who goes around granting wishes?"

"I made a mistake. I love him, Rachel. And I just want him to re-member that." Lola loosened her grip as her expression deflated.

Rachel jerked away from her. She rubbed at the band of red circling her wrist. "Well, despite what you think, I can't help you." *I won't. He doesn't deserve that.*

"We'll see about that," Lola said in her best Southern-belle tone. Her smooth smile slid back into place, covering all traces of her angry desperation.

A hand grazed Rachel's back, fingers skimming across the bare skin above her dress, making her jump.

"Everything okay?" Ashe asked.

Lola laughed. "We're just talking. Nothing to worry about."

"Rachel?"

"It's nothing," she said. Though it was anything but. Lola could ruin the life she was starting to build in Nowhere. Even if no one believed Lola about Rachel's wish ability, they would ask about her brother, her mom. And she didn't want to lie to anyone. Especially not Catch or Ashe. She forced a smile at Everley and Jamie as they approached, grateful for the distraction. "Hey, what are y'all up to?"

Everley tucked her arm through Lola's and held a plate of deep-fried something into the middle of their little circle. "I figured pie was out of the question after the contest, so I got enough fried Oreos and Reese's for all of us, though I don't know which is which. I expect each of you to eat one. And then we're all going to go find a place to watch the fireworks. Together. And we're all going to get along for the rest of the night, no ifs, ands, or buts about it."

"I'm not sure deep-fried sweets have enough magic to make that come true," Lola said to Everley, her voice as sweet as the treats on the tray. She flicked her gaze to Rachel, annoyance sparking in her eyes. "This town is full of mysteries. Secret-keeping pies and now mood-altering candy? Next thing you know, we'll find out that some-one here can make our deepest wishes come true."

"Funny," Everley said. "Now eat. All of you."

Grinning, Jamie grabbed two off the plate and popped one in his mouth whole. Ashe followed suit but handed his second one to Rachel. His fingers brushed against hers with just enough pressure for her to know he'd done it on purpose. When she smiled, it was only partly to convince him she was okay.

"You're staying for fireworks, right?" he asked her.

"Yeah, sounds fun," she said.

Lola pulled away from Everley and gave Ashe a tight-lipped smile. "I understand you wanting to get back at me, Ashe. But at least have enough self-respect not to embarrass yourself in front of all of us."

"Lola!" Everley said. "Happy chocolates, remember?" She shoved the last piece of dessert into Lola's hand.

"I can't stand here pretending to be happy when my husband's clearly not in his right mind. She's done something to him—wished for God knows what—so that he can't see how manipulative she is."

Everley leaned into her friend and whispered, "You know you sound a little crazy, right?"

Rachel's fingers dug into the fried dough encasing the peanut butter cup she had yet to eat. Melted chocolate and peanut butter oozed out of a rip in the side and dribbled down her fingers. Everley offered her a napkin and an apologetic smile. *Just ignore her*, the smile said. But Lola's words roared in Rachel's ears.

"Stop it, Lola," Ashe said.

"She's not who you think she is. If you knew the truth, you wouldn't be defending her." Lola pointed at him, bits of greasy dough flaking off the fried candy as she jabbed at the air with it. Her red-painted lips pressed together, as if for just a second she considered keeping what she knew about Rachel to herself. "Just ask her about the wishes. See what she says."

"Maybe we should get her out of the heat," Jamie said to Everley, with a concerned look at Lola.

As Everley reached for her, Lola twisted away so she faced Ashe. "This has nothing to do with the heat and everything to do with Rachel ruining lives one wish at a time."

"You want to talk about wishes? All right, fine." Ashe shook off Jamie's restraining hand and scowled at him. Jamie held up his palms in resignation, muttering, "It was worth a shot" to Everley, who frowned at everyone. Ashe continued, ignoring the interruption. "I wish you would just eat that damn Oreo so it would shut you up for a change."

Rachel stiffened, her free hand curling into a fist in the soft fabric of her dress. She stepped back as if she could run away from the wish, but Ashe's warm hand pressed between her shoulder blades stopped her. Holding her breath, she scanned the air for a slip of paper. The rest of the festival continued on around them, music pumping from the speakers and people dancing and laughing and drinking despite the hot waves of tension emanating from their small group.

A few seconds later, a flash of white appeared over Jamie's shoulder. She looked away from its lazy spiral, silently repeating, *Ignore it. Don't prove her right.* Ashe tapped his fingers on her back, drawing her attention from the wish.

"I think we're gonna go. Jamie, Ev, we'll catch up with y'all later," he said and pulled away from Rachel long enough to give them both one-armed hugs. "You ready, Rachel?"

"Yep," she said, already turning to leave. She couldn't get away from this wish quickly enough.

Then Everley pulled her back and into a full hug, putting Lola—and the wish that had caught in her hair—right at Rachel's eye level over Everley's shoulder. She squeezed her eyes shut, but the words had already registered.

She tried to think of something else—anything else—but her brain refused to comply. As if some small part of her thought Lola deserved whatever happened after threatening her and spilling her secrets.

Lola bit the Oreo in half and held up the remaining portion as proof that she had done what Ashe wanted. "Happy?" she asked him.

"Not yet," Ashe said. He grabbed Rachel's hand to get her moving.

Watching Lola, she wondered how Mary Beth, one of the most selfless people she knew, could be related to someone so spiteful.

Lola ate the rest of the Oreo in one bite. She stopped mid-chew, her eyes darting from Ashe to Rachel. A strangled sound—something between a cough and a cry of pain—escaped the small part in her lips. Black crumbs rained down to stick on the flawless skin above the neckline of her dress.

"Lola?" Rachel asked, realizing the effect of the wish could cause serious harm. She reached out, her hand grazing Lola's forearm, but Lola jerked away from her.

Everley patted Lola's back a couple of times. "You're not supposed to inhale it, hon."

Lola's eyes widened and darted around the faces watching her. Her fingers left red marks on her skin when she pawed at her throat. She bent forward, her hair swinging down to shield her face, and stumbled into Everley as she struggled for breath.

"Hey, are you okay?" Everley asked. She hit Lola on the back again, a sharp slap of skin on skin.

"Someone, get her some water," Rachel said loud enough for the groups of people clustered near them to hear. A few people looked over at them, but no one moved to help. "Ashe," she said, not sure what she was asking of him.

He dropped his hand from Rachel's shoulders and stepped toward Lola, while Jamie ran off to find a bottle of water. Ashe slipped an arm around Lola's waist to keep her upright, and her fingers clutched at his shirt, pulling him closer.

Rachel drowned out Everley's soft murmurs telling Lola that everything would be okay. She ignored the fact that Ashe had yet to say anything at all. *Please don't do this. Let her be okay.* She checked that they were focused on unblocking Lola's airway and plucked the wish from Lola's silky hair. The bobby pin that had held the wish in place pulled with it, ripping out a few strands of hair with it. Lola whipped her head up and managed a half cough, half yelp. Rachel crumpled the paper in her fist and shoved it into the mess of chocolate and peanut butter in her napkin.

After a few seconds, Lola's quick, wheezing breaths filled her ears. Jamie rushed back, cracking the top off a water bottle before he even reached them so some water splashed onto his shirt. People turned to watch him jog by, eyes widening when they saw Lola's red face and teary eyes. Ashe released his grip on Lola and backed away, stuffing his hands in his pockets. He kept his eyes on the ground, even when Lola coughed and coughed, a deep hacking sound that grabbed the attention of even more festival-goers.

"Here, drink this," Everley said. She took the water from Jamie, pressed the bottle into Lola's shaking hands, and helped guide it to her lips.

Lola took slow sips, punctuated by a whimper each time she paused. Her cheeks remained bright pink, her eyes wide with shock.

"All good?" Jamie asked. When she nodded, his smile shifted from concern to relief and he swatted Ashe's shoulder with the back of his hand.

Ashe still didn't say a word, but at least his jaw had unclenched. Rachel quickly tossed the napkin and wish into a nearby trash can and closed the few feet of space between them, still trying to catch her own breath. Ashe tilted his head toward her, worry pooling in his eyes until he blinked it away.

People crowded around them now. Pushed in closer so their arms and shoulders bumped and their whispers tangled together like the soft droning of bees. Curiosity rolled off of them in hot waves, turning the air thick and hard to breathe.

Rachel tugged at the top of her dress as a drop of sweat slid down her neck and disappeared beneath the fabric. "Are you okay?" she whispered.

"Yeah, you?" he asked.

"I'm just glad she's all right."

Lola locked her accusing eyes on Rachel. "You did that. You almost killed me." Her raspy voice silenced the onlookers.

Shaking her head, Rachel said, "I didn't—"

"You made Ashe's wish come true just like I said you could. They saw you do it."

Rachel flicked her eyes to the trash, to the wish hidden within.

"No, Lola, *you* did that," Ashe said. He threw up his hands and faced her, shoulders tensed for a fight. "What I saw was you pretending to choke, to prove some ridiculous point you're trying to make. That's pretty damn low. Even for you."

Lola swayed back a step as if he'd slapped her. She steadied herself with a hand on Everley's arm and looked at him, mouth parted but no words coming out.

"Ashe," Jamie said.

"She wasn't faking that," Everley said, cutting off whatever sense Jamie was going to try to talk into his friend. "Whatever just happened was a very bad coincidence. Right, Rachel?"

"I guess," she said. Nerves shook her voice, but she hoped it was too quiet for anyone to notice.

"It was not a coincidence," Lola said. She shot a look around the crowd still hovering near them. "She can make wishes come true whether she admits it or not."

Ashe cocked an eyebrow at her, smiling at the people over her shoulder like he thought the sun had addled her brain. "Whatever you say, Lola."

"You don't believe me? Ask her about what she did to her brother."

Rachel's breath caught in her throat. Whatever words she might've said to contradict Lola stalled on her tongue. She didn't look at any of them before walking away. Her heels stuck into the grass with every step, and the back straps dug into the blisters, stinging her raw skin. But she didn't stop. She couldn't watch as Lola tore down the life she'd been building with one well-placed blow.

# 16

Rachel struggled to catch her breath as she made it to the road, which had been closed to traffic for the festival. The street was filled with lawn chairs and blankets. Kids played duck-duck-goose and tag while their parents chatted and nursed cups of beer. Rachel picked her way through the jumble of metal and cloth and body parts. Despite her hurry, she was careful not to step on anyone's hands or toes. She murmured an apology every few steps until she broke free on the other side.

"Wait up," Ashe called.

How long had he been following her? She tossed a quick glance over her shoulder. He still had a few blankets to go before he was free of the mass of people slowing him down. She ducked down the first street she came to. It was familiar, but all the homes in downtown Nowhere looked familiar, with their Victorian styles and lazy wrap-around porches. In her frustration, she couldn't tell if she actually knew where the street would lead.

She cursed Lola for trying to blackmail her. And for forcing her to run away from Ashe when she should've been sitting with him on a blanket somewhere waiting for the fireworks to start. Waiting to see if there was something more to this jumble of feelings growing between them.

Rachel shoved the thought from her head and pulled at her dress, which twisted around her thighs as she walked.

Ashe jogged to catch her, his shoes slapping against the pavement. "C'mon, Rachel. You're not gonna make it all the way home in those shoes. And if you do, you're gonna regret it."

"I can't do this right now, Ashe," she yelled back to him. But she paused long enough to remove her shoes.

It was all the time he needed to reach her. He circled around in front of her and stopped. "She had no right to blame you for what happened. And I don't know how she found out about your brother, but saying what she did was completely uncalled for."

"Who cares what Lola says? It's not like anyone will believe her." *I can't let them believe her.*

They walked on in silence.

The smell of barbecue smoke diminished the farther they got from the park. The first firework vibrated through her, and Ashe ran a hand down her arm when she jumped at the loud boom that followed. When he stopped to watch the next one from someone's front yard, she tried to keep walking. He linked his fingers with hers before she got out of reach and pulled her back.

"Just wait. Please?" he asked.

The fireworks burst above them, dousing everything from the treetops to the grass in shades of green, red, blue, and gold. They had to crane their necks to see the biggest ones. His hand was warm in hers. Solid, like a lifeline. She wanted to say something to let him know she wasn't mad at him, to share some part of herself so he would see she didn't want him to give up on her.

So she let part of the truth slip out.

"My brother disappeared when he was four. I didn't handle it well, so my parents put me in therapy but it only helped so much. And my family fell apart because of it. I had to leave because being there I was just making things worse," Rachel said.

The worry lines stretching out from his eyes deepened when he said, "I'm sorry."

"Me too."

"Was he ever found?"

"No." She was thankful when his fingers slipped from her hand.

When the show ended a few minutes later, he nudged her shoulder and said, "We can cut in between these two houses and come out across from Catch's."

Ashe led her through the narrow side yard and around the enclosed garden that offered more weeds than flowers. He picked one of the moon flowers that stretched over the fence. Its long petals were soft and pale in the moonlight. Rachel's fingers brushed his when he pressed it into her hand. A jolt from the brief contact buzzed through her.

She followed him through a wall of oleander twice as tall as he was and out onto Catch's street. It was quiet with most of the neighborhood still downtown. The light on the front porch spilled into the yard. Rachel tiptoed across the asphalt that was still warm from hours of being tortured by the sun. "You don't have to walk me all the way up. I think I can take it from here," she said.

He reached the front gate first and opened it for her. He followed her up the walk and onto the porch. Leaning down, he cupped her face in his hands, his fingers following a line of freckles on her left cheek. "If I didn't walk you to the door, I wouldn't get to do this," he said and pressed his lips to hers.

The kiss started light, soft. But after a few seconds he took it deeper, pinning her to the door and coaxing her mouth open. He tasted like hops and sun-ripened plums. Her hands gripped the front of his shirt as she stretched onto her toes to get a little closer. He traced his thumbs along her jaw and down her neck.

She sighed against his lips.

Pulling back, Ashe rested his forehead against hers, giving them both time to catch their breath.

"That was—" he started.

"Not fair," she finished for him, her voice shaking. She couldn't allow things to go anywhere between them. It didn't matter if the kiss was due to the wish or because somehow he actually liked her. If she let things progress, she'd have to tell him all the things she was keeping from him. Or lie.

She released his shirt and inched back so their bodies were no longer molded to each other.

His shirt was wrinkled and damp where her hands had been. He tugged at the clinging fabric. "Maybe not. But I think we both needed that."

"What I need and what I want are completely different," Rachel said.

"So, you're trying to tell me you don't want me to kiss you again?"

Rachel pressed her lips together, the taste of him lingering. "I didn't say that," she said. His amused eyes challenged her. Rachel ducked her head, her hair falling between them.

Ashe splayed a hand on the doorjamb near her head but didn't touch her. "You know as well as I do that it was going to happen sooner or later. Now it's out of the way."

She didn't have to look up to know he was giving her the self-assured half smile that made her skin tingle. His keys rattled when he fished them out of his pocket. He reached around her and unlocked the door. Her hand slipped on the knob as he leaned in again. She held her breath and shivered when his mouth hovered next to her ear.

"But I'm thinking we should do it again," he said. He opened the door and straightened, letting his eyes roam over her as she stepped inside the house. "Good night, Rachel."

"Good night, Ashe." She pulled the door closed behind her, refusing to let her happiness be anything more than a momentary thing. No matter how much she might want to believe that Ashe could fall for her—that she could fall for him right back—and have it all be easy, normal. If Lola was threatening to expose her before, Rachel could only image what lengths she would go to if she knew Ashe had kissed her.

# 17

The lightning flashed across the small swatch of steely sky she could see from her room. Rachel counted to five before the clap of thunder rattled the window. She'd been staring at it for the better part of an hour. Her mind jumped between replaying her confrontation with Lola to her kiss with Ashe and back again. Both situations made the room feel so stuffy she was having a hard time catching her breath. And both left her just as confused as to what to do about them.

So she started making deals with herself.

*If Ashe comes over for breakfast, I'll tell him I just want to be friends.* Her heartbeat stuttered at the thought.

*If it thunders again before the rain starts, I don't have to tell Mary Beth about Lola. I don't have to accuse her of telling Lola all of my secrets.* She waited, her whole body tensed as the storm slowly rolled on outside. The thick clouds stagnated, refusing to be bullied by the wind.

Her sweaty fingers left streaks on the phone screen as she opened and closed her favorites list again. Mary Beth's picture flashed on screen, reminding her how much she missed her best friend. Just because she called Mary Beth didn't mean she had to say anything she didn't want to. She hit Call before she could chicken out.

"Hey," Mary Beth said when she picked up.

"Hey yourself," Rachel said. "Sorry for calling so early."

"Lucky for you I was already awake. Everything okay?"

Rachel sank back into the covers. Hearing Mary Beth's voice intensified the tension knotting in her shoulders. *No, I'm not okay,* she thought. *I had a run-in with your completely immoral sister. She knows who I am, knows what I can do. She tried to blackmail me into helping her get Ashe back. Oh, and Ashe kissed me last night. Which may or may not mean something.* Instead she said nothing. She tugged the sheet up and hugged it to her, closing her eyes against the obstinate storm.

"Staying silent is not the way to convince me that you're okay."

"I'm fine," Rachel said after a few more seconds.

"Yeah, I so don't believe you. Please tell me what's going on."

"I've just been thinking a lot about family lately." She rolled onto her side. It had yet to rain or thunder again. She still didn't know whether or not she should tell Mary Beth about Lola. "Do you ever miss them? Your parents and sister?" she asked. She squeezed her eyes shut and held her breath to calm the nerves that waged war in her stomach.

"I don't think about them much."

Rachel couldn't stop thinking about Michael. Even when she tried to force him out of her head, he refused to go. "But if you had the opportunity to see, say, your sister again, would you? I mean, if she suddenly showed up on your doorstep, what would you do?"

"Where is this coming from? Is it about *him*?" Mary Beth asked. She never said Michael's name, as if that would somehow make what Rachel had done to him less real.

"No, it's not about Michael," Rachel said, grateful it was the truth. "And you don't have to talk about them if you don't want. I shouldn't have brought it up."

Mary Beth sighed. "Honestly, Ray, I don't know what I'd do. I guess it would depend on why she was there and what she wanted. It's been so long I'm not sure what we would say to each other. Or if she'd forgive me for shutting her and my parents out."

Rachel would trade almost anything for a second chance with Michael. Even if he couldn't forgive her, at least she would get to apologize. Maybe Mary Beth and Lola deserved the same opportunity.

The wind whipped against the side of the house, rattling the windowpane. Rachel waited for a sharp clap of thunder that didn't come. "But would you give her a chance, if she found you?" she asked.

"Probably. Maybe. I honestly don't know. You and Geoff and the girls are my family now. That's more than enough for me." She whispered something Rachel couldn't make out. Violet's muffled voice called "Hi, Ray" in the background, then Mary Beth was back. "I might be able to take a few days off soon. I could come and see with my own eyes that you're okay."

Rachel shot up, her heart thumping in her chest at the thought of Mary Beth discovering Rachel had kept something as big as finding her sister from her. "You don't need to do that. It's a really long drive by yourself, especially if it's just for a weekend. I'm fine."

"Did you really just turn down an opportunity for me to come visit? We haven't gone this long without seeing each other since we met. Are you sure there's not something else going on with you? You know you can tell me if there is, right?"

A few fat drops of rain pelted the window like gunfire. Mary Beth was right. They were each other's family. And that was enough. "There's nothing to tell. Promise."

She had been so focused on whether or not to tell Mary Beth about Lola that she'd forgotten to be nervous about seeing Ashe. Now that Rachel was almost to LUX, her heart rate spiked as she spotted his truck parked out front.

*It's not a big deal. It probably meant nothing.* But she didn't look in the window as she passed the side of the shop where he was working.

She hadn't even put her purse beneath the counter before Everley gripped her arm and spun her around.

"Interesting end to your first Brews N Cue, huh?" Everley said, leveling her with a grin. "I can't believe you didn't tell me. If I wasn't such a nice person, I'd be really pissed at you."

Rachel touched her fingers to her lips. She could still feel the intensity of Ashe's kiss. Just remembering it made her light-headed all over again. She glanced through the opening into the other half of the shop. Two men sprayed pale-gray paint onto the walls in long, even strokes. The humming from the sprayers drowned out their conversation. If Ashe was there, he was staying out of sight.

"It's not that big a deal. It only happened once."

"Really? Lola said you've been doing it since you were little." Everley peeled a sticker from the sheet of labels and squared it up on the lid of a mason jar. She swiped her thumb across it to affix it.

"Wait, you're talking about what happened with Lola?" Rachel asked.

"I was. But now I feel like we should be talking about something else. If you're keeping another secret from me, I might have to fire you. Spill," Everley said.

Rachel's hand twitched, knocking the pile of lids over. They clattered to the floor in a series of soft, metallic pings. Crouching, she picked up the lids one at a time and willed her hands not to shake as she set them back on the counter. "Sorry," she managed.

"About the lids or something else?"

Rachel walked around Everley and grabbed the pink, ruffle-edged apron from a hook behind the counter. "You don't really believe Lola, do you?" She laughed and rolled her eyes like the whole thing was ridiculous despite the nerves twisting in her stomach.

"Oh, don't look at me like that. It's not such a far-fetched idea, especially not in this town. I'm not saying it wasn't a coincidence or that you hurt her on purpose. But she swore to me she wasn't lying. And she had no reason to stick to her story if she just made it all up to get Ashe's sympathy."

Her ability might be perfectly acceptable by Nowhere standards, but that didn't mean anyone would support Rachel if they thought she used it to hurt people. And if Lola got her way, that's exactly how this would play out.

"C'mon, Everley," she said, an edge of fear seeping into her voice. This couldn't happen. People could not believe what Lola was saying about her. She knotted her hands in the large front pocket of the apron to hide their shaking. "You know if she has you on her side she has a better chance of getting other people to believe her too."

Everley slung an arm over Rachel's shoulder and pulled her close so their temples touched. "You know, I get it. I probably wouldn't tell anyone either. I'm sure they'd be all over you asking for things non-stop. Probably stupid stuff too. There are so many people out there with no imagination. Now me, I'd wish for something good like the ability to give my lotions real healing powers so I could actually help people."

"Wishing for it might not do you any good." Rachel shifted out of her hold.

"No, don't tell me that." The hint of annoyance in Everley's voice didn't register on her face. She smoothed down another label without looking up. "It's not a coincidence that you came into my shop when you did. I'd just been thinking about how badly I needed to find some help. I mean, I was literally making a mental list of the traits I wanted when I saw you outside and I just knew. There was something about you that just screamed you were the person I was waiting for. Like the universe sent you to me on purpose."

"I got lost, Everley. There's nothing else to it."

Everley dropped a lid down with a sharp slap. "You know better than to think I'd believe that. This town is full of lost things and people."

"You know, most people would think being able to make wishes come true was the unbelievable option," Rachel said.

"Most people don't live in Nowhere. A lot of strange things happen here, Rachel. And I've come to realize that life is much more fun if you think anything's possible."

*Not always. Sometimes it makes life really damn hard.*

Rachel turned as someone entered the shop. A blast of hot air and a string of excited barks from a dog somewhere down the sidewalk slipped inside with Ashe. He stopped just inside the door, his T-shirt stretching tight across his chest. He ran a hand through his hair, then lifted his gaze to meet Rachel's. Her heart reacted before her brain, pounding at just the memory of his lips on hers the night before.

"Can we talk for a minute?" he asked.

"Sure," Rachel said. She caught Everley's curious stare and looked away. "Let's go to the other side."

"Don't leave on my account. I promise not to listen," Everley said, her eyes sparkling with curiosity.

"I don't believe that for a second." Ashe winked at her as he passed her.

"Go on, then. Have your secrets. But see if I don't find out anyway."

Rachel touched Everley's arm and said, "I'll be back in a few minutes."

She followed Ashe into the nearly finished addition. Most of the time, she only caught glimpses of the progress when Everley or Ashe held open the plastic sheeting to talk. The brown paper covering the front windows and door kept the light in the room dim. She took in the calming neutral color of the walls and the dark wood floors peeking between gaps in the drop cloths.

Ashe hooked a hand around the doorway molding of a small room at the back of the space and let out a sharp whistle. The two painters looked at him over their shoulders without pausing their work. "I've gotta talk to Rachel for a few minutes. Don't bother us unless one of you is dying."

They chuckled and turned their smirks back to the wall in front of them, nodding their agreement.

"In here," he said to Rachel and motioned her into the room.

More paper was taped to the window that looked into the rest of the space, giving them as much privacy as a room with no door could. She wiped her sweaty palms on her apron and leaned against the thick wood counter. When Ashe stepped close enough to brush her hair back from her face, she tilted her head back to see him.

"You okay?" he asked.

"I'm good."

"If you say so."

"How do you think I should be?" she asked.

He hooked his thumbs in his front jeans' pockets. "Pissed. At least that's what I'd be if someone was starting to spread rumors about me."

"There's nothing I can do about it. Even if I personally told everyone in town that it's not true, it won't stop them from wanting it to be real." *It won't stop it from being real.* She dug her nails into her palms to keep from saying the thought out loud.

"Probably not," he said, a smile tugging up one side of his mouth. "But here's the thing. If we let Lola think she's winning, she'll leave us alone."

Rachel wanted to curl into him and bury her face in his neck. To tell him how much it meant that he was on her side. She settled for straightening so that only an inch of air separated their bodies.

"Listen, about last night," Ashe said, pausing to look down at her. He rubbed the back of his neck as if he was trying to work out what he wanted to say. "I didn't mean to kiss you. Well, obviously I did mean to, I just hadn't *planned* on doing it. We'd had such a good day, and I've let Lola ruin enough of mine already."

Of course he wasn't interested in her. She hadn't wanted him to kiss her simply because Catch wished for it. But kissing her because he was angry at Lola was so much worse. Her chest was tight when she asked, "So, it was a pity kiss?"

"No, more like an I-know-I-shouldn't-but-this-will-make-everything-better kiss."

"If you say so," Rachel echoed back at him.

If she'd been paying more attention, she would have seen it coming.

He had her trapped again. With her back against the counter, the wood pressed into her spine. She put a hand to his chest. His shirt was sticky from the heat. Or maybe it was her palm. Her brain was too muddled for her to tell. When he leaned down, she didn't move. Couldn't, even if she'd wanted to.

His breath was hot on her skin as he persuaded her lips apart. He slid his hands along her jaw, pulling her closer. She pushed up on her toes and pressed into him. She kept her eyes locked on his. He seemed to take it as a challenge and grazed her bottom lip with his teeth. His stubble scraped her skin as he trailed kisses underneath her jaw. Her heart pounded faster, and she couldn't stop the soft moan that escaped.

When he finally straightened, he smiled at her. "Figured I should show you the difference so that next time I kiss you, you'll know I mean it."

She blinked at him, willing her head to stop spinning. She pressed a hand to his chest. If he'd kept it up much longer she was sure she wouldn't have been able to stand at all.

The dimple in his cheek deepened as the smile slid into a self-satisfied smirk. He put his hands around her waist and lifted her like she weighed no more than a pile of rolled-up building plans. He set her on the counter so they were closer to eye level. "That's better."

He kept a firm hand on her hip. His thumb traced lazy circles on a small patch of skin just above the band of her shorts.

"I just want to put it out there that I like you, in case there's anyone else," Ashe said.

"There's not," Rachel said before she thought better of it.

"Good."

He kissed her again, slower this time. The light pressure of his lips on hers had her body yearning for the intensity of a few moments before. The desire simmered in her chest, warming her body as it spread. Her eyes fluttered closed, but her pulse still raced. She dug her nails into the wood and leaned back to break the kiss. "Maybe this isn't the best idea."

"Maybe not, but I'm willing to risk it," Ashe said. He squeezed her knee to get her to look at him.

"I'm not sure I am." Rachel took a deep breath. She willed her pulse to slow and tried to ignore the fluttering in her stomach. "My life is messy and it seems to spill over onto whoever's around me. I don't want to make things worse."

"You're not going to," Ashe said.

"You don't know that."

"Life is shitty sometimes, Rachel. But what good does it do to run away from everything because you're afraid of something bad happening?"

She shook her head, unable to meet his eyes. She wasn't just afraid of something bad happening. She was afraid of being the cause. Again.

She couldn't live with hurting anyone else. "I know you're right. It's not rational. But I can't help it."

"Listen, I'm not looking to jump into anything serious. So, let's just enjoy the fact that we like each other and not put any pressure on ourselves to make it into something else. What do you think?"

"I can try," she said. "But if things get to be too much for you—"

"I'll run for the hills," he said, drawing a cross over his heart and smiling.

She rested her forehead against his chest and smiled. How could she say no to that?

# 18

The lamp was on in the den when Rachel got back to Catch's place. She contemplated trying to sneak upstairs, but if she wanted to keep her secrets from getting out—and have the possibility at a normal life—she'd need Catch.

Catch sat in a squat leather chair catty-corner to the fireplace. Despite the muggy heat that poured in through the windows, she had a blanket draped across her lap as she read a cooking magazine.

"I need your help," Rachel said. She leaned against the doorway, jamming her hands in her back pockets to keep from fidgeting.

"Okay, I'll bite. What do you think I can help you with?"

"A pie. It doesn't matter what kind."

"Is it for you?"

"Yes."

Catch stuck her finger between the pages of the magazine and closed it, keeping her narrowed eyes on Rachel as if she could read the secret on Rachel's face. "What have you got to be keeping secret?"

Nerves sparked along Rachel's skin, and she dropped her gaze to the floor. Her heart beat frantically at the thought of admitting everything to Catch. "Will it work if I don't tell you?"

"You know the rules. You want my help, you tell me what's bothering you and who you plan on feeding my pie to."

"It's not for you or Ashe, if that's what you're worried about."

"I'm not. I've only known one person stupid enough to try and use my own pies on me. I was married to the bastard. Luckily, he was smart enough to get himself killed and leave me the hell alone," Catch said, her tone calm, almost amused.

Catch was probably the only person Rachel knew who could get away with joking about someone's death being a good thing.

"But back to you. Whatever it is you're hiding, you know I'll find out so you might as well tell me now and let me help you."

Rachel bit the inside of her cheek. Catch was right. If Lola started running her mouth to more people about what happened to her at the barbecue festival, Catch would find out anyway. The only way to keep the town from turning against her was to stop Lola before she could convince them Rachel hurt her on purpose.

"I need the pie for Lola," she said.

"You think I'm gonna help you keep *her* secrets?"

"Of course not. I need her to keep mine."

"What does Little-Miss-Has-No-Heart have on you?" Catch asked, slapping the magazine onto the side table.

Stepping into the room, Rachel let out a steadying breath. Then the words spilled out. "I can do things like you can. But instead of binding secrets, I make wishes come true. But I don't always have a handle on it, so sometimes things don't go right. And Lola is threatening to tell everyone all about it."

Catch took the admission in stride, betraying no hint of surprise. "Well, that's an interesting little tidbit you've been keeping all to yourself. You didn't think that maybe I could help you sooner so that it wouldn't be an issue if someone found out?"

"I know. I'm sorry I didn't tell you, but it's not something many people know. And the ones that do know never really believed it." Instead they institutionalized her for a month and then kept her in therapy for years. That wasn't a worry this time around. But being forced to leave Nowhere when she was just finding her place in it—when she was seriously tempted to stay for good—could be just as devastating.

She rocked back on her heels and met Catch's curious look. "I don't know how many people Lola's told, but if I can stop her from telling anyone else, maybe I can do damage control until I can figure out how to keep the wishes under control. Do you think that'll work?"

"Let's find out." Catch braced her hands on the arms of the chair and pushed herself up. She swayed on shaky legs. After a few seconds, she steadied and slapped at Rachel's arm when she offered it. "The day I can't make it to the damn kitchen on my own is the day you can call Hubert down at the morgue to come collect my body, dead or not."

There was a defeated edge to her tone that took away some of Catch's usual bite.

To keep from going down a path neither of them wanted to think about, Rachel said, "Huh, I didn't realize the morgue offered retirement home services." She waited to make sure Catch wasn't going to fall.

"At least the company there wouldn't talk back." Catch swatted Rachel again as she shuffled past her toward the kitchen.

A ball of dough was already waiting on the counter. A glass pie dish, canister of flour, rolling pin, and paring knife sat next to it, almost as if Catch had been expecting this.

Catch rolled the dough in a circle, testing its malleability. She picked at the plastic wrap covering it. Her swollen knuckles made her small hands look frail. She dumped the ball onto the counter with a loud thump.

"Well, make yourself useful. Grab that stick of butter and rub down the pie dish. Make sure to coat it evenly," Catch said.

Rachel smeared the softened stick of butter on the side of the glass in long, even strokes and swirled it across the bottom. When she held the dish out for inspection, she received a grunt in return. She set it on the counter and asked, "What do I do next?"

"There's a derby pie filling already in the fridge that I didn't get to earlier. That work for you?"

"That's fine." Rachel removed the walnut, chocolate, and bourbon mixture from the refrigerator and stirred it when Catch thrust a wooden spoon at her. "So, how does it work?"

"You've got to concentrate on the secret, repeat it in your mind until it's the only thing you can see, feel, smell."

Rachel thought about Michael, about her parents, about how she'd ruined everyone's lives with a careless wish. She thought about how Ashe and Catch would never again trust her if they knew the truth, what damage she could really do. She held her breath. Five seconds passed, then ten. She blew it out and waited.

After another few rolls, Catch peeled the crust from the table and dusted it with a shake of flour before draping it in the buttered pie dish. She pressed it into the corners with her wide thumbs, smoothing it up the walls and over the lip so the excess hung jagged-edged and thin around the rim.

"Then, when your mind is so full of those words you think it might burst, you dip your brush in some melted butter and write the words across the bottom of the pie." She handed Rachel a small glass ramekin with a tablespoon or so of butter in it and said, "Put that in the microwave for eighteen seconds."

Rachel obeyed. She watched the bowl spin in a lazy circle. She started to open the door when the butter bubbled and popped, but Catch's bark of "Leave it!" had her jumping back.

"It's not gonna bite you," Catch said.

"No, but you might," Rachel mumbled.

"Only if you mess up my pie."

Rachel let the microwave beep three times and turn off before she pushed the door release button. She removed the butter. It spit at her, a few drops searing the back of her wrist. Setting it on the counter, she wiped her hand on the towel hanging from a drawer knob.

"So, now I just write it?"

"Now you write," Catch said, sliding the pie dish toward her.

Holding the hot bowl in one hand, Rachel painted the words *I wish Lola would keep my secrets*. Her hand was steady as she wrote. The butter pooled on the surface until the words were unintelligible.

———

Rachel had been ignoring the worry niggling at the back of her mind as the pie baked. But when the oven timer wailed, she could no longer put off asking the question.

"How am I going to get Lola to eat this when it's done?"

Catch passed the oven mitts to Rachel, not getting up from her stool. "If she's already talking about you, she's gonna be suspicious when you show up with a pie. You'll be lucky if she doesn't throw it in your face."

"So no words of wisdom or helpful tips from all your years of doing this?"

"You can't force someone to eat it. But you can trick them, if your conscience can handle it."

Rachel's conscience already had so much weighing on it she wasn't sure how much more it could take. But there really wasn't another option.

Once she had the pie on the cooling rack, Rachel dropped back onto the seat next to Catch. She tapped her foot on the bottom rung of the stool. "What would I have to do?"

"You'd just have to give her the pie and let her think I've changed my mind about helping her."

Rachel sat up straight, her foot slipping to dangle a few inches off the floor. "You want to use Ashe as bait?"

"In a broad sense of the word. But as he won't actually be involved, I feel less bad about it," Catch said. She wrapped one arm around her stomach like she had a stitch in her side and twisted to face Rachel.

Rachel mentally added it to the list of symptoms she'd seen Catch exhibit over the past few weeks. All together, they didn't add up to anything good. But Catch had already released her grip and set her face in an expression that said she wouldn't suffer any more questions about her health. So Rachel refocused on the problem at hand. "Would you really be okay doing that? Do you think she deserves that?"

"Either you want your secrets kept or you don't, Miss-Doesn't-Want-to-Get-Her-Hands-Dirty."

"I do, it's just—" Rachel started.

Catch hissed out a breath between lips pulled tight over her teeth. "Just nothing. I'm not saying I won't get a little satisfaction out of lying to her, but it will get you the results you need. You've just got to convince her that to bind a secret that big she has to eat some of the pie too."

It took a few more minutes of convincing before Rachel gave in. She still wasn't comfortable lying to Lola, but as she couldn't come up with an alternative, it was the best option she had. So she sat there while Catch called Lola and told her to come collect her "damn" pie.

When the soft rap of knuckles sounded on the front door less than an hour later, she shot a nervous glance at Catch and picked up the still-warm pie. The scent of rich chocolate and perfectly browned crust lingered in the kitchen. Light spilled from the lamp at the end of the driveway. The little bit that reached the porch made it hard for Rachel to see Lola's face as she paced. Rachel slipped outside, forcing Lola to pull up short.

"I'm here to see Miss Sisson," Lola said. She gathered her hair in her hands, twisting it into a thick knot like Mary Beth always did when she was nervous. She looked past Rachel into the house, her lips parted as if she couldn't decide if she wanted to say something more.

"She sent me to bring this to you," Rachel said, her voice shaking slightly. She held out the pie with a steady hand, but Lola didn't take it.

"I'm doing fine, by the way. After you wished that I'd choke."

"I didn't wish that. I didn't wish anything. And I'm sorry it happened."

Lola's eyes narrowed. "And I'm supposed to believe you?"

"I don't care if you believe me. I'm just here to give you the pie, which Catch said you wanted." Rachel stepped back toward the door, gripping the handle with her free hand. "But if not, I'm more than happy to leave you out here with your accusations while I take the pie back inside."

"No, wait."

Rachel dropped her hand and met Lola's conflicted stare.

Lowering her eyes, Lola said, "I do want the pie. I know Miss Sisson doesn't want to hear this, but will you please tell her thank you."

"I'll tell her."

Lola took the dish, careful to avoid contact with Rachel. "I'm scared Ashe's dad won't eat a pie if I'm the one bringing it to him. Maybe I should find someone else to give it to him to make sure it works?"

Rachel jerked back and bumped into the door. The glass rattled in the quiet that stretched between her and Lola. *No. His own father?* "Please tell me he's not—"

"Oh, my God." Lola pressed a hand to her lips as if she could pull the words back in. Shame bloomed on her face a bright pink as she dropped her gaze to the porch. "Catch didn't tell you, did she?"

"No, she didn't." When she thought it was just some random guy, Rachel could justify letting Lola think the secret would never come out. But Ashe's dad? A secret that big was not something she wanted to be responsible for letting out. "And I can't let you eat that."

"Excuse me?"

"It's not about Ashe," Rachel said, guilt building hot and thick in her chest.

Lola's eyes narrowed and she shifted the pie out of Rachel's reach. The foil cover crackled as her fingers dug in tighter. "The hell it's not. It's not my fault Catch didn't tell you what the pie was for, but you don't get to take it back just because you don't like that Ashe is involved."

"I mean the pie won't do what you think it will. It won't help you with Ashe because Catch didn't make it. I did. And I can't let you eat it knowing that you think it's for something else."

"I should've known that's not what this pie was for. But I thought maybe you'd convinced her to make sure Ashe didn't find out. I saw the way he looked at you the other day. The way you looked at him. I thought maybe you cared enough about him to not want him to get hurt."

Rachel leaned into the cool glass of the storm door behind her. She thought about how just hours before Ashe had kissed her, and she'd kissed him back. "I do care about him. And I'm sorry for letting you think the pie would help make things better with him."

"You do realize that I could just wish for everything to go back to the way it was, for Ashe to forget what I've done and to love me again?" Lola said. She slid a hip onto the porch railing, balanced the pie next to her, and shook a cigarette out of a pack. Lighting it, she added, "And you'd have to make it come true."

"I can't just make things happen because people want them to, no matter what your sister said."

"Mary Beth wouldn't have told me that about you if it wasn't true."

*She shouldn't have told you at all.* But that was back before she and Mary Beth only had each other to rely on. Back when Mary Beth still wanted her sister in her life. Rachel drummed her fingers against the storm door. "When exactly did she tell you all this? I thought you hadn't talked to her in years."

"It was one of the last times we talked. She seemed to be getting better so my parents let us talk on the phone once a week. It might have been a long time ago, but I still remember what she said."

"How could that possibly be true?"

"If Catch can make secrets stay secret with pies, what's to say you can't make wishes come true?"

"Because it's a crazy idea, Lola," Rachel said, hoping she would see that. She turned away from Lola when the cigarette smoke blew into her face. "My crazy idea. Why do you think I was in therapy?"

"Same reason my sister was. You lost someone you loved and you couldn't handle it." Lola shrugged, taking another drag on her cigarette. "She told me about your brother and some of the things you would do for the other patients. You made Mary Beth's nightmares go away."

That was the one thing Mary Beth had ever outright wished for. At first she'd held fast to the belief that the wishes that came true for the other girls were just coincidences. But after months of waking up in a cold sweat from images of her best friend dying in the car crash—while Mary Beth, the driver, walked away with only a con-cussion and a few scratches—she'd finally whispered her wish to Rachel the next day in therapy. And Rachel had taken care of it, and Mary Beth.

"Just because those things happened doesn't mean I had anything to do with them. I can't do what you're saying I can."

"All right, then, I wish Ashe—" Lola said.

"No," Rachel blurted. Even though she would have to read the wish for it to happen, she refused to take any chances where Ashe was concerned. She waved a hand through the smoke and thought she saw Lola suppress a smile. "Wait."

"If you can't make it come true, what does it matter if I say it?" Lola's tone was condescending, her lips twisted into a smug smile.

Rachel took a deep breath to keep her voice from shaking. "It doesn't," she lied. "Say it if you want. But I won't be responsible if any-thing bad happens. That's all on you." She hoped the threat of making things even worse between Lola and Ashe would keep Lola in line.

"I want Ashe to forgive me because he wants to. Not because I made him," Lola said. She stubbed her cigarette out on the bottom of her shoe. "And just so you know, I didn't say anything to make things hard for you. I just miss Ashe. And I miss my sister. And you're the best chance I have of reconnecting with her."

"So you thought you'd threaten me to get me to help you?"

"Not my finest hour, I admit. But seeing you with Ashe on top of realizing you got to spend months with my sister when I wasn't allowed to just made me snap. I mean, what makes you so special that you get to be with the people I love?"

Nothing. Rachel knew that. She didn't deserve them, but neither did Lola. "This isn't really doing you any favors."

"Just think about it." Lola gave Rachel a sad smile, then strutted down the sidewalk to her car, leaving Rachel even more confused. It was easy to hate Lola when she was the cheating mean-girl she was used to seeing. Less so when she talked about missing Mary Beth.

The pie sat on the railing, untouched. Rachel snatched it up, won-dering what in the hell she was going to do now.

# 19

Rachel held a lighter to the ring of shrink-wrap she'd slipped over the cap of a lotion bottle as a mother and daughter volleyed differing opinions back and forth. They argued about which scent would make the best sweet sixteen present for a friend, what made LUX products organic, and whether or not the daughter could go out with some boy named Tommy that weekend. No matter what the mom said, the girl responded in typical teenage fashion—contradictory for the sake of being contradictory.

"Telling me I'm wrong isn't helping your cause," the mother said. She held out a candle for her daughter to sniff. When the girl pinched her nose, she snapped the lid back on. "Don't ask me about him again."

The girl rolled her eyes, heavily lined in black, then stormed out of the shop, the bell clanging as the door slammed shut in her mom's face. Shoving the candle back onto the shelf, the mother followed and jerked the girl to a stop when she caught up with her on the sidewalk. They faced each other, neither one ready to admit defeat.

Rachel heated another cylinder of plastic, shrinking it onto the lid of the lotion bottle as the argument she could no longer hear continued to rage outside. She kept expecting them to move somewhere more private—that's what her mother always did whenever they had argued about Michael—but they remained in full view of anyone nearby.

Averting her gaze, she noticed a scrap of paper sandwiched between the clear layers of shrink-wrap on a bottle she had already sealed. She rotated the bottle to see what had accidentally gotten caught—and how she hadn't noticed it before. The paper read *Some days I really wish you weren't my mother.*

She didn't have to hear the girl say the wish to know she was the one who had made it. The vehemence on the girl's face as she stood with her arms crossed over her chest said it all.

Rachel flinched though it was already too late. Her elbow collided with the bottle of lotion she'd just sealed, which smacked into the bottle next to it, knocking them both to the floor. The glass shattered, dousing the air with the scents of juniper berries and lime as the lotion poured out.

Squeezing her eyes shut, she willed the wish not to come true. *Don't ruin this family. Please don't ruin this family.* She turned back to the window, knowing she could do nothing to stop it.

The mother's expression had hardened, her lips pulling into a thin line. She responded to her daughter, words pouring out in a rush, then immediately clasped a hand over her mouth, her coral-colored fingernails bright against the sudden paleness of her cheeks. Whatever the wish compelled her to say to her daughter left her too stunned to move. She didn't even reach for the girl, who backed up step by step until a few feet separated them. She didn't move when her daughter turned and ran.

Rachel rubbed out the goose bumps on her arms. The woman's confession must have been hurtful, but at least she was still there. Rachel hadn't made her disappear.

Leaving the lotion to puddle around the shards of glass, she eased the door open and met the woman on the sidewalk. "Are you okay?" she asked.

The mother rounded on her, eyes shiny with tears and jaw clenched. "This is all your fault," she said. She spun around to chase after her daughter, who was already halfway across the park, nearly running into Ashe and Jamie in her haste.

"Did something just happen?" Ashe asked. He skimmed his fingers over Rachel's wrist where her pulse jumped, then led her back inside.

She couldn't look at him. Didn't want to see on his face what she'd seen on so many others. Disbelief. Fear. Blame.

"Just some long-buried secrets being blabbed because I happened to be in the vicinity when the daughter wished for something she shouldn't have," Rachel said, the guilt too fresh to be covered with a lie.

"She's just upset, and after what happened with Lola you're a convenient scapegoat."

No matter how much she wanted it to be different, wishes didn't come true around her for no reason. This was all her. She stuck her shaking hands into the front pocket of the apron.

"What's going on?" Jamie asked, confused.

"It's nothing," she said.

"Okay." He stretched the syllables out so the word hung in the air between them. When she didn't elaborate, he said, "Well, then," and raised an eyebrow at Ashe for an explanation that didn't come.

Rachel turned her focus to the empty sidewalk for a few seconds, ignoring the part of her that yearned to confess everything and have Ashe tell her that what she could do with wishes was fairly normal by Nowhere standards. Then she spotted the slip of paper getting soggy in the pool of spilled lotion.

Normal people didn't ruin total strangers' lives.


Not ready to face anyone yet, Rachel walked through the yard instead of going inside when she got home from work. She wove between the trees, stopping only when she reached the decaying plum tree at the back of the lot. She held her breath against the stench emanating from its corpse. The cracked, crispy leaves had finally fallen off. The spindly branches were broken and hung at odd angles like dislocated joints. She snapped one off. The gritty bark stuck to her hand, and she flicked it to the ground, then scratched at the brown flakes clinging to her skin. She glared at the plum tree as if she could speed up its demise by sheer will.

She jumped when someone banged on Catch's back door in a series of angry raps. Hugging the back side of the trees, Rachel crept closer, unseen.

The mother of the girl whose wish Rachel had made come true a few hours before crossed her arms over her chest and kept her eyes trained on the kitchen through the window. She straightened her shoulders, then took a step back when Catch appeared a moment later.

"You said my secret was safe. That there was no way Genevieve would ever find out. You promised me," the woman said, her voice catching on the last few words.

Catch slapped a palm on the door casing, blocking the entrance. "Now hold on there, Delia. I told you the same as everyone else who comes to me for help. The secret is always yours to tell. I have no control over what you do or don't say."

"But I didn't want to tell her! The words just came out without my permission. Like *that girl* used a wish to control my body and made me say things before I could stop myself."

"Do you mean Rachel?"

The woman swiped her overlong bangs back from her face where they had fallen when she nodded. "Of course I mean Rachel. She was there when Genevieve wished I wasn't her mother, and then she did whatever it is she does with wishes and forced my secret out. I heard she made Lola Riley almost choke to death at the barbecue festival the same way. It's not right what she's doing. Hurting people and revealing things that don't concern her."

Rachel sucked in a sharp breath at the accusation. The scent of the plum tree burned her throat. A silent reminder it held a secret too. One that could come out as easily as this woman's had if Ashe made the wrong wish around her. She choked back a cough, pressing her hand to her lips to keep the sound from giving her away.

"Don't go blaming Rachel for something you let slip in the heat of the moment. One coincidence doesn't mean she's responsible."

"If she keeps on the way she is, she'll put you out of business."

"That's funny. I don't remember you paying me for my services. Or anyone else, for that matter," Catch said. "Lord knows y'all are getting the better end of this whole deal. But if you want to trade, believe me, I'd happily swap my *payment* for your secrets."

"It's only a matter of time before she sets more secrets loose. We'll see if you're still defending her then." With that, the woman stomped back down the porch steps and left.

Rachel stayed in the shadows of the trees until Catch shut the door. The warm breeze had carried most of the rotten plum smell away, but enough lingered in her lungs to burn when she whispered, "I'm so sorry."

# 20

When Rachel walked into the kitchen the next morning she was surprised to find it empty. She stared at the dormant oven as if she'd stumbled into an alternate reality. She scanned the room for anything else out of place. The lights were off and the back door was unlocked. The coffeepot was full, the red power light burning. Catch's usual mug sat empty on the rim of the sink where she'd washed it the morning before and left it to dry.

She startled at a muffled sound coming from the hallway that led to Catch's bedroom. She ducked her head around the corner. A shaft of murky light cut through the darkness. As her eyes adjusted, she could make out the edge of a bed through the opening in the door. She walked a few steps closer and waited.

"Son of a bitch," Catch grumbled from somewhere inside the room.

Rachel hesitated.

The sound of retching followed.

She nudged the door open and crept into the room. The lights were off, the curtains cinched shut. "Catch?" she called. The door to the attached bathroom slammed closed. "Are you okay?"

"Haven't you ever heard of privacy?" Catch called through the door.

"I'm sorry. I heard you and thought you might need some help."

"What? You want to get sick for me?" she asked. The toilet flushed. "By all means, go right ahead."

Rachel moved closer to the door, keeping her voice soothing. Keeping her worry at bay. "Can I get you anything?"

Catch gave a weak laugh. "A stronger stomach."

"I'm fresh out of stomachs."

"That's a shame."

All of Catch's small symptoms she'd seen but brushed off in the past few weeks flooded her mind. What if this was something serious and she'd just let it get worse by not pushing Catch to admit something was wrong sooner?

"I can get you some water or a cold washcloth. Maybe some crackers if you think you can keep them down," Rachel said.

"I don't think any of that's gonna help at the moment."

"Okay. But I'm staying out here in case you need anything."

Rachel sat on the floor in front of the door. The carpet was old, fraying where it met the baseboards, and she traced the flattened loops of fabric with a fingertip. She guessed the carpet had once been navy, but now it was a dull bluish gray. The dark wood furniture in the room absorbed what little light seeped through the curtains. She rested her head against the doorjamb and waited.

Catch threw up twice more. Then she was silent for so long that Rachel considered forcing her way in or calling Ashe. After checking her watch for the eighth time in two minutes, she knocked on the door.

"Rachel?" Catch said. Her voice was faint.

"Yeah?" She scrambled to her feet and gripped the cool doorknob.

"I don't think I can get up."

Rachel opened the door and found Catch half-sitting, half-lying on the floor. Catch wasn't stuck that Rachel could see, but she was so pale her skin was almost translucent. The purple veins created roadmaps up her thin arms. Her knuckles were white as she gripped the edge of the toilet.

Crouching down, Rachel slipped her hands under Catch's arms to lift her. She was even lighter than she looked. When they were both standing, she settled her hand on Catch's waist and took slow, shuffling steps to the bed. Rachel lowered her onto the edge, then helped her lie down but didn't let go. "Do you want me to call a doctor? Or Ashe?"

"That boy's got better things to do than make a fuss over me," Catch said. And for a second she sounded like herself. Strong and in control.

"Just because he's busy doesn't mean he won't find out you're sick."

"I'll be better before he does."

"Don't think so, Catch. You know how I knew something was wrong?"

"You're nosey."

Rachel went to the bathroom and poured a glass of water. When she returned to the bedroom, she pressed a glass into Catch's shaking hand and held it until the tremors stilled and Catch took a small sip. "I knew something was wrong because there are no pies in the oven," Rachel said.

"Damn it. I knew I should have done a couple anyway." Catch slid a leg over the side of the bed. The other one was sluggish, and she used both hands to haul it off after the first.

"You're not getting up. And you sure as hell aren't going to bake, so get that thought out of your mind right now."

"What? Are you gonna go do it for me?"

Rachel picked up one of the pillows and plumped it between her hands. She set it back in place, smoothing the pillowcase. "If you won't let me tell Ashe, and he'll know something's wrong if there are no pies when he shows up this afternoon, then that's really our only option, right? But I'll only help you on one condition."

"And what's that, Miss-Bossy-Pants?" Catch asked. But she let Rachel tuck her legs back under the covers.

"I want to know what's wrong with you," Rachel said.

"I've got a stomach bug."

She wouldn't get a straight answer out of Catch by calling her on what was most likely a lie. Maybe letting her worry show would. "Seems pretty bad. You're sure that's all it is?"

"I'm seventy-eight, for Pete's sake. Don't you think I know what a virus feels like?"

"If you're lying to me, I'm going to . . ." But she couldn't come up with a threat strong enough to make Catch tell her the truth, so she just left it at that.


She'd called in sick to work, knowing she couldn't leave Catch alone. Not with how frail she looked or how she'd given up arguing with Rachel after only a minute.

The sunlight flashed off a sheet of tinfoil as Rachel ripped it off and pressed it around the pie she'd made. The glass dish was still warm but did nothing to chase away the cold, hollow feeling that had haunted Rachel since she'd found Catch that morning. No wish had appeared with words that would link Catch's sudden sickness to Rachel, but she couldn't help feeling like it was somehow all her fault. She wrapped her fingers tighter around the pie and whispered, "God, I hope this isn't because of me."

After checking on Catch and finding her still asleep, Rachel went back to the kitchen in case she woke up and needed anything.

She came out of a daze when Ashe walked in sometime later. A jolt of nerves danced up her arms as her conversation with Lola pushed through her worry for Catch. She now had the answer to the one thing he wanted. As much as she didn't want to keep Lola's secret, she didn't want to see Ashe hurt. She rubbed at the hairs that stood on end along her skin.

"Ev said you had a migraine earlier. Feeling better?" he asked when he reached her. He tucked a stray hair behind her ear.

Her heart beat frantically at the simple touch. When her brain kicked in, she stepped back. "Mostly, yeah," she said in a hushed voice.

"You still look a little flushed." Ashe pressed the back of his hand to her forehead, then her cheek. A dusting of flour floated in the air from her skin when he broke contact. "This doesn't have anything to do with what happened yesterday, does it? I mean, you're not making yourself sick over what people are saying, are you?"

"No," she said, and wondered how many others were blaming her for wishes like the mother had the day before. "I'll be okay, but thanks."

He pushed up on the counter and sat just close enough that he could absently toy with the ends of her hair that escaped the hasty knot. His fingers skimmed the back of her neck. He dropped his gaze to the wooden spoons and knives she'd left soaking in bowls of water. The soapsuds had long since dissolved and the water turned tepid. "Does Catch know you've been messing in her kitchen?"

Her eyes darted down the hall toward Catch's room and then settled back on him. "What makes you think I have?" Rachel asked, one worry instantly replaced by another.

"I left a dirty fork on the counter once and had to eat pie with my fingers for a month."

"Your problem was that you got caught."

"Always was," Ashe said. "So, any chance I get to try some of whatever you made?"

"Maybe." She turned on the tap to reheat the water in the sink. Her arm brushed his leg as she squirted fresh soap into the water.

He trailed the back of his fingers across her bare skin and smiled when she playfully swatted his hand away. "What if I do the dishes? Can I get a piece then?" he asked. He jumped off the counter without waiting for a response and, caging her between him and the sink, dunked his hands into the blazing water with hers.

Rachel stiffened against him, then forced herself to relax. His rough hands slipped over hers, fingers tangling in the popping bubbles. She nudged him back a few inches and turned to face him. Water dripped from her hands onto the front of his shirt.

"I could probably make that happen," she said. "But shouldn't you be at work?"

"I had a few meetings early and things are almost finished at Everley's, so I figured I could take a break and come check on you."

"Who has meetings before seven thirty in the morning?"

"You know when I went to work today?" He tilted his head down so their eyes were closer to level.

"I was just up and noticed you were gone already," Rachel said, shrugging. Hoping he didn't see the truth of his words on her face.

Ashe dropped a spoon back into the sink. "I think you purposely looked to see if I was there. That you were hoping I was so you could come over," he said.

Ashe looked over her shoulder. Whether he was looking for Catch to come out and interrupt them or praying she wouldn't, Rachel couldn't tell. He caressed her cheek, rubbing his wet thumb back and forth on her jaw.

"You think a lot of yourself, don't you?" Rachel asked.

"Sometimes. But I think a lot of you too."

"I guess you got tired of the dishes and decided to try and sweet-talk your way to some pie?"

"I can do both," he said, releasing her.

Rachel reached around him and snagged a knife he had already washed. Before he could argue—or pull her to him again—she scooted out of reach, unwrapped one of the pies, and cut two slices. The orangey insides of the peach pie were dotted with specks of dark red. The sweet, tangy scent teased her tongue as she breathed it in.

"What else did you put in it?" Ashe asked.

"Raspberries," she said and dumped the knife back into the water. "It sounded like a good combo. But in case it sucks, we're gonna eat it instead of sending it to the coffee shop with the others."

"Didn't Catch take some over already? She usually does that first thing."

Biting her lip, Rachel kept her back to him. Hoping her voice was steady as she lied to him, she said, "These are for tomorrow."

"Right. 'Cause whatever is going on with her today is gonna keep her from baking in the morning too, huh?"

"She's fine, Ashe."

"Never said she wasn't. So, are you gonna tell me what's wrong or do I have to go back there and see for myself?" he asked, nodding toward Catch's closed bedroom door.

Rachel leaned on the counter next to him, letting her hip settle against his. She hooked her finger through an empty belt loop on his jeans. Not that it would keep him in place if he decided he didn't like her excuse. "She's not feeling well. She said it's just a stomach bug and didn't want you to worry." It was as much of the truth as she could share without feeling like she was betraying Catch's confidence.

"If it's just a bug, why would I worry?"

"Because you're you," she said. She met his stare, allowing all the pain and loneliness and longing she usually kept buried beneath layers of fierce independence pour out of her.

All she could think about was how he could break her if she wasn't careful. And how maybe finally letting someone get close enough to her to do that wouldn't be such a bad thing.

# 21

The piece of paper stuck to the windshield of Rachel's SUV was too large to be a wish. Ashe hadn't come by for breakfast, and she jogged the last few steps at the prospect of the note being from him. The top edge curled from the humidity, obscuring the message scrawled in thick red marker. She smoothed out the paper, her hand stilling on the wiper as she raised it to free the note. The words wiped the half-formed smile from her face.

*We all get our secrets bound for a reason. It ain't your place to let them out no matter what someone else wishes.*

She'd tried to be so careful to avoid wishes, especially since the incident in Everley's shop. But a few still slipped through her defenses. They'd even started to invade her dreams so she'd wake up with a light sheen of sweat coating her skin because she'd turned a shy boy invisible and wished away a young woman's unwanted pregnancy. But those had just been dreams. Nightmares, really. Unless somehow she was making wishes come true in her sleep without meaning to.

Unlocking the car, she jumped inside and tossed the note onto the passenger seat. She sat there for a few minutes, key dangling uselessly from the ignition, and stared out into the backyard. The trees danced in the breeze, their leaves flipped upside down, a sure sign of an oncoming storm. Despite the heat outside, a chill raced up her bare arms to settle at the base of her neck.

"I'm not letting these secrets out. It's not possible," she told herself, her voice loud in the silence of the car. "This is just about that woman blaming me the other day. That's all it is."

She kept the windows down as she drove into town, hoping the muggy air would help, but the sensation still hadn't dissipated by the time she circled the square looking for a parking space. Pedestrians walking along the sidewalks and lounging on park benches and pockets of green grass turned to watch as she passed. They narrowed their eyes and cupped their hands around their mouths to shield their conversations as if she could somehow hear them across the distance.

Rachel found a spot a block down from LUX. More people stared as she made her way down the street, head held up, eyes focused on the stretch of concrete in front of her. A small cluster of people blocked the shop's entrance. Their voices, like the dull drone of bees, ticked up in pitch as she neared. She made for the construction entrance and a stocky woman in what more closely resembled an old tablecloth than a dress blocked her path.

"I see you decided to show up today," the woman said in a shrill voice.

"Did you think one day off would make us forget what you can do?" another one asked.

Tucking her hands in her back pockets, Rachel met their hard stares with one of her own. "I needed a day off to deal with an illness."

"Something else you caused?" the first woman, Georgia something, asked.

"No," Rachel said.

"Yeah, but would she admit it if she had?" another woman asked.

"Doesn't matter," the lone man in the group said, scrubbing a hand over his sparse beard. "We know the truth now."

A fortyish woman with a severe widow's peak and sharp cheekbones, whom Rachel recognized as one of Everley's regulars, added, "Yeah, and because of her, lots more people are learning the truth about things whether we want them to or not." Her clipped words hung in the air for a moment as the rest nodded their agreement.

"It's not my fault," Rachel said. After the last few wishes had tricked her into reading them, she had been even more careful not to read anything before she was confident it wasn't a wish. Whatever this was, she wasn't responsible.

"So you're telling me that I just happened to tell my sister that the antique time clock she's always wanted didn't get ruined in the fire at our mother's house like I told her but is instead sitting in my living room?" Georgia fisted her hands on her round hips, causing the fabric to swish around her thick ankles. "Because I've had that clock for seven years and she's never called me on my lie. Not until yesterday when she dropped in for a visit and said our cousin Mabel told her about you and it got her to thinking. And you know what she did after she wished to know the truth about the clock, she went right over to Mother's and took the apothecary table we've been squabbling over for years home with her out of spite. And Mother just sat there and let her."

Rachel shifted her weight from one leg to the other, resisting the urge to walk away. "At least she didn't wish for the clock back."

"That would've been better than this. Now she wants to know what else I've been keeping from her. And what's gonna happen if she wants to know where her no-good husband ran off to a few years back or what Mother's spent our inheritance on? Am I gonna be forced to tell her and break her heart all over again?"

"I—I don't know."

"Well, that's comforting," one of the other women said.

Then they were all talking at once, accusing Rachel of letting the man's son know he'd sold their family farm on the outskirts of town. Of making one of the women confess to her mother that she'd been swapping out her prescription pain pills with sugar pills to keep her from getting high on a daily basis, which promptly resulted in the mother threatening to have her daughter arrested for possession of a controlled substance if she didn't stop. Of granting another woman's wish to know if her husband was faithful and learning he'd only kept his vows for three months after they married over twenty years before.

Whatever was behind these wishes coming true, it wasn't her. Couldn't be her.

Unless somehow her ability was changing. Getting stronger so that she didn't even have to know the wish existed for it to come true anymore.

How could she keep people safe if she didn't even know what she was doing to them?

Rachel crossed her arms over her chest and dug her nails into the soft flesh on the backs of her arms. She forced her face to remain calm, the picture of innocence, though none of them would believe it. When Everley ducked her head out to see what was going on, Rachel mumbled a quick apology about still not feeling well and fled.

By the time Rachel got back to the house, she'd made up her mind. The longer she stayed in Nowhere, the more secrets would come out. And everyone would blame her whether she was at fault or not. So she had to leave.

Even if leaving was the last thing she wanted now that she'd finally found somewhere that felt like a home should.

Even if she had nowhere else to go.

She snatched up the latest wish that had manifested on the drive from LUX from the passenger seat and crammed it in the glove compartment unread. The wind caught the car door when she opened it and she flung it shut behind her. The force of the wind railed against her, shoving her along the stone pathway to the back door.

Catch was in the kitchen, eyes narrowed and mouth ticked up on one side in concentration. Her pallid skin hung loose on her face and she sat on a stool while she crimped the edges of the pie crust instead of standing like usual when she baked. "You better not be skipping out on work again because of me."

"This one's all on me," Rachel said.

"Care to enlighten me?"

"I overheard you talking the other night about that woman's secret getting out. She was right. It was my fault."

"If you heard me, then you know we aren't responsible for what other people do or say once they've asked for our help. We can't make them do anything they don't want to."

"That may be true for you, but not for me. Wishes can make anything happen. *I* can make anything happen, and the whole town knows it."

Catch rolled her eyes, the skin wrinkling around them with the movement. "Oh, let Lola talk. I have to believe most people are smart enough not to listen to a single word that comes out of her lying lips."

"It's not just Lola." Rachel dragged a hand through her hair and fisted it at the base of her neck, twisting her hair into a thick knot that sent a spark of pain along her scalp. "There were half a dozen people waiting outside LUX for me this morning. Accusing me of making them spill their secrets and demanding that I fix it. But I don't know how. I've never been able to control what I can do, and I can't seem to escape wishes here. Even when I don't mean to make them come true, they still do somehow. They're everywhere, and they're all making things worse."

"Do you think my pies always worked out well in the beginning? No. I had to learn—sometimes the hard way—how to control it. What we do, it's as much a skill as an innate ability. Like any other talent, we have to practice if we want to get better at it."

"How am I supposed to practice thinking? Because all I have to do is read a wish and it comes true. And more often than not, it goes wrong. There's no ritual like with your pies that I can keep working at until I get it right."

Catch's coffee cup clanked against the counter when she set it down. She frowned at it and then at Rachel. "Did you ever consider that it goes wrong because *you* don't believe it will go right, Miss-Always-Expecting-the-Worst?"

"You know that saying, 'Seeing is believing'? Well, I've seen enough bad results to not expect something good to happen when a wish is involved."

"And that's exactly why you can't get a handle on your ability. You don't trust it. It'll never work the way it's supposed to if you don't believe it can. Don't believe that *you* can."

Rachel leaned her elbows on the counter, wringing her hands. "How can I trust myself, Catch? If it weren't for me, all the secrets you've covered up for people would still be secret. And now that people know that I can undo what you've done with one wish, they won't stop until everything's out in the open and everyone in town is miserable."

"That's a little dramatic, don't you think?"

"Maybe. But that doesn't mean I'm wrong."

"Then what are you going to do about it?"

"The only thing I can. Leave," Rachel said.

It took Rachel even less time to pack up her belongings in her attic room than it had when she'd left Memphis. Catch didn't try to stop her, just watched from the front porch as she loaded a few boxes and her duffel bag into the back of her Pathfinder. Rachel didn't wave goodbye, and neither did the old woman who had become like family to her over the past month. She resisted the urge to run across the lawn and throw her arms around Catch. Partly because Catch was not the hugging type and partly because Rachel wasn't sure she'd be able to leave if she did. She looked away, breaking eye contact, and reversed out of the driveway.

After being diverted by an accident blocking Main Street, Rachel took what looked like a shortcut to the highway she'd come into Nowhere on, according to the map she pulled up on her phone, but it dumped her out on a winding stretch of road that went on for miles. Oak trees infested with thick strands of spongy moss flanked the road. In places, the branches had stretched across it and twined together so it was impossible to tell where one tree ended and the other began. With the dark clouds of a summer afternoon storm amassing above in varying shades of gray, it looked more like a tunnel than a country road.

Fields of cotton plants stretched out behind the oaks on both sides. Every mile or so a long dirt driveway cut up the fields to the road.

When the flash of white appeared on the seat beside her, she swatted the wish to the floorboard. She pressed the gas pedal harder and sped through the tunnel of green and brown and gray, desperate to reach the town limits and be on her way to wherever came next.

But nothing ever came next. She seemed to be driving in circles without ever passing a turnoff for any other roads.

By the time Rachel pulled off into the brown half-dead grass underneath one of the oaks, it was almost too dark outside to see the farmhouse set way back on the property. Thunder cracked, and a few seconds later the sky opened up, releasing a burst of rain so thick the road was obscured from view after a few feet. The car vibrated around her from the force of it.

She checked the map on her phone again. It showed three streets she should've passed already and another two a few miles ahead. Not that she'd be able to see them even if she continued driving.

"Damn it!" She cranked the windshield wipers and squinted into the rain. "Just let me go," she said. A slash of lightning and deafening boom of thunder answered her plea.

Rachel's fingers trembled on her phone keys. She pulled up Ashe's number and sent him a text message: *Stuck on Old Gin Road. Come help?* Her windows fogged up as she struggled to calm her breathing while she waited.

Ashe arrived ten minutes later, his headlights slashing through the darkness. He parked his truck behind hers and jogged through the rain to her passenger-side door. A gust of wind and rain rushed into the car with him. He slammed the door and shook water from his hair.

"What are you doing way out here?" he asked.

"I don't know. I don't even know where 'way out here' is."

Pointing out the driver's-side window, he said, "That house there, that's the one I built for my parents." The sprawling house commanded the farmland from the crest of a hill, all wide windows and pale-gray paint that blended into the sky. "Not that that tells you anything about where you are, but it's odd that you'd wind up right in front of it by accident."

"I was trying to leave," she said.

"Leave?"

She dug her thumbnails into the leather of the steering wheel. "They're all so mad at me, Ashe. And so scared of what else I might do. I'm undoing everything Catch has done just by being here. I don't mean to. I don't *want* to. But I can't make it stop so I have to go."

"You're not making any sense. You were just going to leave without saying bye to anyone?"

"I didn't want to risk anyone changing my mind. And I know you well enough by now to know that you probably could have."

His lips curved in a half smile. "Where were you planning to go?"

Rachel ignored his use of past tense. "To another town. Any other town where there aren't so many secrets."

"Good luck with that."

"I'm serious. I can't stay here. Not with however many years' worth of secrets Catch has kept hidden and how many wishes people throw out there hoping to get an answer. It's too much." She dropped her head to the window, letting the coolness of the rain on the outside of the glass calm her. "But every road I take leads me back here. Even the roads I know for a fact will take me away from town somehow dump me right back in the middle of nowhere. I didn't even know Nowhere had an actual 'middle of nowhere' until today. Yet here I sit, unable to escape it."

"So you're lost?"

"Yes, but that's beside the point. I can't leave."

He took her hand, rubbing circles on the back with his thumb. "Okay."

"No, it's not okay. It is the farthest thing from okay," she said.

"I'm not going to tell you I understand what's going on, because clearly I don't. But this storm is getting pretty nasty and with you as upset as you are, you do not need to be out driving in it. Why don't you come back to Catch's tonight, and we'll figure out what to do in the morning. When everything's clearer."

She gripped his hand, squeezing it tight to her chest where her heart threatened rebellion. "One night won't make a difference. They'll still all blame me in the morning. And by then there'll probably be even more of them to add to the list. I have to go before that happens. Please just help me find a way out of here."

"You can't let a few people convince you that everyone's against you. Whatever's happening, whatever they're making you think is your fault, can't be fixed by running away. Like you said, one night won't make a difference. Come back with me and I promise I'll help you figure this out."

The SUV shook again, the surge of wind pummeling it with a heavy sheet of rain. Lightning flashed in the distance followed by a loud crash of thunder a few seconds later. Ashe was right: She wouldn't make it anywhere in this weather or this mood.

"Okay," she said.

"I'll follow you home," he said and shoved himself back out into the storm.

*Home.* The word twisted in her gut. *Not anymore.*

# 22

Ashe followed her back, but when Rachel turned onto Catch's street, he continued to his own. She sat in the car for a moment, trying to settle her nerves. The rain had all but stopped now, as if the town was appeased by her decision to stay.

The air between her car and Catch's house was so thick with humidity that Rachel struggled to get a full breath. She coughed in an attempt to expel the slightly rotten flavor that lingered on her tongue as she made her way to the back door.

"Didn't make it very far, I see," Catch said when Rachel walked inside. She didn't bother to look up from her baking, but her tone scolded as much as a reproving look would have.

"I'm not in the mood to fight with you again," Rachel said, dropping her purse on the counter.

Catch's head snapped up, and she locked her watery blue eyes on Rachel's. "Good thing, Little-Miss-Runs-Away-from-Every-Damn-Thing."

Rachel fought the urge to smile. "Why? Are you worried I might win the argument?"

"No. I'm just hoping it means you might be in more of a mood to listen," Catch said and slapped her palm on the lump of dough she'd finished rolling into a ball.

"I've been listening. And you know what I've heard? Most everyone in this town is scared of me. They don't want me here, and I can't blame them."

"Oh, don't listen to those idiots. They don't know what they want. You need to listen to the town itself 'cause Nowhere isn't through with you yet. Or did you think you just happened to get lost in a town the size of a peach pit?"

Rachel had guessed as much, but hearing it said out loud—as if being magically trapped by a town was an everyday occurrence—made the hairs dance on the back of her neck. "Are you saying the town won't let me leave?" As much as she wanted to believe that the town itself wanted her to stay as much as she did, the idea that some outside force could keep her here unnerved her.

"What I'm saying," Catch said, letting a little annoyance tinge her words, "is that you are here for a reason. And it'd be a shame if you were too scared to ever find out what that was."

"I'm not scared for me."

"Like I told you earlier, you've gotta trust in your ability if you want it to work right."

The sidewalk was blissfully abandoned as Rachel turned the corner, bringing LUX into view. She fast-walked toward the door and slipped inside without incident.

"Hey," Everley said, drawing out the word. Her smile was as easy as it had always been, no trace of annoyance or fear tightening her lips. Skirting around the counter, she pulled Rachel into a one-armed hug. "What happened yesterday? Are you okay?"

Rachel squeezed her back quickly, then extricated herself. "I'm sorry. I know I shouldn't have bailed on you like that. I just needed to get away. From *everything*."

"Don't worry about it. Everybody has days when they just can't deal with people another second. But after Ashe filled me in this morning on what's been happening, I totally get it. So, seriously, are you okay?"

"Not really. But I don't know what else to do yet."

"Do you want to work today? Get your mind off everything for a while?"

"If you still want me to," Rachel said.

Everley reached behind the counter, grabbed an apron from the hook, and thrust the frilly pink fabric at Rachel. A thick curl spilled onto her cheek and she tucked it back into the mass with the rest. "Why the hell wouldn't I?"

"Oh, I don't know. Maybe because half the town thinks I'm out to ruin their lives?"

"I'm pretty sure it's more like ninety percent."

"Even better." Rachel knotted the apron ties around her waist and stowed her purse beneath the counter. Straightening, she met Everley's eye. "Listen, you know I can't stay in Nowhere after all this, right?"

"That's just ridiculous. You're not going anywhere."

"Not for lack of trying, that's for sure."

Everley rolled her eyes.

"Once I can leave town, I will. I *have* to. But I promise I won't bail again. And I'll find you a good replacement before I go," Rachel said.

"Just give it some time, Rachel. People will come around once they have a chance to see all the good you could do, and you'll look back at all of this and think, 'It was pretty damn stupid of me to think I had to leave because of all that shit.'"

"Doubtful." But Rachel smiled anyway. After what happened with Michael, she swore she would never make another wish for herself. But if she did, that one would be close to the top of her list. Staying in Nowhere.

She turned as a customer entered. The squat woman with short dark hair curling around her face fanned herself with a magazine as she sagged back against the door. The air gurgled as she heaved it out of her open mouth. When she pushed away from the door, she left damp splotches on the glass.

"It feels like heaven in here," she said.

Everley eyed Rachel before saying, "And you haven't even gotten started yet. We've got a talcum powder that'll make you forget you were ever hot and sweaty. Rachel, why don't you grab a sample and show her?"

"Sure thing." Rachel smiled, grateful the woman hadn't turned and immediately walked out upon seeing her.

Running her finger across the labels, she read the various scents—pear and peony, juniper berry and lime, coriander and olive tree, orange and fennel, ginger and lemon, vanilla and pineapple—and tried to pick the one that fit the woman best. She carried a jar of the juniper-berry-and-lime-scented powder to the woman, unscrewed the lid, and motioned for her to hold out her hands. She shook out a fine mist. The scent was crisp and cool with just a hint of sweet.

"Go ahead and rub that in," she instructed.

The woman's rings clinked on her thick fingers as she massaged the powder into her skin. "I hadn't really planned on getting anything," she said, her gravelly voice a few notches above a whisper. "I was just looking for a few minutes somewhere it was cool. But she knew that, didn't she? Your boss. She knew I wouldn't leave without this." She lifted her hands to her face and sniffed before swiping the back of one hand across her forehead.

"She's good like that," Rachel said.

The woman glanced outside as if debating if the twenty-dollar price tag was worth it. She rubbed her hands together again, her smile melting into a twisted scowl. "Maybe I should just wish this damn heat away. It would certainly be cheaper."

"Please don't."

"But could you actually do it?"

Rachel's hand shook, spilling powder onto the floor. "I don't know." *I really have no idea what I can do.*

While Everley went to talk to Ashe about the progress of the construction, Rachel tidied the shop.

The air conditioner buzzed steadily in the background as she added slices of cucumber and oranges and a few cups of ice to the water containers and updated the welcome message with the daily special—two-for-one bath bombs—on the sandwich board sign in pink and green chalk. When the bells on the door chimed half an hour later, she forced a smile, determined not to let any more of the townspeople's accusations get under her skin.

Lola crossed the store and stopped a foot away from Rachel. She gripped her purse straps with both hands. "Hey, can I talk to you for a minute?" She glanced around the shop, her eyes lingering on the workroom where Ashe and Everley were debating two different glass light fixtures.

"I'm working," Rachel said, turning her attention back to the inventory.

"Does that mean you can't listen?"

Sighing, Rachel lifted her gaze and waited.

"I know I wasn't the nicest to you the other day, but I didn't mean for things to get so out of hand with everyone blaming you for everything," Lola said.

"Is that supposed to be an apology?" She bent down and opened the cabinets underneath the shelves where they kept the extra inventory. She loaded her arms with mason jars filled with lemon-sugar scrub. She shivered as the cool glass pressed against her skin.

"No. Everything I said was true, so I have nothing to apologize for," Lola said, taking a few jars from Rachel's grasp and lining them up on the shelf. "But that doesn't mean I'm enjoying what's happened because of it."

"You don't have to pretend with me, Lola. We both know you're just saying that so I'll change my mind and help you with your sister."

"Fine. It's not all out of the goodness of my heart, but I'll do whatever I have to to find Mary Beth. I want that more than anything."

Rachel knew that feeling. She would give almost anything to get her brother back. Had tried to make countless deals with the universe over the years. So far nothing had been enough for the universe to take her up on it. "Even more than Ashe?"

Lola's eyes flashed with anger at being forced to choose. Instead of answering, she said, "If you'd just tell me how to get in touch with her, I would owe you. Big time. I could maybe even help end your pariah status."

Before Rachel could tell Lola she'd think about it, Ashe stepped into the room. One of the lamps dangled from his hand. It swung slowly back and forth. It caught the sunlight and sent shafts of light streaking across the floor.

"Everybody playing nice?" he asked. He looked at Lola when he said it.

She pressed her lips together into a thin line and rolled her eyes. Something about the expression was so Mary Beth that guilt burned in Rachel's chest for not immediately telling Mary Beth about her sister.

"We're good," Rachel said.

"Let me know if there's anything I can do to help you make up your mind," Lola said.

"I will."

After Lola left the shop, Ashe continued to hover. He set the light down and leaned against the wall that separated the two parts of the shop. His shirt was wet with sweat in spots and his jeans had dark handprint stains where he'd wiped dirt from something onto his thighs.

"Can I ask you something?" Rachel asked.

"Sure."

"It's about Lola." She closed the gap between them and stopped less than a foot away from him. "If you don't want to talk about her I understand, but I'm not really sure what to do about something and if anyone would know how she'd react, it would be you."

"I'm not so sure about that, but I'll try," Ashe said.

"What do you know about her sister?"

"I know that she had one. Not that she ever talked about her. But I saw a picture once and figured it was her sister." Ashe fidgeted with a ribbon on one of the bottles of lotion. It unraveled in his hand. "I'm a little surprised she told you. She doesn't even like you. Sorry. I didn't mean it like that."

"Don't worry about it. It's no secret that I'm not her favorite person." Rachel reached over him and retied the satiny ribbon.

"Why did she tell you about her sister, then?" Ashe asked.

"She thinks I know her. And she wants me to help her contact her."

"Do you? Know her, I mean?"

"Yes," Rachel admitted. "But I don't know if reuniting them is a good idea. They haven't spoken in a decade for a reason, and I don't want to break any trust or make things worse."

Ashe leaned against the wall again and stared out the window, lost in thought for a moment. "Can I ask *you* something?" he finally asked, turning back to Rachel.

"Sure," she said.

"Is her sister's name Mary Beth?"

"I thought you said Lola never talked about her. How do you know her name?"

"After Lola moved out, I found a box of her stuff in the attic," Ashe said. "There was a whole stack of letters addressed to Mary Beth Beaumont, but there was no address. It looked like she'd been writing them for years. I even found one of our wedding invitations in there."

"Did you read the letters?" Rachel asked.

"I was tempted, but no. It was just something else she'd kept from me and I didn't want to know what it was. They're still up there if you want them."

"I don't. But it helps knowing they exist. Thanks."

As much as Rachel hated having something in common with someone who had betrayed both Mary Beth and Ashe, those letters proved that Lola had never given up on finding her sister. And that was one thing Rachel understood deep down in her core.

# 23

When Rachel walked into the kitchen and found Catch asleep at the island, knife in hand, she swore under her breath. She'd been so caught up in her need to get away from all the wishes in town, she hadn't stopped to think what the stress of all of these secrets coming out could be doing to Catch's already run-down body. Ignoring her sense of self-preservation, she woke Catch and offered to deliver the six pies that were already lined up on the counter with yellow sticky notes affixed to the aluminum foil identifying the recipients. It took twenty minutes of persuading and the threat of calling Ashe to convince Catch she could handle both the pies and the potential accusations. In the end, Catch was too worn out to keep arguing.

And then there was no way to back out.

She looked up each address and marked them on a map before she left the house. There were four home deliveries and two to the coffee shop down the street from LUX. *Could be worse*, she thought as she loaded the pies into the back of her car and wedged them into place with rolled-up towels she pilfered from Catch's linen closet.

No one answered at the first two houses, though cars sat in the driveways and music hummed through open porch windows from a radio or TV somewhere farther back in the house. Rachel left the pies on the welcome mats, knocked one last time, and ignored the shadows that danced behind curtains as she jogged back down the sidewalk. At the third house, the front door slammed shut, forcing the screen door to swing out, then smack back against the casement with a loud *crack* before she'd even made it halfway across the yard. The sound made her jump. Readjusting her grip on the flimsy disposable dish, she contemplated dumping the pie right there and laughing as the deep-red cherry pie filling seeped out onto the ground. But being spiteful would get her exactly nowhere. So she continued to the house and knocked.

"You can just take that on back with you," a voice called from inside. "I'll just throw it away if you leave it here."

Rachel peered into one of the windows flanking the front door. An elderly woman—Barbara, according to the sticky note—with a tight perm and a lined, sagging face looked back, gray eyes sharp and focused. Leaning closer to the thin pane of glass, Rachel said, "It's from Catch."

"I know who it's from. But who's to say what you've done to it."

"Nothing. I promise."

"I still don't want it," Barbara said.

"I'm going to leave it anyway. Throw it away if you want, but you'll just be wasting a perfectly good pie."

*And perfectly good magic.*

She set it on the small wrought-iron table, clenching her jaw to keep from saying the words out loud and fueling the rumors even more.

By the time she arrived at Elixir, the coffee shop that sold Catch's non-secret-keeping pies, Rachel was tempted to call Ashe or Everley and have them run over to carry the pies inside just to avoid another confrontation. Instead, she balanced one pie on her left hand and the other on her forearm and swung open the door. Heads swiveled her way, and whispers raced from table to table. It was impossible to distinguish between "wish" and "witch" at that low volume. She took a deep breath and held it all the way to the counter.

"Listen," the manager, Janelle, said as Rachel set down the pies. "If anyone sees you delivering this, we won't be able to sell any of it."

"You've got to be kidding me. All I'm doing is delivering them. I didn't help make them. I haven't done anything to them."

"I'm not saying you did, but people are more than a little freaked out by what's happening. Whether it's because of you or not, it doesn't matter. They need someone to blame so they don't have to feel bad about the things they've done and you're an easy target. That's the reality of the situation right now."

Rachel's fingers tightened on the pie dish, pressing indentations into the aluminum. "So you're not going to take them?"

"I'm going to make a show of turning you away, and then you're going to come around back and drop them off where no one can see you," Janelle said, her voice dropping to a whisper.

"All right. Thanks."

She turned, careful not to make eye contact with any of the patrons, who watched the whole exchange over the rims of their mugs and peered around flimsy sheets of newspaper.

It took Catch until the next day to find out how the deliveries had gone—or hadn't gone, in most cases. Rachel would've joked that it must be a record for the longest amount of time something had been kept from Catch if the old woman hadn't barged into LUX and smacked Rachel across the butt with a rolled-up menu she must have accidentally carried out of Elixir in her haste to get to Rachel.

Everley raised an eyebrow at them and, smirking, guided a customer toward the body sprays at the back of the store. Not quite out of listening distance, but at least as far away as they could get without leaving the building.

"Did you think letting them get away with treating you like you were nothing would make them decide you weren't so bad after all?" Catch asked, leaning in so her breath blew hot against Rachel's face.

"I was hoping the town would see I wanted to leave as badly as everyone else wanted me gone and it would let me go."

"Hogwash. You want to be here as badly as the town wants you here and you know it."

"Well, it's not like that's doing me any good. In case you haven't noticed, things aren't getting better."

"That's because you aren't trying, Miss-Wouldn't-Know-What-to-Do-with-Happiness-If-It-Hit-Her-in-the-Face."

Rachel picked at a nail protruding a quarter inch from one of the shelves. Whatever had been hanging from it had been sold or moved to better display it elsewhere. "Excuse me for not wanting to be hit in the face. Even if it is by happiness."

"Don't get smart with me." Catch fought the twitch in her face that might have been the beginnings of a smile. "Encouraging their idiotic behavior won't change their minds. And it sure as hell won't help you get control over your ability. So cut it out. And you," Catch said, pointing a bony finger at the customer with Everley, who was known for her love of gossip, "pass this along for me. I'm going on strike for anyone bad-mouthing Rachel or spreading rumors about her. That means no more pies for anyone trying to run her out of town. They don't want her magic, they don't want mine either. And make sure they know that's coming directly from me 'cause if any one of them shows up at my door asking for my help, I'm likely to beat them senseless with my rolling pin for my trouble."

"Yes, ma'am," the woman said, eyes wide with the promise of a new story to share. Her smile faltered when it landed on Rachel, but she dragged it back into place. "For what it's worth, I'm happy to have her stick around."

"Thanks," Rachel said and smiled back at her, hoping more people would come around.

# 24

Catch turned away a half dozen people over the next week after word got back to her that they weren't playing by her rules. The more word spread about her boycott, the less openly antagonistic people were to Rachel. They still whispered behind her back and switched to the opposite side of the street when they saw her coming, but the direct accusations had tapered off. Not that she ventured out into town for more than work these days, much to Catch's irritation.

Summer finally seemed to be releasing its sticky grip on the town with a subtle dip in temperature. The windows had been open for days, the scent of blooming honeysuckle and fresh-cut grass drifting in on the breeze. When Catch and Rachel were home, they kept the front door open too.

"It's your turn," Rachel said to Catch when the doorbell chimed.

Catch wiped her hands on a towel and tossed it on the counter next to the dough Rachel was rolling out. A puff of flour danced in the air. Catch shuffled out of the kitchen, grumbling under her breath about it being her damn house.

"I thought you knew better than to show your face here again," Catch said to whoever stood at her door.

"I'm sorry, I—"

Rachel couldn't hear the voice well, so she set the rolling pin aside and moved to the doorway leading into the dining room. She still couldn't see who was on the porch, but she could hear better.

"I thought you were someone else for a second. Someone I'm not real fond of," Catch said. She put her hand on the knob, but didn't open the screen door. "But since you're not her, what can I do for you?"

"I'm a friend of Rachel's. Are you Catch?"

This time the voice was clear. Unmistakable.

"Maeby!" Rachel yelled, obscuring whatever Catch said to her. She shot through the dining room, rattling the china in the buffet, and threw her arms around Mary Beth before the door was fully open. "You're here."

Mary Beth braced a hand on the porch railing to keep them from both falling down the steps. Laughing, she said, "You never gave me a firm answer about visiting, so I just decided to show up."

"I'm so glad you did. You have no idea." Rachel gave her another squeeze before stepping back.

Mary Beth looked Rachel over, her eyes narrowing as she did. Then the worry ebbed enough for her mouth to twitch into a quick smile. "You just got flour all over me."

A fine white powder clung to the amethyst fabric of Mary Beth's shirt. "That's what you get for showing up without calling first," Rachel said, grinning.

"This way I knew you couldn't blow me off," Mary Beth replied.

"I like her," Catch said from the doorway. "I don't know who she is, but I like her."

"This is my best friend, Mary Beth *Beaumont*. Maeby, this is Catch Sisson."

"You do know I haven't been a Beaumont for almost six years now, right?" Mary Beth said.

Rachel bit her lip. She knew the name would register and trained her eyes on Catch, silently begging her not to say anything about Lola. "I know—"

"What are you now?" Catch interrupted.

"I'm a Foster."

"Well, it's nice to meet you, Miss-No-Longer-a-Beaumont. C'mon in." She held the door open and cracked a small smile when Mary Beth thanked her.

Rachel pointed out the rooms on the main floor as they walked toward the kitchen. She promised to give Mary Beth a full tour later. She told her to drop her bag anywhere, as if the home was as much hers as Catch's.

"Let me know if you see it start to move," Mary Beth said. She wedged the suitcase between the legs of the stool at the island. Sitting, she said, "I had to forcefully remove Violet from the car twice, so I wouldn't put it past her to stow away in my luggage."

Rachel's laugh came easy. Just having Mary Beth there settled some of the restlessness and gnawing tension she hadn't been able to shake since the townspeople turned on her.

"As much as I would have loved to see her, I'm kinda glad it's just you. We haven't had it be just the two of us since—"

"Since Geoff."

"I was going to say since you ditched me for some guy, but same thing," Rachel teased. She redusted the rolling pin with flour and flicked droplets of water onto the dough to keep it from drying out.

"Yeah, but at least I didn't leave town. Or the state. Be glad I didn't just wish you home." Mary Beth covered her mouth as if she could force the words back in.

"It's okay. Catch knows."

Catch whipped her head around to glare at her. She thrust her hand on her hip. "I know what?"

"About the wishes," Rachel said.

"Oh," Catch said. The pie in the oven sizzled when she opened the door to drape a foil crust cover around the edges. The room filled with the scent of sweet cherries and caramelizing sugar. Nodding at the pie as if it was doing a good job of baking itself, she asked Mary Beth, "Do you make wishes come true too?"

"No, I was just your standard so-depressed-I-needed-to-be-medicated teenager. And with my family, spending most of my time crying out on the side of the highway where my best friend had died was not acceptable behavior, so they sent me to therapy to get over my issues and keep me from embarrassing them more."

"Sounds like them," Catch muttered, adding, "Okay, you two, go on and get outta my kitchen. I've got things to finish up and you're distracting me."

Rachel smiled at Mary Beth to let her know that was a normal reaction and to not take it personally. Leading her back through the house, she bypassed the sitting room in favor of the cool breeze on the front porch.

"Is it happening again?" Mary Beth asked as they slid into the rockers. "The wishes?"

"Yeah. They had stopped for so long it was easy to tell myself they were gone for good. But then I came here and it's like the floodgates opened," Rachel said, staring at a splintery groove in the arm of the rocking chair. She traced it with her fingertip. The wood was sticky with humidity and left a smudge of dirt on her skin. "I've picked up the phone so many times in the past week to call you, but I didn't know how to tell you what's been going on here without you sending someone over with a straightjacket." She smiled at the lame joke.

Mary Beth's throaty laugh broke the tension. Looking sideways at Rachel, she said, "That's not the kind of thing you let strangers do. At least not to the people you love. I've got one in the car just in case."

Rachel reached out and linked her fingers with Mary Beth's. "That's true love right there."

"Damn right," Mary Beth said.

"So, you're not going to disown me if I keep using my ability?"

"I want you to be happy, Ray. And whatever does that, I'm okay with. I've been telling you for years you needed to move on from all the baggage you've been carrying around. Maybe this is a step in the right direction."

"You think I've moved on?"

"Well, not in a bad way. Not moved on from me or anything because that's just unacceptable. But moved to a better place emotionally. And, not that it's my first choice, but you could stay in Nowhere if that's what you want," Mary Beth said.

No she couldn't. Not if everyone in Nowhere kept blaming her for everything that went wrong. But if Rachel could find a way to control her ability like Catch said, then maybe.

"You'd really be okay if I didn't come back to Memphis?" Rachel asked.

"Define okay."

"You know, able to perform basic human functions. Actual happiness is out of the question if I'm not there, but as long as you can put on a brave face for Geoff and the girls, I'll be able to go about my business without any worries."

"I'm sure I can muster up something to fool them," Mary Beth said with a laugh. "But I don't want it to seem like I'm trying to talk you into this. Especially if you want to come home. 'Cause I'd be all for you packing up your things and driving back with me this weekend."

Rachel looked up at the rumble of an engine. Ashe's truck slowed on the street. Music blared through the open window, the metal thumping from the bass. He reversed and pulled into the driveway, kicking up gravel and dust. The engine cut off and the music died.

When he skirted around the hood of the truck in charcoal suit pants and a button-up shirt with the sleeves rolled halfway up his forearms, Rachel had to look twice to make sure it was Ashe. He glanced up and saw her, his tired expression morphing into an easy grin.

Mary Beth let out a soft whistle. "Hello, hot neighbor. I see baking's not the only thing you've picked up while you've been here," she said under her breath.

Rachel forced herself to look away from him. "It's not 'picked up' so much as 'fell in a whole pile of complicated with.'"

"More like a whole pile of hormones."

Ashe jogged up the porch steps and ran a hand through his hair. When he saw Mary Beth, he froze.

"Oh, wow. Hi," he said. He stared at her, lips parted and eyes sparking with recognition. "I'm Ashe."

"Hey," Mary Beth said, drawing out the word into two syllables. She glanced at Rachel, eyebrows raised.

Rachel's skin prickled with heat despite the cool breeze. She pushed up from the chair and the rock shifted under the right runner, so she had to lurch forward to avoid slamming into the house. Ashe caught her as she stumbled to her feet. He rubbed his fingers up and down her arms.

"This is—" she started, staring at his chest, the top of his fraying collar.

"Mary Beth. Yeah, I got that," he said. He tipped Rachel's chin up. He pushed a strand of hair back from her face and met her eyes.

"My best friend," Rachel finished.

"Your best friend is . . . ?"

"Yeah."

"Guess this means you're not free for dinner," he said, releasing her. "Can we talk later?"

Goose bumps sprouted on her arms where his hands had been. "Yeah."

"Rachel," Mary Beth said from behind her. "What's going on?"

"I'm sorry," Ashe said. He half-waved at Mary Beth before heading down the sidewalk to his truck. He looked back at her just once, his shoulders slumped and the tension pinching his mouth into a thin line, before he closed the truck door behind him.

Mary Beth grabbed Rachel's hand and jerked her back into the chair. Her nails dug into the soft underside of her forearm. Rachel tucked a leg under her and took a deep breath.

"There's something I need to tell you. I should've told you a while ago, but, I don't know, I guess I just didn't want you to not come visit because of it," she said.

"You've already made up your mind to stay permanently," Mary Beth said.

"Not what I was going to say." She started rocking. The chair grated against the wood planks beneath, scratching softly. Taking a deep breath, Rachel blurted out, "Your sister's here."

Mary Beth's smile melted away. "Shit." She scanned the yard as if expecting Lola to jump out from behind a tree or lamppost. "How is she here?"

"She lives here, Mae. She's been in Nowhere since your family left Memphis."

"Since they left me, you mean?"

Rachel nodded. It wouldn't do any good to remind her friend she was the one who told them to leave her alone in the first place. That she hadn't wanted to believe them when they said everything would be fine again if she'd just put the accident behind her and move on. That she had refused to see them so many times they finally gave her exactly what she'd wanted.

"How do you even know it's her?" Mary Beth asked.

"Lola recognized me from one time when she visited you. She asked me to help her get in touch with you. But she doesn't know that we're still friends. I didn't tell her anything."

Mary Beth gripped her hand, squeezing hard until Rachel looked at her. The flecks of gold in her hazel eyes intensified when she said, "She hasn't tried to get in touch with me in ten years. Why would she want to see me now?"

"I have no idea. But it shouldn't be too hard to find out," Rachel said.

# 25

It took the better part of breakfast, but Rachel managed to pry directions to Lola's apartment out of Catch the next morning, along with a mumbled "Don't come crying to me if this don't work out." Catch's eyes flicked to Mary Beth, who, hands shoved in the back pockets of her jeans, shifted her weight from one foot to the other and back again.

They made the five-minute drive to downtown in silence. The building was older and similar enough to the two on either side that Rachel had to check the number again to make sure they picked the right one. The stone front was faded and chipped. The topiaries in large cement planters on either side of the door had been cut to resemble corkscrews.

Mary Beth clutched the back of Rachel's shirt and tugged her to a stop. "I don't think I can do this," she whispered. "It's been so long. I'm a totally different person now."

"Listen, you were both young enough not to have a choice before. Now you can decide your relationship on your terms." She unhooked Mary Beth's fingers from her shirt and they walked inside.

The spacious lobby didn't match the outside. It was classy and sleek and still somehow reminiscent of the original building. The inset ceiling painted in a steely gray accented by white crossbeams and the arched doorways of the elevators all but screamed Ashe had renovated the building. The more she was around him, the easier it was to pick out his work.

They continued up the curving staircase to the third floor. The paneled white doors all had brushed-nickel numbers affixed to them. Rachel stopped when they reached the corner unit. She looked at Mary Beth and hesitated.

Mary Beth was staring at the door like it was the only thing keeping her safe. Her cheeks paled. "You knock," she said.

Rachel waited another few seconds to make sure Mary Beth wasn't going to faint, then knocked.

Lola cracked the door just far enough to see out.

Rachel didn't even try to smile. "Can we come in for a minute?"

"Depends. Who's 'we'?"

"Me and Mary Beth."

"She's here? She's here now?" Lola stammered. She nudged the door wider but clutched at the edge before it opened far enough to see inside. She turned and looked at something in the room. "Can you give me just a second?"

Rachel nodded, and the door shut in her face.

Mary Beth slipped her hand into Rachel's and held tight. "Is there anything I can say to convince you to go in there with me?"

As happy as she was to be able to help her friend find some closure with her sister, a speck of jealousy had wormed its way into her heart. She would never have that with Michael. And she couldn't sit there watching Mary Beth and Lola reconnect and pretend like it wasn't eating her up inside.

Forcing herself to stay focused on her friend, she said, "It'll just make things even more awkward if I do. You'll be fine. I promise. Text me if you need me. And there's wine and pie back at the house if you need it."

Mary Beth hugged her. "I don't know how I've survived without you for almost two months."

"Back at ya," Rachel said.

When the door opened, she didn't want to let go of Mary Beth's hand. She gave it a squeeze for reassurance and stepped aside.

Lola's eyes sparkled with tears. She looked at her sister, her glossed lips turned up in a tentative smile. "Sorry. I thought it would be better to see you for the first time when I wasn't in my pajamas," she said.

"I wouldn't have minded," Mary Beth said.

"Your hair's so short."

"Yeah, I guess." Mary Beth tugged on the ends. "It's good to see you, Lola."

"You too. You have no idea how good," Lola said. She smiled the first genuine smile Rachel had seen from her. "Come on in." She held the door wide for them and grabbed Rachel's wrist before she could walk away. Her grip was light, just enough to make Rachel pause. "I know you didn't do this for me, but thank you," she whispered.

Rachel stepped back into the hall, letting Lola's hand fall away. "I know what it's like to miss someone you love and thought you had lost forever. I couldn't stand in the way of y'all getting each other back."

If she couldn't know how good it felt to have that moment happen with Michael, at least she could give it to her best friend.


After leaving Mary Beth to talk with her sister, Rachel went to find Ashe. She owed him an explanation. And an apology.

She passed through the bubble of cool, calming air in front of LUX and took a deep breath as the feeling faded when she reached the entrance to the new space. She hesitated on the sidewalk. Ashe stood by the far wall, scribbling something on a note taped to the new paint. He looked up, saw Rachel. His face softened as he pushed a stray strand of hair off his forehead. She plucked at her shirt that stuck to her balmy skin as she walked inside.

"I'm sorry I didn't tell you about Mary Beth," she said.

Ashe tapped the clipboard against his palm and raised an eyebrow at her. "So, Lola's long-lost sister is your best friend. Only in Nowhere would that make sense."

"Catch said something about Nowhere being one hell of a lost and found and it being inevitable. I didn't quite follow it then, but I get it now."

Ashe leaned against the wall separating the retail space from the new workroom. The light from the workroom brought out the sharp blond highlights in his hair. "She has this theory that all sorts of lost things end up here. Stolen paintings that have been missing for decades suddenly turn up in someone's attic or garage sale. Bags of money tumble out from behind drywall during a home renovation. Wedding rings that disappeared down a drain or slipped off at a beach fall out of books at the library. And people passing through town on their way to who knows where end up staying, like Nowhere was where they were headed all along."

He nodded to her, a hint of a smile playing on his lips.

"Do those things really happen, or is that just some line to keep the tourists hanging around a few more days?" she asked.

"You didn't plan on staying here, and then when you tried to leave, you couldn't. If you had, Mary Beth and Lola might not have ever found each other again, so you tell me."

Rachel brushed her hand over the velvety cream-colored fabric of the chaise lounge. "Do you think that's the only reason I'm here? Not that giving Mary Beth a second chance with her family isn't enough. But maybe I'm stuck here so that I can find something I've lost too?"

"Stuck?"

"You know what I mean."

"I thought you liked it here."

"I do, Ashe. But I'm not exactly in the running for citizen of the year. Do you know how much it sucks to be in a place where almost no one wants you? A whole lot, in case you were wondering."

"Sounds to me like that's a very convenient excuse to get the hell out of Dodge and never look back," he said.

"I won't say that's not part of it. But I've tried to leave and the town wouldn't let me. So maybe if there's nothing else for me to find here, it will and I'll know Nowhere isn't where I'm supposed to be."

Pushing off the wall, Ashe walked to her and took her hand. He circled her around to the side of the chaise, nudged her onto it, and squatted in front of her. He rested his forearms on her knees, holding her hands between them. "I think if you want to find something badly enough, you can make it happen here."

"You don't know how badly I hope you're right," she said.

A wish started to form in her mind, and, closing her eyes, she willed it away.

Sitting in the kitchen, Rachel picked at the crust of the toasted tomato and mozzarella sandwich Catch had served for lunch. A chunk of it fell off and scattered crumbs on the counter as it broke apart. She hid the bits of crust under the edge of her plate with her pinky and took a bite before Catch could snap at her for playing with her food.

It had been more than three hours since she'd left Mary Beth at Lola's. The only text Rachel had gotten said Lola would drive Mary Beth back "later." And though her conversation with Ashe had calmed some of her nerves, she hoped that the extended visit meant things were going well between the Beaumont sisters.

Catch had already cleared their plates and started amassing ingredients for the next pie when the front screen door creaked open.

"In the kitchen," Rachel called. She turned on the stool and held her breath. "Well?" she asked when Mary Beth reached them.

She sat on a stool next to Rachel, slipping her arm around her waist tightly. Leaning her head on Rachel's shoulder, she said, "It was weird. I mean it was good, but it was also so weird."

"Maybe I should've kept my mouth shut?"

"No. I'm glad you didn't."

"Are you sure?" Rachel asked.

"There was so much I wanted to ask her, so much that I wanted to know about her life," Mary Beth said. She released Rachel and slouched onto her elbows. "But at the same time I didn't want to tell her about Geoff and the girls. I did, eventually, because she saw the wedding ring and asked. But the whole time, all I could think was 'I don't want her to tell our parents.'"

"After everything you've been through with them, it's understandable."

Catch stopped adding ingredients to the glass bowl and pointed her wooden spoon toward Mary Beth. "You're being cautious. In my opinion, that's not a bad thing. That girl's had years to find you and she didn't. That's gotta tell you something."

Mary Beth sighed and sank lower onto her arms. "She's not the only one to blame. I didn't try to find her either."

"Ashe said there's a box of letters she wrote to you but never mailed in his attic. Want me to have him bring them over?" Rachel asked.

"If it's okay with Lola that would be great. Reading them might help me figure out what to do now. I'll text her and let you know."

Slamming the refrigerator door, Catch glared at them both. "I hope she's more trustworthy toward you than she was toward Ashe." She ripped the paper from a stick of butter, exposing the top half, and rubbed it along the pie dish. "But things have a way of coming out in Nowhere, as Rachel can tell you. They'll find out you're here if you don't do something about it. I can make you a pie, if you want."

Rachel put a hand on Catch's arm. "No."

"What? My pies are fine for everyone else, but not your friend?"

Mary Beth's stool creaked as she leaned forward. "What exactly are we making a pie to do?"

Catch shook off Rachel's hand and narrowed her eyes, making the wrinkles bunch up on her forehead. "To keep your parents from knowing you were ever here."

"You can make people forget things with pie?" Mary Beth looked both confused and intrigued.

Catch nodded. "It's a gift," she said, her voice carrying a sarcastic tone.

"Okay, then I guess I want to make a pie . . ." Mary Beth's voice trailed off.

"That's what you want, isn't it? To have your parents leave you alone?"

"Yes. But . . ."

"Well, go on, spit out the rest," Catch said when Mary Beth met her stare with her wide eyes.

"What if I change my mind? I don't want this pie to make it so I can't ever contact them."

Smiling, Catch said, "Things can always be undone. You just have to know the loophole. In this case, you are the loophole and can spill your own secrets anytime you like."

*Always.* The word spread through Rachel's body like a jolt of electricity, vibrating her nerves and making her blood pump faster. When Catch met her eyes, she asked, "Even a wish?"

Could she really find a loophole to bring Michael back? To set things right with her dad? She'd never been able to do it on her own. But with Catch's help, maybe she could find a way to fix everything she'd ruined.

"Yes. Even that." Catch's mouth twitched almost as if she was in pain. "Now, let's bake Miss-Wants-to-Stay-Anonymous a pie, shall we?"

# 26

The kitchen was empty when Rachel went down to start a pot of coffee before Mary Beth hit the road. A pie was already baking in the oven, and the scent of blueberries and vanilla made her stomach growl. A bowl of fluffy white cream sat on the counter covered in plastic wrap next to another bowl containing plump, dark blueberries.

The first hint of sunrise was just visible through the trees outside as Rachel scooped coffee grounds into the filter. The yard was still, no breeze shaking the leaves or birds pecking at the fruit. When something thudded on the back porch, she almost poured the water on the floor instead of into the coffeemaker. She whipped around and accidentally banged the pot against the side of the counter. She hugged it to her chest as Ashe pushed through the door.

"God, you scared the shit out of me," Rachel said. She threw him an annoyed look, then inspected the pot for cracks and, finding none, dumped the water into the reserve and powered on the coffeemaker.

"Sorry. Didn't realize you'd be down here so early," he said. He shut the door and set a thick bundle of yellowing envelopes on the island. "I brought those letters over for Mary Beth."

"Oh, thanks. I meant to stop by and get them last night after Lola said it was okay, but I kinda just wanted a night alone with Mary Beth."

"Good visit, then?"

"Really good."

Smiling at her, he dunked a blueberry in the bowl of cream, then popped it in his mouth. "Want one?"

Rachel raised an eyebrow at him and settled onto a stool at the island across from him. "What if Catch has plans for those?"

"She doesn't." He grinned at her and ate another one.

"What makes you so sure?"

"She knows better than to leave stuff on the counter unattended if it's not fair game. You should know that by now."

"Very true." Rachel took the berry he held out to her and swiped it through the cream. It tasted almost as decadent as the sweet, fruity scent pumping from the oven.

Resting his elbows on the counter, Ashe stretched across it so his face was a foot away from hers. He slid his hand beneath hers, trailing his fingers along her palm, down to her wrist, and back up again. "Mary Beth didn't convince you to go back to Tennessee with her, did she?"

A rush of heat spread up her arm from his touch. She flicked her fingers over the underside of his wrist and lifted her gaze to meet his. That confident smile she'd grown so used to over the past two months drew her attention down to his lips. "Is this your way of saying you agree with the town and don't want me to go?"

"Well, it'd be much harder to kiss you if you left." He closed the distance between them, cutting off whatever reply she might've had with his mouth.

Rachel's bare feet pressed into the bottom rung of the stool as she leaned even closer to him.

"Oh, I see how it is," Mary Beth said from the darkened dining-room doorway. Rachel jumped and had to steady herself with a hand on Ashe's shoulder to keep from slipping off the stool. "You sneak out of your room at zero-dark-thirty so you can make out with a cute guy in the kitchen instead of seeing me off?"

"It's almost seven, Mae. And I came down to make you coffee." She stroked her hand down Ashe's neck, smiling at him, then sat back down. "This was just a perk."

Shuffling into the room, Mary Beth hugged Rachel from behind. "Coffee? You're the best."

"I'm pretty sure you own that title. By the time you get home, you'll have spent half as much time on the road as you did in Nowhere."

"Yeah, but I got to see you, so it'll be totally worth it."

Ashe poured three mugs and held one out to Mary Beth. "Sugar's on the counter in the blue canister and cream's on the top shelf of the fridge."

She wrapped both hands around the mug and inhaled the steam rolling off her coffee. "Black's good." She slid onto the stool next to Rachel at the island where the stack of letters Ashe had brought over waited. She lifted her eyes to Ashe, who leaned against the counter on the other side. "So, you're my brother-in-law."

Ashe shrugged, the corners of his mouth tugging down. "At least for a little while longer."

"I'm sorry about that. I know it can't be an easy thing to go through."

Rachel rubbed circles on Mary Beth's back, offering what support she could for the awkward conversation happening around her.

"Can't say I'd recommend it," he said.

"I know it's really none of my business, but is there any way Lola deserves a second chance?" Mary Beth asked.

With all the trust issues Mary Beth had with her own family, Rachel knew she wouldn't even be asking if she'd known Lola had cheated on Ashe with his dad. But that was something she hoped neither of them ever found out. That knowledge could cut the final thread holding together Ashe's relationship with his dad and sever any chance of Mary Beth and Lola building any sort of real connection again.

"Not from me, not for what she did. But that doesn't mean you should write her off." Ashe straightened and pushed off the counter to lean closer to her. "Listen, I'm sure it must be weird for you to suddenly find her after all this time. And to not know what kind of person she's turned into. But the only way you're going to get to know her again is to try. For what it's worth, I think that's something you both deserve a shot at."

Rachel mouthed *thank you* when he smiled at her. She rubbed the ribbon binding the envelopes between her fingers and pulled the stack toward Mary Beth. "And if you say something you wish you hadn't, just let Catch know and she'll take care of Lola."

Ashe tossed Rachel the oven mitt seconds before the timer buzzed. "Is that what this pie is for?"

"No, we made that one yesterday. Seeing Lola I could handle. My parents, not so much," Mary Beth said.

Rachel pulled the pie from the oven and set it on the wire cooling rack just out of Ashe's reach. The top crust was gold with a ring of darker brown covering the scalloped edges. Dark purple filling bubbled out of slits in the top. She looked up and caught Mary Beth watching her, a small smile playing on her lips.

"What?" she asked.

"You just seem so at home here. Not just in Catch's kitchen, but in Nowhere in general," Mary Beth said. "I feel tons better about going home knowing that you're happy here."

Rachel pressed her knuckles to her chest, the thought of not being able to stay in Nowhere making her heart beat faster.

Work had been slower than usual with people purposely doing their shopping on Rachel's days off. Not that she minded the break from unwanted wishes and glares. But the monotony of cleaning and straightening day after day without the social interaction she'd come to love was wearing thin.

She looked up as the bell jangled and a woman entered. Her faded brown dress was at least two sizes too big and hung on her bony frame like an unwanted hand-me-down. Dirt and years of wear had turned her sneakers gray. She jolted when the door clicked shut behind her. "Hi, Everley," she said.

"Hi, Helen," Everley replied.

Helen twisted her fingers together and wouldn't look either of them in the eye. "Um, could I have a minute alone with Rachel?"

"Sure. Rachel, I'm gonna go check in with Ashe. Holler if you need me." Everley eyed Rachel and slipped into the other side, only looking back once with her eyes narrowed in an are-you-okay kind of way.

Turning back to the woman, Rachel stuck her hands in her back pockets, and feeling the wishes she'd stashed there, immediately removed them. "I'm not really able to help you with much unless you want me to ring you up. For everything else, Everley's your girl."

"No, it's not a cream or anything." The woman looked around and, seeing they were alone, she continued in a hushed voice, "I heard you can . . . can make things happen. Is that true?"

"I'm sorry, but—"

"Please, before you say no, I can pay you. Not much, but I have a little set aside for emergencies, and I think this would qualify as one, don't you?"

"I'm not even sure what we're talking about, Helen," Rachel said. *Please don't do this. Just walk away.* She attempted a smile but wouldn't meet Helen's pleading stare.

Helen pulled a wad of bills from her pocket and thrust it at Rachel. "Please help me. I just wish we weren't losing our home. My husband, Ricky, made a deal to sell our farm—the land, the animals, the house—all of it. He didn't even tell me before he did it."

"I'm sorry."

"It's my fault he did it. I got sick and the medical bills were too much and the bank wouldn't let us take out any more loans. But that land's been in his family for generations. Farming is all he's ever known. We can't survive without it. Can you do whatever it is you do and help us get it back? Or at least keep it tied up legally for long enough that we can find a way to afford to get it back ourselves?"

Rachel pressed the money back into Helen's clammy hands. She bumped into the display table and a bar of soap tumbled to the floor with a slap. They both jumped back a step. "You don't know what you're asking," she said.

"Please. If it's not enough money I can try to get some more. I'm not asking for you to fix everything that's gone wrong for us. Just this one thing. I'll never ask you for anything again. Cross my heart."

"It's not that simple, Helen. It might not work out the way you want. You'll be better off saving that money so you can find a new house, new jobs."

Helen's eyes were glassy when she looked at Rachel. "I'll save it in case you change your mind." She clenched the money in one fist as she left.

The bell warbled as a piece of paper dislodged and fell out. When Rachel picked it up, there were tiny black words bleeding into the soft fibers of the paper. She flipped the lock on the door and stuffed the paper in her pocket with the rest.

Everley came back in a few minutes later. "Is Helen okay? She looked upset."

"She's worried about her family," Rachel said.

"Yeah, she's been a mess since Ricky sold the farm. Worried herself sick and lost a good ten pounds. Doc Jensen tried to put her on antidepressants, but she refused to take them. Said she'd be fine once the lawyers worked things out and they got their deed back. What did she think you could do for her?"

Rachel shrugged.

"Don't do that. She obviously came to you for a reason."

"She wanted me to grant a wish. And I told her I couldn't help her," Rachel said, staring out the window in the direction Helen had gone. The street was bare but for the heat vapor that rose from the asphalt distorting the road.

No matter what Rachel did, she couldn't get Helen's plea to save her farm out of her head. She was so distracted at dinner that Catch got fed up with her and took her bowl of bow tie pasta and chicken to her bedroom. Rachel left her half-eaten dinner on the counter.

Something flashed white outside the kitchen window. The sky was growing darker blue, but there was still enough light for her to see. Her car's windshield was covered in what looked like feathers. The small strips of white fluttered and danced in the wind. When she walked out on the back porch, she heard a faint rustling, like wind through leaves, but scratchier.

Rachel tripped over a rock, but the fist-sized gray stone didn't budge. Catching herself on the railing, she noticed a scrap of paper sticking out from beneath it. She bent and tugged the paper out. She nudged the rock with the toe of her shoe and it fell off the side of the deck as if it weighed nothing. The note read: *I wish my parents would get back together.*

The paper slipped from her fingers. Like the rock, it refused to move despite a strong gust of wind that rattled the papers clinging to her car.

"What do you want?" she shouted at the empty yard. "Why are you doing this?"

Rachel charged down the steps, the wishes buzzing like a swarm of cicadas. She lifted the wipers and swept her arm over the slips of paper. A few of the less desperate wishes dislodged and took flight. They flitted through the air and landed in a neat pile at the back door. The rest remained glued to the glass.

She pinched one between thumb and forefinger and peeled it off. *I wish my Grams was still alive.* She pulled off another. *I wish I knew why my friends don't like me anymore.* And another. *I wish everyone could see through his charm to the amoral creep beneath.* And another. *I wish I didn't resent the baby for taking over everything in our lives.*

Grabbing them by the fistful, she stuffed them in her pockets. When her pockets bulged, she cupped her shirt and dumped the rest into it.

"Okay, okay," she said when a half dozen more floated down from the gutters and settled on top of the rest. "I'll try to help."

She remembered the desperate twist of Helen's mouth when she begged for Rachel's help. *I wish Helen's farm belonged to her family again.* She hugged her arms across her chest and closed her eyes.

*Oh, God, please let me help her. Please, please, please don't let this wish go wrong.*

Rachel stopped at the back door, scooped up the last stack of wishes, and locked the door behind her, hoping she wouldn't end up regretting what she had started.

# 27

Catch had two pies completed and another one in the oven by the time Rachel made it downstairs for breakfast. With the ceiling fan off again and the oven going full tilt, the kitchen was stifling. Despite that, Catch wore a cardigan over her fruit-stained apron. She was still pale and grimaced every third step as she moved around the kitchen collecting ingredients for the next pie.

"You might want to check the front page," Catch said. She pointed to the newspaper she'd left on the counter.

Rachel took the glass of orange juice Catch handed her and sat at her usual spot at the island. Ashe's seat was empty. She tried not to feel disappointed. She'd seen him in passing at work, but they hadn't been alone together in days. She wasn't sure yet if that was a good thing or not.

"Did you give a tell-all to the paper?" she asked.

"I'm not in the business of *sharing* secrets, Miss-Smarty-Pants. But you should've given Lola that pie when you had the chance."

"Oh, no. What did she say?" Rachel's juice sloshed over the side of her glass when she knocked it in her haste to get to the paper. She unfolded the cover. A picture of a man she didn't recognize took up half the page. His smile looked out of place on his gaunt, stubbly face.

The headline read, FARM DEED REVERTS TO WILBANKS FAMILY AFTER PAPERWORK MISFILED.

Her hands were sweaty. The newsprint rubbed off on her fingers as she continued to read.

> When asked about this miraculous turn of events, Ricky Wilbanks, 38, gave credit to a woman he's never met for giving his family their farmland back. "My wife said she asked a woman to help us after I'd been conned out of the farmland that's been in my family for four generations, like a handful of other down-and-out families in Nowhere. Apparently this woman can make wishes come true, or something," Wilbanks explained. "Helen heard about her after someone else almost died because of a wish at the local barbecue festival and tracked her down at that fancy beauty supply shop where she works. She begged the woman to wish for us to keep our home. I thought it was some scam to take what little money we had left, but she didn't want the money. I don't understand how it works, I'm just glad it did." Both declined to name this "wish doctor." But whether it was divine intervention, karma, or just luck of the draw, Wilbanks is thankful to still have a home to go back to with his wife and children tonight.

"I assume they're talking about you?" Catch said.

Rachel continued to stare at the article as if the letters were going to rearrange themselves into words that said she'd accidentally turned the property into unusable swampland, the wish gone awry. But the black type continued to say the same thing.

The Wilbankses had their home back.

The wish had worked.

She smiled at the plate Catch set in front of her, the scent of the egg-and-pepper pie so spicy it made her eyes water.

"Do you know who he was talking about? The one who conned them in the first place?" Rachel asked.

"If I had to guess, I'd say Ashe's worthless father. He's handled a number of property sales in the past few years. All in the same area out by the piece of land Ashe built that fancy new house on for his parents. Rumor has it, most don't remember why they wanted to sell in the first place, but it was too late to do anything about it. I wouldn't put it past him to try and charm someone out of something he wanted."

"Why would he want the land?"

Catch jerked one bony shoulder up in a half shrug. "Who the hell knows. Probably has something up his sleeve to get him more money and influence."

"I remember Ashe saying something about his dad having the ability to charm people. Kinda like your pies and my wishes," Rachel said.

"I'd say what he can do is more of a curse for the rest of us," Catch said, slapping at the paper. "Anyway, I'm a little surprised you're not asking me to hide this."

"Could you really make them all forget I was behind it?"

"Not after that. There's too many people that know now. I couldn't cover it up without some serious consequences." Catch clutched at her side and sucked in a sharp breath. She glared at Rachel, effectively warding off any questions about how she was feeling. "It wouldn't work the way you'd want it to."

"What do you mean?"

"Changing something that big always has side effects. Asking that many people to forget one thing could erase that thing altogether. Not just from their memories, but from other people's memories as well," Catch said.

Rachel's heart pounded in her ears. Catch's lips continued to move, but the words didn't penetrate. She latched on to the small thread of hope dangling in front of her.

*If Catch can make people forget me, maybe she can make them remember too. Maybe she's my loophole to get Michael back.*

Catch dug her fingers into Rachel's shoulder and shook. "Are you hearing me, girl?"

"Sorry," Rachel said. Blinking, she tried to clear her head. "I was just wondering, once someone's forgotten, is there any way to bring them back?"

"That's tricky business. You'd best not get yourself in a position that we have to find out," Catch said. She dropped a fork next to the plate of breakfast pie that was going cold on the counter in front of Rachel. "Now quit asking me about things you've got no business asking and eat your damn breakfast."

A young girl waited in Catch's front yard, half-hidden behind the hydrangea bush. Her dark hair and green shirt blended into the garden as if she were one of Catch's prize-winning plants. But the flowers swayed in the breeze—and the girl stood motionless, staring wide-eyed at the house.

Rachel peered out again, hoping it was a trick of the light.

"She's been out there for an hour," Catch said. Her voice rang with the same annoyance she'd had at breakfast.

"What does she want?"

"You, I'd expect. If she wanted a pie, she woulda come to the back door already."

Even from the safety of the foyer, Rachel could see the desperation as plainly as if it had been tattooed on the girl's skin.

"How do you do it?" Rachel asked.

"Do what?"

"I know you like helping people and don't mind them coming around at all hours of the day, but I don't know if I can do that."

Catch reached around her and pulled the cord on the blinds. The slats clicked shut. "Maybe you shoulda thought of that before you went and got yourself on the front page of the paper."

"I didn't do it on purpose. Get in the paper, I mean."

"Lots of things happen that we don't mean. Doesn't change the fact that they happened. You'll have to figure out what you're gonna do the next time someone asks for your help."

"What should I do about her?" Rachel asked, gesturing to the young girl still half-hidden in the front yard.

"Since she doesn't look like she's going anywhere, I'd suggest you talk to her."

Shielding her eyes from the blinding morning sun with her hand, Rachel headed to the yard. "Can I help you with something?" she asked the girl, who now stood at the edge of the driveway.

The girl couldn't have been more than seven or eight. Her hollow cheeks stretched thin and her legs were bone and skin, no muscle to speak of. "I hope so," she stammered.

"You know, ringing the doorbell might've gotten me out here sooner."

"I didn't want to bother you." The girl hugged her arms across her chest. She raised her eyes to Rachel's. Sniffling, she tried to keep her composure. "Mama told me not to come, but I just wanted to thank you for saving my home."

Rachel took a step back and toed the gravel driveway. "You're Helen and Ricky Wilbanks's daughter?"

"I'm Jody."

"I'm really glad you don't have to move out of your house."

"Thanks. Me too." Her timid smile revealed two missing teeth on the top row. "Mama said you didn't want anyone to know it was you, but I heard her telling Daddy how you live with the lady who makes the pies. That's how I knew where to find you. But I won't tell anybody."

"I appreciate that," Rachel said, returning the smile.

The girl turned to leave, then looked back at Rachel. "I think you should tell people, though. There are lots of people who need help—not just with keeping their homes—and if they knew about you, their wishes might come true too. And that would be really good." She raced off before Rachel could respond. Her sneakers ground against the gravel in the driveway for a few seconds, then she reached the pavement and picked up speed, leaving Rachel to question how good things really could be if she let them.

———

All morning at work, Rachel couldn't stop thinking about what Mary Beth had said about her being at home in Nowhere. She hadn't wanted something to be true that badly in a long time. Not since Michael first disappeared and she was desperate to believe he had been real. But most of the townspeople were still of the opinion she could only bring trouble.

Somehow Everley had convinced Rachel that making some of the wishes she'd been collecting come true would help her show the naysayers that she not only belonged in Nowhere, but that they needed her too. Everley had also offered up her home as the place to do it. At the time, it had made sense. Now, curled up in a plush chair in Everley's living room, Rachel couldn't remember why.

Since she'd left her shoes in a cubby by the front door, she tucked her bare feet under her and sank farther into the cushions.

Dropping into the chair next to Rachel, Everley asked, "Will it ruin anything if we have some wine?"

"I don't think so. Actually, it might mess things up if we don't drink," she said, hoping a little alcohol would calm her nerves.

Everley uncorked the bottle and poured two glasses of pale white wine. "To making wishes come true." She tapped the rim of her glass to Rachel's. Wine sloshed over the edge and dribbled down the glass. After wiping it off, she licked her thumb clean. "All right, so how does this work exactly? Is there a chant or spell or something you have to say?"

"I just have to think about it. That's how it's always worked before," Rachel said.

"Okay. What can I do?"

"Pick one." She held the box of paper slips out to Everley like they were selecting a raffle winner.

Everley swished her hand around the box. The papers shuffled against each other. She pulled one out with a triumphant flourish. "Any way I can test one? You know, just so I can see it work since these will happen to people who aren't in my living room?"

"I don't know, Everley. I've done that before and it never worked out right."

"Just something little. Unimportant. Please?"

Rachel's stomach fluttered. She took a sip of the wine. "Tell me what you're thinking, but don't actually wish for it yet. I get to veto it if I don't want to do it, okay?"

"Okay, okay. How about another bottle of wine."

"That's one I can live with."

Rachel looked at the open bottle sitting on the table. The label was slick from the condensation beading on the green glass. She wished for a second one sitting on the top shelf of the fridge next to a double slice of chocolate raspberry cheesecake. The air fluttered around her, and a crisp white piece of paper landed in her lap.

"Did it work?" Everley asked.

Reading her own wish sent a thrill through her she hadn't felt since she was little. "Go check the fridge." She twisted her fingers together to keep them from shaking and held her breath.

Everley gathered her skirt in one hand and launched off the pillow. Her bare feet padded on the floor as she jogged to the kitchen. "Oh my God! It totally worked. You just imagined a bottle of wine out of thin air."

"There should be some cheesecake too," Rachel called.

"Holy shit. Cheesecake!" Everley peered at her around the doorjamb, her smile half awe, half jealousy. "This is amazing. *You* are amazing."

Rachel smiled back at her and laughed. *Maybe this will work. Maybe I can make everything right.*

Everley left the wine in the fridge, but carried the cheesecake into the living room with two forks.

Glancing at the box of wishes, Rachel asked, "Okay, what's first?"

Everley unfolded the wish she'd pulled earlier and laughed. "Oh, this is gonna be fun. Someone really wants Deborah Anne to find a husband. Any man will do. It really says that, see?" She passed the wish to Rachel, who tried to keep her face straight despite her friend's infectious laugh.

"Let's hope she means that because I don't get to pick the guy. I'm just the messenger."

Rachel's fingers shook as she took the paper. She closed her eyes and wished. The wind gusted again, fluttering her hair and sending a chill up her spine.

"How will we know if it worked?" Everley asked.

"I guess we just have to wait and see if Deborah Anne starts going around town with a new guy."

Everley dug deep into the box again and said, "I've got a good feeling about this one."

"Don't make me regret doing this with you," Rachel said.

"I can be serious. Watch. Okay, this person wishes—" She dissolved into a fit of giggles.

Rachel snatched the paper from her.

"I'm sorry, I'm sorry," Everley said, holding her stomach while she laughed. "But how am I supposed to keep a straight face when someone's wishing to marry Nathan Fillion? Not that I blame her for wanting it, but not even you can make something like that happen, can you?"

"It doesn't always work out the way people want. Like this person will probably meet and marry another guy named Nathan Fillion or someone who's into cosplay, but not Captain Tight Pants himself."

Everley laughed harder, then when she caught her breath, asked, "But you have some control over it, don't you?"

Rachel put her wineglass down, suddenly feeling light-headed. "Not really. I don't get to shape the wishes. They are whatever the wisher wants them to be. I'm just the conduit."

Everley dropped the wish onto the table, looking closely at Rachel. "We can stop if you want."

It was tempting. Part of her—the part that was still bitter about not being able to wish Michael back—yearned to pack up her stuff and pretend that she was just like everyone else. Like she couldn't change people's lives just by wishing things were different.

But she'd done that before. It hadn't done her any good. And if

Catch was right, Rachel had to finally commit to her ability if she wanted to gain control.

"No, it's okay. I need to do this. But maybe we skip that one since I'm doing this to help people, not disappoint them. What's next?"

Instead of selecting another wish, Everley asked, "Are you sure? I don't want you to feel like you have to do this." She fingered the stem of her glass, rotating it so the wine danced up the sides.

"I'm good. I promise," Rachel said. She leaned forward and picked another wish from the box. Taking a deep breath, she read it out loud. "So, it looks like this one wants State to have a winning season. Do you have any idea what sport they're talking about?"

"Football. This time of year, it's always football. March? Now that's a whole 'nother story."

"See, it's a good thing you're doing this with me, or I might've ruined some poor team's chances."

Everley toasted the air. "To me, then."

"I'll second that," Rachel said and pulled the next wish from the box.

"I can't wait to see how everyone reacts when their deepest wishes start coming true. They're going to fall over themselves to beg your forgiveness for being such asshats to you. It'll be glorious."

"I'm just doing this to put things right. Do some kind of good in case I have to leave. Maybe get some of the land back from Max." Everley made a low growling sound at the mention of Ashe's dad. Rachel nodded in agreement. She added in a lighter tone, "And make some frivolous wishes come true in the process."

"You're not going anywhere. I refuse to let you," Everley said.

Rachel flicked the wish she still held, hoping it contained a weightier wish than the first few. "I promise to wish you a very good replacement on my way out of town."

Everley took another long drink of wine and smiled at her over the rim. "And I promise to wish for you to stay right here."

# 28

Rachel had been sober enough to know she shouldn't drive home. But when Everley suggested calling Ashe to come get her, she knew she was still buzzed enough to do something stupid. She settled for walking the mile and a half back to Catch's.

She stopped at the end of the driveway, just before the yard disappeared into the darkness of night. A warm breeze sighed against her skin. The leaves laughed quietly as the current tickled them. For a second, maybe two, the air smelled sweeter, like the trees were wooing her. Squinting into the darkness, Rachel contemplated ripping a peach from the branch and sinking her teeth into its fuzzy flesh, letting the sweet juice run down her chin and fingers.

She jumped when a shadow moved in the yard. Her fingers slid from the box of wishes she had clutched to her chest. It dropped to the ground and dozens of white paper scraps lifted and flapped in the breeze. They rustled like insect wings.

"I was beginning to wonder if you were coming home at all tonight," Ashe said. He reached out and plucked a wish from the air.

"Shit," Rachel said.

"Afraid I'd sneak up to your room and read them?" he asked, waving it at her. His eyes sparkled in the moonlight, a mischievous glint that irritated and seduced all at once.

She stretched up on her toes to catch a wish that fluttered by his head. "No."

"Need some help?"

"I've got it," she said, grabbing at another one that floated by. It drifted through her fingers.

"I'm actually pretty good." He lunged and caught two in one hand. "Scott and I used to run around trying to catch leaves before they hit the ground. Hell, who am I kidding, we still do that. After-Thanksgiving dinner ritual." He picked another one out of the air inches from her fingertips.

"Fine. Just don't read them, please," she said. She reached for another one and laughed when it crumpled in her fist.

"Deal," he said. She grinned at him and popped a kiss on his lips. His fingers closed around hers when the wind kicked up to keep the paper in her hand from taking off again. When he leaned down to turn her playful kiss into a real one, she didn't pull away.

Tart remnants of fruit from whatever pie he'd eaten that evening clung to his tongue. It mingled with the wine on her own. Stepping back, he said, "Did you spill a bottle of wine on yourself?"

"No. Most of it's in me," Rachel said. She stumbled a bit, laughing, and Ashe steadied her.

"I'm gonna kill Everley for letting you drive home. Then I'm gonna kill you for actually doing it."

Rachel patted his chest. "Oh, calm down. I walked. Everley and I might've gone through a few bottles, but we're not stupid."

"Why didn't you just stay there?"

"She was calling Jamie to see if he wanted to have a sleepover. Though I very much doubt they're going to get much sleep. Plus, I didn't trust her with these," she said. She wiggled her hand—and the paper—free from his grasp.

"You ever gonna tell me what those are?"

"They're wishes." She said it so easily she surprised herself.

Ashe bent and scraped one off the ground. He held it in the air where she couldn't reach it, opened it, and read, "I wish my mom would find a new job so she'll be home at night." Folding it back, he handed it to her. "Are they all like that?"

She'd tried not to listen, but the words wormed their way in, sparking her nerves. "Some of them. Others want love or money or a new car. Violet, Maeby's oldest daughter, wished for a unicorn for her last birthday. The best I could do was a horse with an ice cream cone tied to its head. Not that I meant to do it, mind you. It just sort of slipped through my defenses. Violet's kinda hard to resist."

"You're serious?" he asked.

"Well, I couldn't very well get her a real unicorn. Not even I can wish that into existence." Rachel tilted her head back and looked at the stars. "It's so pretty out tonight," she said. The wind whipped a strand of hair across her face.

Ashe reached out and twisted the hair lightly around his finger. She darted her eyes back to his. Releasing her hair, he skimmed the back of his fingers down the side of her face. "I meant are you serious about the wishing thing. You can really do that?"

"What do you think I was doing with Everley all night?" she asked.

"Other than getting drunk?"

Rachel pushed his hand away. "You think I'm making it up?"

"Why don't you prove me wrong?" Ashe said. He met her eyes and saw the challenge take hold. Smiling, he continued, "I'll make a wish and you make it come true. Easy as that."

"Fine. You're on. But help me pick up the rest first," she said.

The wind had settled and the paper littered the grass. In the hazy moonlight, the wishes glowed white. Rachel and Ashe went in opposite directions, scooping the papers up and tucking them into pockets when their hands got full. If Ashe read them as he went, Rachel couldn't tell. The yard smelled too sweet, like the inside of a candle shop. She made a grab for the last remaining pieces and jogged back to the driveway where the air was less potent.

"I think it's getting worse," Rachel said. She held her hand under her nose for a few seconds to hold off the rotten plum smell before stuffing the paper slips back into the box. She glowered at the orchard. "It's like it wants everyone to know."

He followed her gaze. "*What* wants everyone to know *what*?" he asked.

"The plum tree. It wants everyone to know that it's there. That it's not going anywhere and you're just going to have to deal with it." She could imagine how Ashe would deal with learning the man Lola cheated on him with was his father. And imagining it was bad enough. She had no desire to see it play out in real life.

"Is the plum tree evil? I can't see its mustache, so it's a little hard to tell."

"Not everything has to look evil to be dangerous," Rachel said. Her head was a little fuzzy, her throat dry. Ashe looked back at her with eyes so intense she could almost see herself reflected in them. "Are you okay? After all the stuff with your dad charming people out of their farmland coming out, I mean. I heard another two families came forward today. And that his business partner is threatening to send him before the bar."

"I really don't want to talk about him right now."

"But are you?"

"I've known my dad wasn't a decent person for a long time. I didn't know he was that much of a dick, but I'm not surprised. It's a life goal of mine to be nothing like him."

Hugging the box to her chest, she said, "Consider that one checked off the list, then, because you are damn near the perfect guy," and led the way inside. His hand was warm on her back, just above the bottom of her shirt.

The porch light illuminated enough of the kitchen that they could fumble their way through without waking Catch. Rachel reached back and groped for his hand. He slid his fingers in hers as she guided him through the dining room and up the stairs. Their footsteps whispered behind them.

Her breath caught as she entered her room with Ashe a step behind, his free hand now resting on her neck. Pale light filtered in through the window, illuminating a swath of her bed. For a moment she forgot about wishes and wondered what it would feel like to be pressed into the mattress with his body covering hers. When she turned, she could just make out the curious glint in his eyes. She left her hand in his.

He pulled up short and tugged her to a stop. "Still planning to leave town?" he asked, kicking one of the boxes she'd already packed up. He scanned the room, eyes lingering on the few personal items she still had out—her family photo, a unicorn stuffed animal Violet had sent with Mary Beth, a bottle of hibiscus hand cream from LUX.

"People might've calmed down with all the accusing and pitchfork-thrusting, but that doesn't mean they're really okay with what I can do. Or that they want me to stay."

"I want you to stay." Ashe tightened his grip on her hand to keep her from pulling away.

"And I guess I'll just stay locked up in Catch's attic and you'll sneak up and see me when no one's looking?"

"I'd move you to my attic at least. Easier access and all."

Rachel set the wish box on the table and swatted his chest. His laugh rumbled against her cheek as he pulled her into him. "That's so chivalrous of you," she said against his collarbone.

"That's one hundred percent selfish of me. And surprisingly, I'm okay with that."

"Of course you are."

He released her, his smile pulling mischievously to one side. "Hey, you still owe me a wish."

"I know. But I can't promise it'll turn out the way you want."

"So, we'll start small," he said. Pointing at the wishes still in the box, he continued, "Do I need to write it down?"

"No, you just have to think it. The paper will appear on its own."

"Um, okay." Ashe closed his eyes, his dark lashes fluttering as he concentrated. He rubbed a thumb over the back of her hand.

The wish popped into the air a few inches from her free hand. Turning her palm up, the paper settled on her skin with a soft tickle. "I wish Lucy could come home," she read out loud, her voice faltering. "I know you're new to this whole wishing thing, but wishing for another girl is probably not the smartest idea."

He cracked one eye open and laughed at the look on her face. "As much as I love Lucy, you have nothing to worry about. How long till we know if it worked?" The affection in his voice knotted her stomach.

She moved to the door and dropped his wish into the box. "No clue. Why don't you go home and wait until Lucy shows up?"

"I'm good here." Ashe grinned and walked toward her. He backed her against the shelf, stopping just shy of touching her.

She stared at the hollow of his neck and the strip of tan skin that disappeared into his shirt. Fisting her hands at her sides, she stilled everything but her racing heart.

Tipping her chin up with one finger, Ashe said, "All right, let's try something a little more immediate. You know I want you. I wish I knew how you felt about me, you know, ignoring the fact that I just wished for another girl." His crooked smile said he knew he was giving her complete control over his wish, as if he didn't care whether or not she really could make wishes come true.

"You're an ass," Rachel said, but she felt herself melting into him.

Though his desire was intense, the wish wasn't forceful enough to appear. But it was one she could happily oblige. He ran his thumb over her lips, applying just enough pressure to open them. Desire skimmed along her skin. The rush of heat spread from her chest and settled, tingling, in her curled fingertips.

She sucked in a breath and the edge of the shelf dug into her back. Closing her eyes, she tried to ignore the words that urged her to lean into him. To catch his bottom lip between her teeth, and to do all the things she'd been dreaming about with him.

Ashe traced his fingers along her jaw. "You gonna make me say it again?"

Whether it was the wish or the challenging curve of his lips, Rachel couldn't resist. Rising up on her toes, she unclenched her hands and, burying them in his hair, dragged his mouth to hers. Unlike their kiss in the driveway, this one was urgent, demanding. Her body molded to his when his hands dropped to her hips and pulled her closer. His stubble scraped her top lip. Her skin sparked where his fingers snaked under her shirt.

She pulled back long enough to see his eyes hazed over with need. When he gripped her hips harder and lifted her, she wrapped her legs around his waist. He tugged her shirt off and threw it across the room. Despite the fan whirling above, the air was stifling. Her hair clung to her sweaty back. She tried to catch her breath. He moved his mouth to her neck and worked his way down to her collarbone, his lips moving along her skin until she moaned his name.

They made it to the bed in three long strides. His boots thumped on the wood floor in time with her erratic heartbeat. He sat on the edge of the bed, stroking her bare back and finding her mouth with his. Unwinding her legs, Rachel straddled him and flipped open button after button on his shirt.

"Who's Lucy again?" she teased, the words vibrating against his mouth.

The muscles under her hands tensed. His eyes were suddenly a sharp, focused blue as he rested his forehead against hers. He closed his eyes and blew out a shaky breath.

"Rachel, I can't." Ashe leaned back, dragging his hands through his hair. "I know I'm not with Lola anymore, but I'm technically still married and I just can't. It's my fault. You warned me about making a wish and I pushed you anyway. I should've known it would get out of hand."

Disappointment shuddered through her. Her skin flushed as his words sank in. *He thinks I was going to sleep with him because of a wish. God, I'm an idiot.* Rachel eased off the bed without meeting his eye. She turned to retrieve her shirt and saw a hint of color draped over the top two steps. She reached for a pillow to cover herself but pulled back, not wanting him to see how much he'd affected her.

"You couldn't have told me that before you took off my shirt and threw it down the stairs?" She tried to dull the hardness in her voice with a smile.

"I'm sorry," he said.

Wrapping her arms around her waist, she turned away.

"You make it a little hard to think sometimes," Ashe said.

"Then maybe you should watch what you wish for from now on."

Rachel shivered, knowing her current state of undress had nothing to do with a wish and everything to do with simply wanting him.

# 29

Rachel vaguely remembered wishing as she fell asleep that she wouldn't get a hangover. Opening her eyes, she squinted against the early-morning sunlight streaming through the window. A slip of paper balanced on the window ledge above. She blew on it so it danced in the air before landing on the empty pillow next to her, confirming that she was the reason for her lack of a headache and queasy stomach that usually followed a night of drinking too much wine.

She also remembered Ashe's wish from the night before and how he'd ended things. "Thanks a lot," she whispered and sat up.

After she'd dressed, she headed downstairs. The air in the foyer was a few degrees cooler than upstairs. The front door was propped open, letting in a trickle of a breeze and the buzzing of a lawn mower from a neighbor's yard. She stopped on the last step as the back door swished open and clicked softly back into place.

*Ashe. Shit. What if things are weird between us after last night?*

She glanced back up the stairs and contemplated hiding in her room until he'd gone. But that would definitely make things awkward, so she stayed put and listened as Catch greeted him.

"You look awfully chipper this morning, Mr. I-Snuck-Up-to-a-Girl's-Room-Last-Night-and-Thought-I-Didn't-Get-Caught," Catch said.

"I know better than to think you don't know what goes on under your own roof," Ashe said, his tone matching hers.

"Oh, stop your gloating and eat your damn breakfast."

The floorboard at the base of the steps creaked when Rachel continued toward the kitchen.

"I think there's somebody here to see you," Catch said. When Ashe turned toward Rachel, she added, "Wrong way, Romeo. This one's a ginger and is currently running circles in my backyard."

His smile morphed from devastatingly sexy to pure joy before he pivoted to watch a dog playing outside. Her big paws dug into the ground as she darted in and out of the trees, sending tufts of grass and dirt into the air. Ashe eased off the stool, scooting it back so it screeched on the floor, and let out a short, sharp whistle. The dog skidded to a stop and met his stare through the window. She returned a playful bark and raced to the back door. He had it open before she launched herself up the two wooden steps. The dog pulled up short and sat, tail thumping, on the doormat. She lifted her right paw in greeting. Ashe knelt and buried his face in her copper fur. He scratched and rubbed and nuzzled. She nibbled on his hair in return.

Rachel laughed as she watched them from where she'd stopped in the middle of the kitchen. Catch raised one thin, gray eyebrow. The creases around her mouth deepened as she laughed too.

"I was wondering when Carol Ann would send her back. I thought she was holding her prisoner to try and force you and Lola to reconcile?" Catch asked.

"She was," he said with his face still pressed into the dog's neck.

"Guess your brother'll be along in a few minutes too." Catch got out a fresh plate and sliced another piece of pie.

"I'd expect so. Don't think she drove herself here, unless that's part of the wish." When Ashe stopped petting the dog, she nudged his hand with her muzzle. "I missed you too," he said to her.

"I don't remember you wishing for a dog," Rachel said.

He looked up then, his eyes locking on hers over his shoulder. "This is Lucy. Lola exiled her to my mom's a year ago because it turns out she's not a dog person. Apparently Lucy's been set free. That makes two wishes I'm incredibly grateful for. Even if the second one got put on hold."

Stuffing her hands in her back pockets, Rachel ignored the nerves dancing in her stomach at the implied promise of the wish getting fulfilled at some point. "Good for her."

"Good for me." He rubbed his hands under Lucy's jaw, shaking her whole head. Her tags clanked against the metal ring on the collar. Her floppy ears flapped up and down.

Ashe stood, taking his hand off Lucy. She barreled past him into the kitchen and leaped at Rachel. He wasn't quick enough to stop her from placing both paws on Rachel's shoulders and licking her face.

Rachel stumbled back a step. Catching a hand on the edge of the counter, she gripped it as the dog pressed her wet nose to Rachel's neck.

"Apparently she likes our girl," Catch said.

"She's a smart dog." He snapped his fingers, and Lucy dropped back to the floor. Her tail whacked his shins when he strode to her, grabbed her collar, and tried to pull her back outside. "Stubborn as all get-out, but smart."

Rachel wiped at the wet spot on her neck. "It's not hard to see where Lucy gets her manners," she said. She tugged her shirt back down when Ashe stared at the exposed skin below her belly button.

"She better get her furry butt out of my kitchen before I swat her," Catch said. She raised a wooden spoon and smacked it against her bony hand a couple times.

"You heard her," Ashe said. He gave Lucy another rough tug, maneuvering her back outside. He held his hand up for her to sit. She turned her hopeful brown eyes up at Rachel and let out a short bark. "I'm pretty sure that was a 'thank you.'"

"You're welcome," Rachel said. Ashe ran off after Lucy, his laugh and her barks filling the backyard.

The park was packed with tents and tables and people selling fresh fruit, vegetables, breads, bottled marinara sauces and handmade pasta, fresh-cut flowers, organic dog treats, and pies. Rachel would've skipped the farmers' market altogether if Catch hadn't nearly passed out as she loaded the pies into the back of her car that morning.

While Rachel emptied the trunk and backseat, Catch sat in a folding chair glaring at her and mumbling under her breath about how she wasn't an invalid and she could handle selling her own damn pies by her own damn self.

Rachel ignored her. She suspended the chalkboard listing the flavors and prices from the back legs of the tent.

People nodded to Rachel from across the sidewalk and whispered thanks as they squeezed through the crowd that encircled the tent. They stopped in front of her, touching her hand, her arm as they told her she was welcome to stay in Nowhere as long as she wanted. Only one in every five who came to their booth actually wanted a pie. She didn't know who all the wishes she'd granted a few nights before belonged to. She wasn't even sure everyone who thanked her had been a recipient of her gift. But they all seemed to know that she was responsible for returning every plot of land that had been sold under false pretenses to Max Riley back to the original owners. And not one of the wishes had gone wrong.

"Well, aren't you Miss-Queen-of-the-Market today?" Catch asked between customers.

"I kinda gave in and made some wishes come true."

"Some?"

"Okay, a lot. But in my defense, there was wine involved. And guilt. A whole lot of guilt. I guess I just figured what's the point of being able to do what I do if I don't actually do it."

"Told you." Catch's low chuckle morphed into a wracking cough. She held up one hand to keep Rachel away. Her eyes were watering by the time the fit passed.

She handed Catch a bottle of water but knew better than to ask if she was okay. "I'm just glad I could help them. And that Ashe won't have to."

"That makes two of us."

They lapsed into silence again as more people flooded the tent. The wishes accumulated in her pockets and littered the ground.

Despite the breeze, the paper never blew farther than the tent entrance.

Rachel tried harder to sell the pies.

As she handed a middle-aged woman the last peach-raspberry, she glanced into the crowd. A man with a familiar smile caught her eye. Suddenly dizzy, she closed her eyes and took a deep breath. When she reopened them, he was still there, less than a hundred feet away. The guy she saw on her first morning in Nowhere, whom she'd mistaken for Michael. The words of the customers in line turned to a low buzzing in her ears. She grasped the pole to keep steady and stared into the throng of faces looking for the one she'd recognized a moment before.

She found him on the edge of the park, skirting a group of girls who all smiled at him. He sent them a sheepish grin and disappeared into the crowd.

*Michael.*

Rachel's pulse raced. She waited one second, two for him to come back. When he didn't, she elbowed her way through the line of customers. Catch called after her but she didn't respond. She had to find him.

When she reached the spot where he'd disappeared, she paused. Looking left and right, she found a wall of people, faces she didn't know. Then she spotted him again, working his way through the crowd. His deep brown hair was curling at the ends from the heat. He headed to the outskirts of the market, weaving in between tents and people, and was gone again. She chased after him, not caring when she bumped into someone or stepped on a foot. She ignored the questions and curses. She ignored the frantic thumping in her chest until the stitch in her side forced her to stop running. She looked around, desperate to find him.

He was gone. Again.

She groped for the back of the splintery bench she'd stopped next to and collapsed onto it. She thought she heard someone call her name, but her head was too heavy to lift. Hunched over, she hugged her thighs, her fingers digging into the soft grass beneath the bench.

"Breathe, girl. You're gonna pass out if you don't get ahold of your-self."

"I . . . can't," Rachel managed. She closed her eyes as Catch sat next to her and patted her back.

"You don't seem like the type to hyperventilate over nothing, so why don't you tell me what's going on."

She took one ragged breath, then another before she said, "I saw him. I followed him, Catch. He's here. I didn't imagine him. He's here."

"Who did you see?" Catch asked.

"My bro—" Rachel whipped her head up. Her vision spun. Every-thing was a mishmash of grass and concrete, leaves and flesh.

Catch's hand slipped from her back. "Well, don't stop on my ac-count. That was starting to sound interesting."

"I saw Michael. My brother."

"Oh."

Rachel's hands shook so she balled them between her knees. "I wished he'd get lost when we were little. I didn't mean it, not liter-ally. Not permanently. But I did it and he was gone. Just like that. I was the only one who remembered him. My parents thought I'd made him up. And sometimes I thought I had too."

"How old was he when you made your wish?"

"Four."

"And you haven't seen him since, until today?" Catch asked. Her eyes narrowed on something across the square, but when Rachel fol-lowed her line of sight, she only saw Ashe watching them from the front window of Everley's shop. Catch held up a hand, letting Ashe know to leave them alone.

Looking away, Rachel said, "I thought I saw him the morning Ashe took me around downtown. I tried to follow him but he dis-appeared just like today."

Catch swore under her breath. "He left town that day." Her voice was barely a whisper.

"Wait, you know who he is?" She gripped Catch's skinny wrist, and the old woman looked at her with her mouth twisted into a frown.

"There was a little boy who suddenly arrived in town years ago, just walking down the road. He didn't remember his name or where he was from. And he had no idea how he got to Nowhere."

Rachel's breathing had almost returned to normal as she replayed Catch's words in her head. She released Catch and scanned the crowd for her brother again. "He was here the whole time? Living in Nowhere?"

"Seems that way," Catch said, shaking her head. Rachel noticed how gaunt Catch's face was, her skin pale despite the heat. She worried that Catch still seemed sick and briefly thought about telling Ashe, but then Catch continued, pushing the thought from Rachel's mind. "A family took him in when no one came looking for him. He's had a good life. Not perfect, but good. He's a happy kid who thinks he's always been a part of his family."

Rachel swallowed past the lump in her throat and she asked, "Who is he? Please tell me where to find him."

"Now hold on a minute, Miss-Jumping-in-Headfirst. I believe you were meant to come to Nowhere and find him when you were ready. That's probably why the town kept you from leaving a few weeks back. This is what you were meant to find here. But rushing into this without considering all of the ramifications, well, that won't get you what you want."

"I've been trying to get him back for most of my life. You have to help me. Please," Rachel said, her voice catching on the last word.

"I'm not saying no. I'm just asking you to give me a little time and trust me to do what's best for both of you."

Rachel was tired of waiting. After more than fifteen years, all she wanted was to get her brother back. But she knew enough to know that Catch didn't do anything until she was good and ready.

# 30

Rachel sat in a rocker on the front porch, numb. Her brain repeated the same two phrases over and over as she rocked.

Back. *Michael still exists.* Forth. *Catch knows who he is and won't tell me.* Back. *Michael still exists.* Forth. *Catch knows who he is and won't tell me.* Back. *Michael still exists.* Forth. *Catch knows who he is and won't tell me.*

The temperature had dropped a good ten degrees since the rain started two hours before. It fell steadily. Fat drops pinged on the plants, the sidewalk, the porch roof. When the wind blew, a cool mist drifted onto her, making her shiver.

Rachel didn't notice Catch until she pressed a cup of tea into her hands. The ceramic warmed her skin. She held the mug tighter. The scent of whiskey rivaled the chamomile as she sipped the bitter drink. She winced as it scorched her tongue, then her throat.

Catch opened her mouth, but turned away without saying anything. She shuffled back across the porch. The screen door creaked open. "I know this is hard on you, finding out he's been here the whole time," she said. "But there's no sense blaming yourself any longer when he's had a good life."

"How could I possibly forgive myself?" Rachel whispered after the door closed.

After years of others insisting she'd made him up, Rachel had found someone who insisted she'd been right all along. That Michael was as real as she was, and he was in Nowhere.

Rachel lay in bed, still, listening to what sounded like metal scraping against metal downstairs. There was a low rumble followed by more grating.

She'd grown used to the smooth, muted sounds of Catch moving around in the kitchen. This was loud, chaotic.

This was not Catch.

Her mind raced with possibilities. *What if it's Michael? What if he found out who I am and what I did to him?*

Fear rocked through her, making her movements sluggish as she slipped out of bed and made her way to the door on the balls of her feet. Rolling it slowly open, she paused. The blackness below swallowed the small amount of light from the window in the hall, but she went down anyway, her hand gripping the railing to keep from tripping in the dark.

More disembodied sounds drifted up from the floor below. The clanking and banging and scraping were coming faster now, closer together. Shadows raced across the floor and up the walls as the wind harassed the trees outside the window, and she realized she should have grabbed her phone or a flashlight. She plunged into darkness again as she started down the last staircase.

She crept through the foyer into the dining room and paused just inside the entrance to the kitchen. Air rushed out of the floor vents, chilling the tile under her bare feet.

A dark figure stood by the sink.

*Definitely not Catch.* She groped the wall for the light switch. She flipped it and jumped when Ashe whirled around with a knife.

"What the hell are you doing?" she whisper-yelled, at once grateful and disappointed it wasn't somehow her brother.

"Stealing pie," he said. He lifted his hand to shield his eyes from the light. His shirt was unbuttoned like he'd thrown it on just to say he had something on. His bloodshot eyes couldn't focus on hers.

He'd opened half the drawers and a couple cabinets. Whatever he'd been looking for, he hadn't found it yet. "At nine thirty? I thought you and Jamie had a boys' night tonight."

"We did. He and the other guys went home. I wasn't really in the mood."

Rachel understood not wanting company. After learning her brother was somewhere in Nowhere, holding a normal conversation with anyone but him seemed almost impossible. But she couldn't ignore whatever was going on with Ashe.

"So you thought you'd come over here and rummage through the drawers loud enough for me to hear all the way upstairs?"

"I wasn't rummaging," he said. He opened another drawer and shuffled through utensils and measuring cups. "The pie server isn't where it should be."

Rachel opened the drawer where it lived and found it lying right in front. "This pie server?" She smacked his hand with it when he tried to take it from her.

"Ow. What was that for?"

"If you wake Catch up, I will beat you senseless with this," she said.

Ashe took a step back, surprise on his face. "She's in bed already?"

"She wasn't feeling well." To be fair, she rarely felt well these days whether she admitted it or not. "Now give me the damn pie before you make any more racket."

"Sorry," he said, dropping his hands to his side.

Like for Ashe, pie was quickly becoming her go-to comfort food. After the day she'd had, it sounded like exactly what she needed. She took the dish and cut two slices, and red strawberry juice leaked from the edges of the pie, pooling on the plates. She dipped her finger in, then licked it clean. Wrapping the plastic wrap back over the remaining pie, she savored the sweet berry taste that lingered on her tongue.

Ashe dug in the refrigerator for whipped cream, shoving milk cartons and juice bottles into each other on the shelf. He pulled out the can and shook it. Rachel stopped him before he sprayed it. Motioning outside, she whispered, "I'll grab forks. You wait out there."

He nodded.

She checked to make sure Catch's lights were still off. The hallway was dark, her door firmly closed. When she met Ashe on the deck, his head hung off the back of the chair. His eyes were closed, and for a second, she thought he'd fallen asleep. He clutched the whipped cream can to his chest with one hand and cracked one eye open when she sat in the chair next to him. He held his free hand out for his plate. Covering the top crust in whipped cream, he angled the nozzle of the canister toward her.

"Not that much," she said.

"Suit yourself." Ashe squirted one small dollop in the center of her piece.

"Are you okay?" she asked him, after they'd eaten a few bites in silence.

"I don't know. I mean, I should be. I've been pushing for this. A couple weeks ago it couldn't happen fast enough."

"What?" Rachel asked, her fork clanking against the plate when it slipped from her grasp. She'd been thinking the same thing about Michael all day. But whatever Ashe meant, it wasn't her brother.

He took a bite before answering, not looking at her. "Lola signed the divorce papers today."

The pain in his voice sent chills up her arms. Most of the time, he kept his emotions about Lola buried far below the surface. She'd seen glimpses of how Lola's betrayal had affected him, but when he kissed Rachel it was hard to imagine he'd ever wanted anyone else. Even when he'd kept things from getting too physical between them, she'd assumed it was because he refused to break his vows even though Lola clearly had. Now she wasn't so sure that's what had stopped him.

"Oh," she said, thoughts of Michael temporarily replaced by Ashe's pain.

"Yeah." He sighed, took another bite. "I thought I was over it.

Over her. Then she came by work today and said she'd finally done it. Like all of a sudden she's ready to be done with me after months of dragging it out and telling me she didn't want it."

"She didn't say why?"

"Something about seeing her sister again and not wanting to be the type of person who would do what she did to me. I don't really know. I kinda tuned out after she handed the papers over, too shocked to really understand her."

"I'm sorry, Ashe."

"Not your fault," he said.

"No, but I'm sorry anyway." Rachel turned to look at him. All of his usual energy had been drained. He seemed lost. "Want me to leave you alone?"

His lips turned up in a half smile. "If you do, I'll probably just keep wallowing. It's not a pretty sight, I promise."

Rachel hated seeing him this way. He was always so confident and sure of himself. Sure of everything. "Well, we can't have that," she said in an attempt to keep things light.

He set his empty plate on the deck. "You should probably keep me away from the pie too. Unless you want Catch to wake up and find it all gone."

"Now *that* I can do."

"Sorry for coming over and dumping this on you."

"I'm not," she said, turning her face to him. There was nothing she could do about Michael until Catch told her who he was. At least she could comfort Ashe.

Ashe opened his mouth to respond, but ended up sighing again instead.

She waited.

"I really loved her," he said.

She couldn't tell if he was talking to her or merely thinking out loud so she stayed quiet. She set her half-eaten pie on the railing, pulled her knees to her chest, and pressed her feet on the edge of the chair. She stared out into the yard. Something scraped and clawed as it scavenged in the dark. Letting her head fall back against the chair, she stared at the cloudless sky. Stars twinkled in constellations she could no longer name.

After a minute, she reached over, took Ashe's hand, and held it. Neither spoke, just sat together as the night wore on around them.

# 31

Rachel forced herself out of bed at seven, even though she'd only gotten five hours of sleep. Even without sitting with Ashe for half the night, she wouldn't have managed much more. Her thoughts vacillated between Ashe and how to get Catch to tell her who her brother was. She rubbed at her dry eyes, hoping to suppress the dull ache that was brewing behind them. With Catch already up and making noise in the kitchen, she trudged downstairs in search of coffee.

"I see you got into my pie after I went to bed," Catch said. She shoved the pie dish with her knuckles. It scraped on the counter as it slid a few inches toward the edge.

"It was for Ashe," Rachel said.

"And that's supposed to make it okay?"

"I didn't think it was a big deal. I'm sorry."

"Just because I've got a soft spot for the kid doesn't mean he can get away with doing whatever he wants. Same goes for you. This is still my house. I'm still in charge of what goes on here. Got it?"

Rachel nodded. She debated just going back upstairs and letting Catch stew in whatever bad mood had found her. Instead, she thrust the coffeepot back onto the cold burner and turned to face Catch. "Before you go and yell at Ashe too, you might want know that his divorce went through yesterday. And as much as you hate Lola and want her out of his life, he's not quite as okay with it."

Catch doubled over, clutching her middle. "Son of a bitch." She slapped a hand onto the counter to keep upright, her fingers curling into the granite.

Rachel rushed forward and slipped a supporting arm around Catch. She didn't try to move her, just held her until whatever was going on had passed. She could feel Catch's erratic heartbeat thumping against her chest.

Straightening, Catch gripped her hand. "I'm okay," she managed in a trembling voice that undercut any authority her words may have had.

"What's wrong with you, Catch?" Rachel asked.

"Just a cramp. It's nothing." Catch elbowed Rachel in the ribs when she didn't let go.

The oven timer blared, and Rachel stared at it for a moment, unsure what to do. She'd known something was wrong—really wrong—with Catch. And she'd ignored it. Told herself it was nothing because she didn't want to face the fact that the woman she'd come to care about, to rely on like family, might not be okay. Though even if she had tried to do something, Catch probably would've bitten her head off for it.

She finally stepped aside, hoping Catch was strong enough to hold herself up, and removed the pie from the oven. The heat assaulted her face and forearms. After setting the dish on the wire cooling rack, she tossed the pot holders onto the counter.

"At least have the decency not to lie right to my face," Rachel said.

"Somebody put on her sassy pants today," Catch mumbled.

Moving to the stool, Rachel kicked the other one toward her. "What's going on with you? I know you don't like asking for help, but you don't get a choice this time."

"What? You think that just because you came clean with me I have to spill all my secrets too?"

"Yes," Rachel said. "Actually, I do."

Catch settled onto the stool, gripping the edge of the seat. Her shoulders shook slightly, but her voice was steady and serious when she said, "Apparently keeping secrets all these years is taking its toll on my body."

"How bad is it?" Rachel tried to hide her anxiety, knowing from Catch's expression that the news wasn't good.

"Stomach cancer. Stage four."

The words refused to sink in. They rolled around in Rachel's mind, trying to rearrange themselves into something that made sense.

"Stage four?" she asked. "That's pretty serious, right?"

"Next stage death," Catch said, her voice resigned.

"No. That's not an option." Rachel sounded hysterical but couldn't help it. "The doctors have to be able to do something. They can do chemo or radiation or something, right?"

Catch reached over and patted her hand. Her skin was so thin, practically translucent. "It's too late. I'm too old. I told them it wasn't worth trying."

"No," Rachel said again. "I'm sorry. That's not acceptable. I should have done something sooner. I knew something was wrong. Maybe then the doctors could have—"

"I can't be fixed. And there's nothing you or Ashe could've done."

Rachel jerked her hand free and met Catch's eyes, defiance shining brightly in them. "Ashe doesn't know, does he?"

"No. And you're not telling him either."

"I can't keep this from him. And you shouldn't either. Don't you think he's been lied to enough?"

Catch rubbed at her heart. Her stiff cotton shirt rustled beneath her fingers. "That's not a fair thing to say. This is different."

"Only because you're the one who doesn't want him to get hurt this time."

"So, I guess he knows all about your brother, then?" Catch countered.

"I haven't told him because I don't want to scare him off. You haven't told him because you do. That way it'll hurt less when you go. But he's not going anywhere. You're one of the few family members he has left. If you don't tell him, he might not ever forgive you. And neither will I."

Rachel pushed back from the counter and slammed through the

back door. The morning air had turned sour. She sucked it in through her mouth, trying to catch her breath. *Catch can't be dying. I can't lose her too.* She fled to the back of the property line that separated Catch's house from Ashe's. He mowed both yards so there wasn't the telltale line to mark the end of one and the beginning of the other.

The plum tree was now no more than a moldering, leafless stick poking out of the ground to infect the other trees around it. Their leaves had turned brown and curled at the ends. The apples and peaches were speckled with rotting spots and ant bites.

She couldn't let it ruin everything.

Despite its brittle appearance, the tree put up a fight. The bark ate into her hands as she tried to rip it from the ground. She leveraged her weight and nearly sat on the ground as she yanked. Something cracked, and a small fissure opened down the center of the wood. Rachel didn't let go. Even when a thin trail of blood dribbled down her wrists.

"Whoa. Hey, what're you doing?" a voice yelled from somewhere to her right.

She didn't answer. If she stopped now, the tree—with all its disease and destruction—would win. The roots shredded as it pulled free from the earth. The soil underneath was black and slimy with fermenting juice. The stagnant air engulfed her, and bile pumped into her mouth, coating her throat.

"Hey," the voice said again, closer. She knew this voice.

She went to say something, then turned and vomited at her brother's feet.

When she looked up a moment later, he was still there. *Michael.* Blinking, she met his eyes. Eyes that were a reflection of hers. His face was broad with a strong jaw like she remembered their dad's being.

Before she could wrap her mind around how Michael was in Catch's backyard, his hands were on her arms, holding her up. He stepped them both a few feet to the side. "Are you okay?" he asked. In his deep Southern voice, she heard traces of the boy she remembered.

"I'm sorry," she said, crying hard enough to be embarrassed but not being able to stop. "I am so, so sorry. I didn't mean to do it. If I could take it back I would. God, I would undo it in a heartbeat if I could."

"Relax. It's not a big deal. If I'd been the one to pull the tree out and find that shit, I probably would've puked too."

He wasn't making any sense. She took a steadying breath and asked, "Do you know who I am?"

"Yeah. You're Rachel." He slid his hands down her arms to inspect her bleeding palms. "These look pretty deep. We should get you cleaned up. C'mon. My brother's got a first aid kit on the deck." He walked toward Ashe's house, pulling her along by the wrists.

"You're . . ." Rachel trailed off.

"Scott Riley," he said.

The name rolled off his tongue like he'd been saying it all his life. Which, of course, he nearly had.

The pressure built in her head until all she could hear was a shrill ringing that kept time with her racing heart. Unable to look at him, she focused on the dirt and blood that caked her hands. A new rush of bile made her throat clench. She swallowed every few seconds to keep from throwing up again.

"I need to sit," she said. Her weak voice matched the shaky feeling in her knees.

He lowered her onto the top step of the deck. Holding her hands off to the side so the blood dripped onto the deck instead of her shorts, he said, "Can you hold them here for a minute? I just need to run inside and get the stuff. You okay until I get back?"

Rachel nodded, which made her vision blur. For a second, she saw the four-year-old boy with shaggy hair and unconditional trust. She squeezed her eyes shut.

"I'm just gonna grab some water real quick and the kit. Don't pass out on me now."

He came back after a minute, though it could have been ten, she wasn't sure. His footsteps pounded on the wood beneath her, the vibrations pulsing in her wounds. She bit her lip to keep from crying again when he crouched in front of her. His face—so familiar, yet so different—hovered inches from hers.

"How're you doing? Still with me?" Scott asked.

"Yeah," she whispered.

He poured cool water on her hands. Her cuts stung as he rubbed gently with a soft cloth to clean them. She tried not to flinch.

"So, what did the tree do?"

"It was killing the others," Rachel said, her voice a little stronger than a moment before.

"Next time, maybe you should use an ax or some shears. Your hands are pretty cut up."

"I'm fine," she said, hoping it sounded like the truth.

Scott laid a dry towel across her hands and prepared the gauze. He squirted ointment on the bandage and rubbed it in with a Q-tip. His hands were gentle when he wrapped the gauze around one hand, then the other.

A snippet of a memory fought to the surface. She could see his small, careful hands doctoring the front paw of his stuffed dog, Rufus. His eyes had been calm, focused, just as they were now.

He set her hands in her lap, rubbing a thumb over her right wrist. It was such an Ashe move it stole her breath. "Feel any better?" Scott asked.

"Yeah. You were always good at that," Rachel said.

"Good at what?" His eyebrow quirked up in confusion.

"Nothing. I think I must be a little out of it. Sorry."

"Want me to walk you back?" Scott asked.

Rachel leaned her head against the scratchy wood beam of the stair railing. "Is it okay if I just sit out here for a little bit?"

"Sure. I'm supposed to go meet Ashe soon, but I can hang around for a few minutes if you want." He stood and dumped the water from cleaning up her hands over the railing into the grass.

"No, go. You've done more than enough."

His phone buzzed and he answered it after a quick glance at Rachel. "Hey, bro. I'm about to head out. Had a little mishap with Rachel, but she's gonna be okay."

She looked up, startled at the mention of her name. Scott smiled at her.

"She's okay. . . . All right. See you in a few," he said. He sat on the step beside her. His legs stretched two steps below hers. "He's on his way home."

*Oh, no. How am I supposed to keep Catch's cancer a secret from him? How am I supposed to tell him that his brother is also my brother?*

They sat in silence for a few minutes. Her thoughts continued to race, amplifying her dizziness. Rachel closed her eyes against the sharp glare of the sun as her hands continued to throb.

"Ashe seems really happy," Scott finally said.

"Does he?" she asked without opening her eyes.

"Yeah. Everything with Lola messed him up pretty bad. But he seems better since you've been around."

"What do I have to do with anything?"

"He likes you. You reminded him that not everyone has to suck."

Rachel smiled at that and raised her head to look at him. But she moved too fast, and black spots covered half his face as her consciousness ebbed. Terrified he would disappear again, she wrapped her fingers around his forearm. He was solid beneath her grip. His sincere, concerned expression was so familiar that she wanted to cry again.

"You okay, Rachel?" Scott asked.

She shook her head. "If you knew more about me, you wouldn't feel that way. Neither would Ashe. I've done things that hurt people I loved and no matter how I tried I couldn't make it right."

He contemplated this for a moment, sitting beside her quietly, before finally asking, "Did you do them on purpose?"

"No, but the results were the same."

A door slammed, followed by quick footsteps on gravel. Ashe appeared around the corner of the house. His dark sunglasses shielded his eyes, but she could tell he was scrutinizing her to see what was wrong. He nodded to his brother, a silent message to move. He sat next to her and waited until his brother had gone inside to ask if she was okay.

Rachel couldn't look at him. "Yes," she answered.

"What happened?"

"Tore out the plum tree."

"With your bare hands?"

"Yes."

"Let me look." He picked up her hands and set them in his lap. He kept his touch light as he lifted one side of the gauze to examine the damage. "Why?"

"It needed to come out," she said.

"Why didn't you ask me to do it?"

She tugged her hands away, but he closed his fingers around her wrists, keeping her in place. "Contrary to how it might seem, I am capable of doing things on my own. Go see for yourself. The tree's not there anymore."

"I didn't mean it like that. And I'm glad Scott was here to fix you up. If you'd gone back into Catch's looking like you must've looked, you'd have given her a heart attack."

*A heart attack might have been better than what Catch is dealing with.*

The thought sent a sharp pain through her chest. She sucked in a breath and Ashe put an arm around her.

"Ashe—" Her throat tightened, and for a moment, she forgot about the pain in her hands as words crammed in her mouth vying to get out first. "I have to go," she said.

If she let one confession escape, there was nothing left in her to keep all of the others in.

# 32

Locked in her room, Rachel put on her headphones and cranked up the volume on her iPod. The deep bass line pumped through her, making her body vibrate. Lying on the bed, she stared at the ceiling fan. The blades thrashed around in a frantic circle.

She'd always thought finding Michael, apologizing for what she'd done to him, would erase the guilt. Instead it dredged up more memories. And she was too worn out to fight them off. The angry bass and frantic guitar did nothing to drown out an argument she hadn't thought of in years.

Michael had been gone for two months, and Rachel had refused to believe what her parents said. That she'd made him up, that maybe her insistence was more than a little girl's overactive imagination—that maybe she was ill.

On the night they agreed to commit her to the hospital for a month, she'd lain curled up in the hallway with a hand pressed to the cool wall where Michael's door had once been.

"I can't live like this anymore, Roger," her mom had shouted. She didn't seem to care if Rachel overheard.

"Calm down, Cynthia. Let's talk about this," her dad had said, Rachel straining to hear him.

"I've tried that. You don't listen. We have to do something. She's not getting any better, and frankly, neither are we."

The springs creaked on the bed when her father had sat—her

mom was too light for it to ever notice her weight. "We can help her, but we both have to believe she can get better."

"You say that like I'm not trying!" Her mom's voice had risen an octave, verging on hysteria.

Rachel had turned away from the wall. The carpet had pressed a pattern to her left cheek. She'd run her fingers over the hills and valleys on her skin. A strip of pale light slithered under the door.

"No, I'm not. I know you're trying. I am too. We've just got to agree on what's best for her," her dad had said.

"But why does that have to be what you want? It kills me to see her like that. But what's worse, she believes in it so hard that sometimes she makes me second-guess myself and I almost start to believe Michael was real. Whatever is wrong with her, we need to get her some help."

"You really think locking her up for a month is what she needs?" he had said, his voice booming under the door.

"I want her to get well and that's not something we can do. The doctors can. I have an appointment for us to go talk with them on Tuesday and for them to evaluate Rachel."

Rachel shot up from her bed in Catch's house and clamped her hands to her ears. Even through the blaring music, the memory of her parents' voices refused to cease. *Make it stop*, she begged. *Please make it stop.*

She had been right all along.

Maybe if they had believed her, they could've gotten him back sooner. Maybe her mom wouldn't have become so depressed and distraught that she saw killing herself as the only solution. Maybe her dad wouldn't have left them to deal with their unanswered questions and guilt on their own.

The cardboard boxes she'd used to pack up her things, stacked by the stairs, caught her eye. She dug through the top box, tossing aside journals and pictures and sci-fi books that reminded her of Michael. Her hand closed over the cool plastic pill bottle, the gauze on her hands making her movements stiff. She shook out two pills and tossed them back with no water. The pills burned for a few seconds as they began to dissolve in her throat. She let saliva build up and swallowed hard to wash the bitter taste away.

Her knees dug into the floor but she didn't move. She concentrated on the silence seeping through the floorboards and cracks around the door, let it wash over her like the warm rain had the day before. Steadier, Rachel recapped the bottle and stuffed it back in the box. She shuffled to the bed and curled up on top of the covers, wishing for dreamless sleep.

Rachel woke up sweaty and a little hazy. Her hair was tangled around her head like a noose. Coughing, she unwound it and rolled so her head hung over the side of the bed. She had the vague sense that she needed to throw up.

She lay there until the floor stopped rolling beneath her, then she sat up and blinked against the bright light shining in the window. The sun was halfway down the sky already. Standing, she braced a hand on the wall as her vision darkened. When it cleared, she walked to the steps and unearthed the bottle from the box for a second time.

She headed downstairs with the bottle gripped in her gauze-wrapped fist.

The kitchen was empty, but two pies sat on the counter. She listened for sounds from Catch's room. After a few seconds of silence, she opened the bottle and dumped the contents down the drain. She turned on the water and let it run fast and hot.

She slid open the cabinet below the sink and rooted through the garbage, burying the bottle somewhere in the middle.

"I was beginning to worry about you," Catch said from behind her, making her jump.

"Oh, really?" Rachel said, letting the remnants of her anger heat her words. "Because earlier I could've sworn you didn't give a damn about anyone."

"Don't get smart with me, missy. And let me see your hands. Scott said you'd done something to them, but no one would tell me how bad it is. Give 'em here."

Rachel extended her hands. It was difficult to stay mad at someone who was trying to take care of her. "You no longer have to worry about the plum tree."

"Is that why my backyard smells like rotten damn fruit?"

"I was mad. And it was sitting back there mocking all of us. Spreading its poison to the rest of the trees, ruining what good was left. I had to stop it, so I ripped it out."

"And ripped your hands to shreds in the process?"

"Yes."

Tsking, Catch opened a cabinet and pulled out a round tin from Everley's shop. "Put this on twice a day. Should help with the pain and keep it from getting infected."

"Thanks." Rachel peeled off the gauze and rubbed the ointment on her palms. She sighed at the cool sensation that spread from her hands into her wrists. It smelled like lemons and honey. She caught the box of food service gloves Catch tossed her in the crook of her arm.

"Why didn't you tell me he was Ashe's brother?" Rachel asked.

"You weren't ready. If I'd told you yesterday who he was, you would've gone over there and told him that nothing about his life is real. Not his parents, not his brother, not even his name. How do you think either of you would've handled that?"

"But he doesn't even remember me."

"I know," Catch said. She crimped the foil tighter around one of the pies, as if she needed something to keep her hands and mind occupied. "With their bastard of a father dragging the family name through the proverbial mud right now, Ashe needs him. And he needs Ashe. I hope you see that."

Rachel nodded and put on a pair of the gloves. "I'm not heartless."

"Of course you're not. If you weren't the type of girl who would help people get what was rightfully theirs even after they tried to run you out of town, you wouldn't be living in my house. You're a good girl, Rachel. I know you'll do what's right with my boys too."

"I won't say anything about Scott yet." She looked back at Catch until she was sure she had her attention. "But this doesn't mean that I've forgiven you for not telling anyone about being sick."

"Guess it's a good thing you won't be the one waiting at the Pearly Gates, deciding whether or not to let me in, then, huh?"

"If it were up to me, you wouldn't be going anywhere anytime soon."

Rachel sat cross-legged in the center of her bed. Through the window she could see the black spot where she'd torn the plum tree from the ground. The earth was still dark, decaying. But the other trees had come back with vigor. Their fruit was vibrant with color. She could smell their sweet scent through the open window.

She still had no clue what to do about her brother, but there was one thing she could fix. At least she hoped she could. Of all the wishes she'd encountered since coming to Nowhere, this one was the most important. It wouldn't go wrong. She wouldn't let it.

Remembering what Catch had said about her ability only working right when she fully believed in herself, she released the last dregs of doubt, and, closing her eyes, whispered, "I wish Catch didn't have cancer." She repeated the phrase over and over until the words ran together so they sounded like a foreign language. *IwishCatchdidn'thavecancer.*

A wish materialized in the air. She pinched it between her forefinger and thumb, the words shimmering in black ink as the light hit the crisp, white paper.

This wish would go right. She could feel it.

She closed her eyes, forcing her body to relax, and let the room melt away first, then the sounds of the birds outside, so the only thought in her mind was the wish.

*IwishCatchdidn'thavecancer.*

The air blew in through the window, hot and sticky. A bead of sweat rolled down her neck and was absorbed by her bra. She kept her hands locked together in her lap, the paper pressed between them. The deeper cuts were still raw despite the salve Catch had given her. Ignoring the sharp pain that shot through her palms, she clamped them tighter together and refocused her attention.

*IwishCatchdidn'thavecancer.*

When she finally opened her eyes, she had to blink against the bright sun. It took her a moment to realize Ashe was standing on his back deck watching her. He smiled, raised a hand in greeting. She smiled, but stayed focused on her wish. On Catch.

Rachel thought it one more time. Clear and strong, it filled her mind.

*I. Wish. Catch. Didn't. Have. Cancer.*

# *33*

The quilted pie carrier slung on Rachel's arm dug deep lines into her skin. She walked toward Ashe's house like a kid being forced to bum a cup of sugar from the neighbors. Head down, she held her breath as she passed the remnants of the plum tree. Dead leaves and bits of bark crunched under her shoes.

She'd taken the bandages off her hands. The red wounds on her palms throbbed, but at least they were less noticeable than the bulky wraps that made her hands useless.

"A pretty girl and a pie. What did I do to deserve this?"

Rachel's head snapped up. Ashe waited at the top of the steps, leaning on the railing. She wondered if he'd been watching her the whole time. Barefoot and in a wrinkled gray tee and jeans, he looked like he'd just rolled out of bed. His easy smile caused a pang in her heart.

Taking a deep breath to steady her voice, she said, "Mandatory socializing."

"For you or me?"

"Both, I think." Rachel tried her best to smile. "Between your dad's extracurricular activities and your divorce, Catch is pretty worried about you."

He shrugged, but the pain in his eyes gave him away. "I'll be fine. Like I've said, neither are a big surprise."

"Doesn't mean they hurt any less."

"True," Ashe conceded. Then he walked back to the door, leaned inside, and said, "Got a pie delivery out here. Bring utensils!"

Rachel stopped a few feet from the steps. Tightening her fingers around the pie carrier's handles, she winced as the force sent pain through her still-healing palms. But at least it gave her something besides her brother to concentrate on. She closed her eyes as it traveled up her arms. The sun shone red behind her eyelids.

When she opened them, she swayed on the uneven grass, light-headed. Ashe was already down the stairs and a few feet from her before she realized he was there. His gentle hands stroked her arms, her hair. She blinked at him. "I just got dizzy for a second. I'm fine." She brushed the hair back from her face and exhaled a long, steadying breath.

He slipped the handles of the bag down her arm, careful not to touch her injured hand, and trailed his fingers over the red grooves on her skin from the weight of the pie pulling on the straps. He led her to the lounge chair on the deck. The sun-soaked fabric warmed the backs of her knees and the tops of her calves where they pressed against the cushion. She settled in deeper, the warmth comforting.

Setting the pie down on the far end of the cushion, Ashe sat on the chaise opposite her. He cupped her knees, splaying his fingers to cover as much of her skin as possible. He rubbed his thumbs back and forth.

"What's going on with you?" He ducked his head to meet her eyes. "You've been acting strange since the market. And then that thing with the plum tree. Please tell me what's wrong. Maybe I can help."

How could she tell him Catch was dying or his brother wasn't really who he thought he was? How could she tell him that despite all of it, she still wanted him to want her?

"There's nothing you can do, Ashe." She looked down at her lap to avoid his stare. "But thanks."

Scott came out, a roll of paper towels tucked under his arm, plates and silverware clutched in one hand and a six-pack in the other. Lucy bounded out after him and headed for Rachel.

Ashe let out a sharp whistle and the dog froze. "Get the door, Lucy," he said.

The dog trotted back to the door, hopped onto her hind legs, and pushed the door with her front paws. It closed on the first try. Ashe left one hand on Rachel's leg when he removed the pie from the carrier and broke off a piece of crust. He tossed it, and Lucy snatched it out of the air. When he snapped his fingers, she lay down at the foot of the chair.

"Hey, how're the hands?" Scott asked her, setting the paper towels down.

"A little better," Rachel said. "Thanks." She watched Scott while he unstacked the plates and set them on the empty half of Ashe's chaise, wondering if she would ever get used to the shock of seeing him alive and grown. She leaned forward and wrapped a pinky around Ashe's thumb.

Scott popped the caps off of three beers and set them on the small table between the two chairs. He sat next to Rachel, stretching his arms out behind him on the cushion. Narrowing his eyes at Ashe, he said, "I don't think I've ever seen you take this long to cut into a pie. You sick?"

"Delivery girl's a little distracting," Ashe said. But he let go of her leg and reached for the knife.

"I can go back inside if you want." Scott smirked at his brother.

"No," Rachel said. As much as seeing him confused her and brought the sadness to the surface, she hated the thought of him leaving more. "You should stay. You're not interrupting anything."

Ashe shrugged at his brother. He ripped off paper towels and then cut three slices of pie. The raspberry sauce dripped onto the deck. Lucy's claws scratched at the wood as she inched closer and licked at the red spots.

Rachel set her plate on her knees. Gripping the fork loosely to keep her cuts on her hands from reopening, she dug the tines in and broke off a small bite.

Ashe and Scott ate their pieces in four bites each. They both saved a small chunk of crust, which they threw in the air for Lucy.

"So, Ashe told me you want to be a vet. Is that what you've always wanted to do?" Rachel asked Scott.

"Pretty much. Our dad's never really been a fan of pets so we didn't have any growing up, but I always knew I wanted to work with animals," Scott said. Catching Ashe's eyes, he smiled. "I snuck out of the house once to go check on the neighbor's dog that had been hit by a car the week before. Mama didn't know about it, obviously, or I wouldn't have been sneaking out, and she went around closing all the windows and locking the doors because a storm was coming. When I came home I couldn't get in and had to stay outside in the pouring rain because there was no way I was waking her up to tell her what I'd done."

Ashe laughed, tapping the tines of his empty fork against his lips. "Poor kid was curled up on the porch swing, soaked through to his underwear when I found him. He was sick for two weeks after that with pneumonia."

Rachel could see him there, tucked into a ball with his Transformers T-shirt clinging to his little body and his dark hair dripping onto his forehead. The bone-deep recognition sent a chill through her body. She rubbed at her arms to tease some warmth back in. She jolted when Ashe laid a hand on her arm.

"You all right?" he asked.

"Yeah. That just reminded me of something similar that happened with my brother," she said. She leaned her elbows on her knees for support and concentrated on keeping her plate from shaking. "Did your mom find out?"

"Nah," Scott said, eying the pie dish. "Ashe covered for me."

"Scott even gave me his favorite Ninja Turtle figurine as a thank-you," Ashe said.

"Michelangelo," Rachel said without thinking. She'd found the orange-masked turtle abandoned under her bed after Michael disappeared. It was the only thing of his that had remained in the house for reasons she still didn't fully understand. Perhaps because he had given it to her, so it was technically no longer his.

Ashe stared at her. "What did you say?" He straightened, not moving his eyes from hers.

"Michelangelo was Michael's favorite, you know, because of the name," she said, her voice shaky.

"You're not going to tell me he gave you his figurine too, are you?" Ashe asked.

"Is Michael your brother?" Scott asked, saving her from answering Ashe.

She nodded, not trusting herself to speak.

Ashe squeezed her leg to get her to look at him. When she did, his look of concern nearly made her tell him everything right then and there. She shook her head, just a hint of movement to tell him to let it go for now, and brushed her fingers over the back of his hand. She exhaled slowly when he smiled at her.

Scott held out his plate to Ashe for another piece of pie. "Run it off later?"

"Definitely," Ashe said, carving out two more slices. He transferred one to Scott's plate, then he dished himself the other piece. With a quick glance at Rachel's plate—and her barely touched pie—he set the knife down again.

"What? We like pie," Scott said, seeing Rachel's face, the fork halfway to his mouth.

She laughed. "Obviously. I just didn't expect you two to be so much alike," she said before she could stop herself.

"Why's that?" Ashe asked.

"He's not—" She paused to think of something else to say that wasn't *He's not your brother.* Instead she took a small bite of her pie, adding, "He's not here much."

"That's only been the past few years. He's had his whole life to try and emulate me."

Scott snorted. "Emulate, my ass." He took a swig of beer and rolled his eyes. "We've always been like this. Hell, Ashe's name was my first word."

Rachel's stomach twisted. *No it wasn't. My name was.* She swallowed the words down, grateful neither of them noticed her reaction.

"Technically your first word was 'ass,'" Ashe said, laughing.

He knocked his knee against Scott's. Scott slapped his leg away.

"Well, I was trying to say 'Ashe.' Not my fault 'sh' is hard to pronounce when you're little."

"So is 'ch,'" Rachel said. She nudged a raspberry around her plate with her fork. "Michael said my name first too, but the best he could do was *Ray*. Even when he was older he only called me Rachel if he was mad at me."

"Why didn't I think of that?" Scott said. His eyes were bright, mischievous, when he looked at her. Much more like Ashe's than Rachel would have thought.

She blinked and the resemblance vanished, as if she'd imagined it.

"Start now and you'll have to find a new place to stay," Ashe warned.

"Catch would take me in. And then Rachel and I could sit around plotting ways to get back at you for being a jerk." He winked at her.

Rachel smiled in response, hoping neither one of them could see how much effort it took to keep her real emotions locked inside. But the more time she spent around Scott, the more she worried she wouldn't be able to keep this secret for much longer.

Rachel walked into the kitchen the next morning just as Catch was heading to the back door. She called out her name and Catch's head snapped up, locking her eyes on Rachel's. The sagging purple skin under Catch's eyes seemed to grow darker, heavier by the second.

*She's not getting better. Why didn't the wish work?*

She shifted under Catch's annoyed gaze. "Not baking this morning?" Rachel asked, noticing the clean counters and lack of pie baking in the oven.

"Not yet. I've got some things to do first," Catch said. She shook her keys for emphasis as her other hand remained on the doorknob.

"Were you heading to the store? I can go for you if you want, save you the trip. Just tell me what you need." *And save me from seeing Ashe or Scott if they come over for breakfast.*

Catch pursed her lips and grumbled something under her breath. Then she said in a more normal tone, "If you must know, Miss-Asks-Too-Many-Questions, I'm going to the doctor."

"Oh," Rachel said. She tapped her fingers on the cool counter in time with her heart, which sped up at the word "doctor." "Do you want me to come with you?"

"I most certainly do not. But if you insist on being helpful, you can stay here and make a few pies for me to take over to Elixir when I get back this afternoon."

"Must be pretty important if it's going to take all morning."

Catch gripped the doorknob harder, twisting it back and forth without pulling the door open. "Just some tests to check the progress and make sure nothing's spreading. Now you get to work on those pies and stop worrying about me, got it?"

"Yes, ma'am," Rachel said, though she wouldn't stop worrying about Catch. At least not until the wish came true.

She waved bye to Catch, then stood in the kitchen for a few minutes, forcing the events of the past few days to the back of her mind. Then she gathered the ingredients and utensils she needed and started baking.

When the back door opened a while later, Rachel had the potato chip crust for a salted chocolate tart cooling on the counter and a pastry crust for a chess pie underway. She opened her mouth, ready to ask Catch how things had gone, but the words evaporated when Ashe stepped inside.

"Hey," he said. His mouth pulled down in concern, causing lines to form at the corners of his lips.

"Hey, Ashe." Nerves broke free of the calm she'd managed to hold on to since Catch left and rioted in her stomach. She turned her attention back to the dough.

"Still upset about whatever was nagging at you yesterday?" When she pressed her knuckles harder into the dough but didn't respond, he continued, "Yeah, I noticed something was wrong even though you were pretending like it wasn't."

She should've known he wouldn't let it go. And she couldn't be mad at him for it because it meant he cared enough to check up on her. Sighing, she said, "I've just got a lot on my mind. I'll be okay."

"Anything I can do to help?" Ashe stood next to her, ducking his head to make her look at him, and settled his hand on her lower back. The tips of his fingers found skin where her shirt rode up beneath the apron she wore.

"Nope," she said and pressed her hips into the counter to keep from leaning back into him and the comfort he offered.

"C'mon, Rachel. You don't have to deal with it all on your own. Whatever this is, you can talk to me. You know that, right?"

Rachel rolled the ball of dough to the far side of the counter and rubbed her hands so flour and bits of dried dough flaked off and rained onto the floor. "I can't tell you *this*, Ashe."

"Why not?"

"Because once I say it, you can't unknow it. And it will change everything."

Ashe's hand slid from her back, but he didn't move away. "Is it Catch?" A mix of fear and frustration at being kept in the dark turned his voice hard.

Rachel hesitated, chewing on her lip. Until she knew if her wish worked, she couldn't tell him about the cancer. Even then, she'd probably still keep it from him if Catch asked her to. "No," she finally said.

"Then what is it?"

"Ashe, please drop it."

"I can't." He stepped around her and dropped onto the stool on the other side of the counter. His fingers tapped impatiently on the granite. "You're upset about something and it's making things weird between us. I would really like to put a stop to both."

"Why do you have to be so nice? This would be so much easier if I didn't care if I hurt you." She mumbled the last part.

"Yeah, see, that's not the way to make me stop worrying."

Rachel turned away, her fingers fumbling with the knot on her apron. When she got it undone, she set it on the counter, ignoring the thin circle of flour she'd been rolling the dough through. She braced her hands on the counter and leaned on the end of the island so she was only a foot away from Ashe. "Last chance. I'm telling you, once you know this . . . well, it's going to change things."

Ashe stared at her. "I can take it."

"Fine. I found my brother," she said.

"What? Seriously? No wonder you've been so distracted." He covered her hands with his, curling his fingers around her wrists and rubbing the soft skin at the base of her palms. "How? Where is he?"

Rachel fisted her hands under his, and he pulled away. "He's in Nowhere. But he doesn't remember me. He doesn't even remember his name, who he really is."

Leaning forward on his elbows, Ashe drew his eyebrows together, studying her. "What do you mean?"

"Somehow when he disappeared, he ended up here. A family took him in and raised him like he was their own. And no one knows except Catch."

"I'm sure you've noticed that Nowhere is a pretty small town. How would people here not notice that a family suddenly had a young son they didn't have before?" His voice dropped, the pity in his words making it soft and cautious. "Even with Catch's help, I don't see how everyone would forget that."

"I don't know how it happened, but it did," she said. She pushed back from the counter. Her palms left sweat marks along the edge. "Something about how he arrived in Nowhere altered people's memories, altered *your* memories so you think he's always been here."

Ashe stood, the stool scraping along the floor as he moved it out of his way. His eyes narrowed as he studied her. "Wait, what are you saying? Do I know your brother?"

She picked at a spot of dried dough on the counter, then looked up to meet his gaze. "It's Scott." Her voice came out stronger than she'd expected.

"No."

"I know it's hard to believe—"

"That's because it's not true," Ashe said. He crossed his arms over his chest and shifted his weight so he leaned slightly away from her. His jaw tightened, pulling his face taut. "I'm sorry about what happened to your brother, and I get that you want him back. But Scott's not him. You're seeing something that's not there because you want it to be true."

Rachel wanted to yell at him, to tell him he was wrong and he'd see the truth if he'd just open his damn eyes, but she held it all back. She wouldn't want to accept it either if the roles were reversed. Her throat ached from the restraint. "Do you really think I wanted to find him this way? That I'd want to tell you or Scott that this isn't the life he was supposed to have?"

"I know you and Catch think the town brought you here to find him, that it wouldn't let you leave when you tried to bail after everyone found out about the wish thing. But I think you're letting the magic of Nowhere go to your head, making you think things that can't possibly be real. Making you see something in *my* brother that's not there." His voice turned as hard as his face, all traces of his earlier worry gone.

"I'm not. For the first time since I was little—since I wished Michael would get lost and he did—I am one hundred percent sure about what is real. Just ask Catch about Scott. She'll tell you the same things I have."

When Rachel met his eyes, denial stared back at her. A thick patch of goose bumps erupted on her arms and neck, and she rubbed at them with a shaky hand. The silence stretched between them, tingeing the room with doubt.

Ashe stalked to the door, the hard set of his mouth saying that some part of him knew his brother wasn't his at all. "You're wrong, Rachel. I'm sorry, but you're just wrong." He didn't look at her as he walked out and slammed the door behind him hard enough to shake the pies on the counter.

# 34

Catch still wasn't back after lunch, so Rachel took the pies down to the coffee shop herself. She walked them in the front door and even received a few smiles and calls of "Hey, Rachel," from the customers. She returned their greetings, grateful that they'd finally accepted her. Then she wandered around downtown and sat in the park under the shade of an old oak tree to avoid going back to the house and potentially fighting with Ashe again or running into Scott. Everley had given her a few days off to let her hands heal completely, but Rachel thought that she might have sensed Rachel's emotional upheaval and wanted to keep her stress levels as low as possible so wishes didn't go haywire again.

While she appreciated the gesture, it gave her too much time to think. And all she could think about was her brother.

But now Scott was walking toward her, Lucy tugging on the leash a few feet in front of him. He smiled when he saw Rachel. She jumped up from the bench. The desire to hug him battled with the need to run. She froze in the middle of the sidewalk and squinted against the sun. Lucy strained to reach Rachel as fast as she could, and Scott had to use both hands to restrain her.

"Seems like somebody's excited to see you," he said as they got closer.

Rachel's mouth tasted like she'd licked an eraser. Swallowing did nothing but spread the feeling farther down her throat. "Yeah," she croaked.

He looked at her curiously. "You okay?"

"I think the heat's getting to me."

"Do you wanna grab something to drink? I'm sure Lucy wouldn't mind a stop at Elixir. They usually keep dog bones and a bowl of water for the pooches."

Rachel wiped her hand along the back of her sweaty neck, trying to get ahold of herself. "I'll be okay. Thanks."

"Oh, c'mon. I promise we don't bite. Well, I don't, at least." He laughed and ruffled Lucy's fur on her head.

When Scott spoke, she could hear an echo of Michael begging her to play with him. When she nodded and accepted his invite, she prayed she was doing the right thing.

Lucy nudged her muzzle under Rachel's hand as they walked. She scratched her nails in the downy fur under the dog's chin.

"I didn't believe Ashe when he told me at first," he said.

"Believe what?" Her fingers froze in the dog's fur as she thought of all the things Ashe could have told him about her.

"That Lucy liked you. I thought he was just saying it so I'd like you too."

"You'll only like me if the dog does?" she asked. "Wow. Tough crowd."

Scott laughed. "Listen, dogs are pretty good judges of character. Lucy wouldn't go near Lola even from the first day Ashe brought her home. Guess we should've known something was up then."

Scott walked past the entrance to the coffee shop and looped Lucy's leash around the base of a wrought-iron table. He tugged a few times to make sure it was secure. Lucy turned her brown eyes up at Rachel and whined.

Rachel gave Lucy another scratch under her chin and a promise they'd be right back before following Scott through the door. They were greeted by a blast of air conditioning and the hissing of the espresso machine as the barista frothed milk.

"That's a new flavor of pie," Scott said when they reached the counter. The pie display case was already half-empty. He ordered two slices and two sweet teas. "But since it's Catch's, I'm sure it'll be great."

"Actually, I made that one. But I'm not making any promises that it's anything close to great," Rachel said, taking the plates the girl behind the counter handed her.

Scott grabbed the glasses of tea. "Catch lets you bake?"

"Sometimes. Usually she just tells me what to do and stands there like a drill sergeant barking orders at me while I mix things together. But this one she let me do all on my own."

"She told me I had clumsy hands and won't let me near the kitchen if she's baking," Scott said, taking a gulp of his iced tea.

A memory of baking cookies with Michael when they were little flashed in her mind. He'd had more dough on his clothes and smeared across his round cheeks than on the cookie sheet. Rachel fought to suppress the smile—and the words that itched to come out. She couldn't let even something that small slip.

Lucy jumped up and rattled the table, pulling on her leash as they neared. Rachel's hands shook when she set the plates down, and the ceramic clattered against the metal. Lucy bumped her head under Rachel's hand when she sat.

"You're really good with her," Scott said, nodding to the dog. "Did you have a lot of pets growing up?"

"Mom was allergic, so we weren't allowed to have them." She scratched behind Lucy's ears a few times, then clasped her hands on her lap.

"Just a natural, then?"

*Seems to run in the family.* "I guess so."

"Ashe said you're the reason Mama sent Lucy home, but he was a little cagey about how exactly. Want to fill in the details for me?"

"He wished for Lucy to come back," Rachel said. She took a bite of her pie, the saltiness of the potato chip crust and the bittersweet flavor of the chocolate tart lingering on her tongue. Her heart rate spiked as the initial panic at telling someone what she could do tried to take over. She pushed it down with a deep, slow breath. "And like Catch is good at keeping secrets, I'm good at making wishes come true."

"That's cool. No wonder Catch trusts you with her pies. This is really good, by the way," Scott said, halfway through his pie already. "You should convince her to let you bake on your own more."

"I'll try. But you know how stubborn she is," Rachel said. "She won't even let me do her laundry with mine because she says I put too much fabric softener in, even though I measure it with the same cap she does."

A laugh rumbled out of him. He squinted slightly, like their dad had when he laughed hard. "Maybe Ashe should ask for you. She pretends not to listen to him, but most of the time winds up doing what he wants."

"It's good that she's got him."

"It's even better that we've got her," he said.

She thought about Catch's doctor's appointment, how it had run longer than expected, and wondered for the hundredth time if that meant her wish had come true and Catch was well. She wondered if she'd done the right thing by not telling Ashe about Catch's cancer.

She gulped sweet tea, forcing the guilt back down. "Were things not great at home?" Rachel asked, quickly adding, "I'm sorry. That's pretty personal."

"It's okay," Scott said, shrugging. "Sometimes it was bad. But I was lucky. I always had Ashe to look out for me and take me over to Catch's when it got to be too much. And she'd feed us pie and let me pretend to examine her cats for made-up diseases. They were persnickety little things, but they put up with me pretty well. Mostly because I'd give them my corncobs to chew on after dinner, but I like to think it was because I was good with animals even back then."

Lucy pawed at the ground. Her nails scraped on the brick patio. The table wobbled as she paced back and forth and around their chairs.

"Hold your horses," Scott said to her. He worked on the knot she had pulled tight in her attempt to get free. "If you'd just sit still this would be a lot easier."

"Sit," Rachel ordered. Looking Rachel in the eye, Lucy obeyed.

"Thanks," he said. He got the leash loose and nearly tripped over the dog when she darted in front of him. "We'll be right back."

Rachel watched as he jogged after Lucy, then nearly jumped out of her seat when she realized she had company. Lola stood behind the vacated chair, wearing large dark sunglasses and a frown. Her hair was swept back from her face with crisscrossed bobby pins, and her silk tank top in a pale blush offset her milky skin.

Glancing toward the cafe's front door, Lola asked, "Is Ashe with you?"

"No," Rachel said. Turning away from Lola she scanned the park but couldn't see Scott or Lucy circling the grass. "Scott. He just took the dog for a walk."

Lola shifted her weight and for a moment, Rachel thought she was about to leave. Instead, Lola plucked off her sunglasses and stared at Rachel, her golden eyes sparkling with a soft smile that cracked her usually hard demeanor.

"I got an email from Mary Beth. She sent me pictures of the girls. They were dressed like really creepy angels," Lola said.

Rachel paused, trying to decide where Lola was going with this. "Yeah, Geoff's a sci-fi fan. He dressed them up as Weeping Angels for Halloween last year."

Lola laughed, shaking her head. "I don't even know what that means."

Rachel smiled thinking of Geoff, with his tech-speak and geek addictions, and Lola, with her impeccable fashion sense and old-fashioned beliefs, trying to get through a dinner conversation. But Lola had to have a fun, kind side if Ashe and Everley liked her. *Hidden way, way down deep.*

"Neither did the girls. All Violet knew was that she got to be scary and that was good enough for her," Rachel said.

Lola gripped the back of Scott's chair, her French-tipped nails curling against the black iron. "I hate that I don't know them, that

I've already missed out on so much," Lola said. "I know I was horrible to you before, but I just—"

Lucy's growl was low and threatening. It was more warning than vicious, but Lola jumped regardless. She moved behind Rachel's chair, her hands grazing Rachel's back as she stumbled in her heels.

Scott stood there, letting the dog scare Lola.

"Lucy," Rachel said in a soothing voice. "Be nice."

The dog eyed Lola suspiciously but stopped her growl. She sat and laid her head in Rachel's lap.

"Everything okay?" Scott asked, his harsh tone clearly directed at Lola. He pulled out his chair but didn't sit.

"Yep. Just talking," Rachel said, patting Lucy's head.

Lola shifted to the left, toward Scott and farther away from the dog. Her lips twitched into a half smile. "Hi, Scotty."

His face was hard, his eyes dark and glaring. "My brother might be nice enough not to tell you to get lost, but I'm not. So, take your cheating ass someplace else and leave us alone."

"I'm sorry," she said. She touched Rachel's shoulder as she started to walk away. "I know I can never repay you for what you did, but if you ever need anything, you'll let me know?"

"Yeah. Thanks," Rachel said, giving her a small smile.

After Lola was gone, he retied Lucy's leash and looked up at Rachel with an unreadable expression. "What did you do for her?"

"I gave her the chance to make something up to someone she loves," Rachel said.

"Ashe?"

Lucy lifted her head and looked around at the mention of his name. Her big brown eyes followed people on the street, and, coming up empty, she lay down on the ground with a dejected thump.

"No," Rachel said. "I don't know if Ashe told you or not, but my best friend is Lola's sister. They hadn't spoken in years and I put them back in touch." Rachel dropped a half-inch piece of her crust in front of Lucy's nose. The dog's tongue darted out and licked it up within seconds.

"After everything she's done to Ashe, I can't believe you'd help her." Scott's voice was rough, just this side of angry. He wasn't look-ing at her anymore when she glanced up.

"This had nothing to do with him. Mary Beth deserved the chance to get her sister back if she wanted."

"If Lola treated her sister like she treated Ashe, your friend was probably better off without her. She doesn't deserve to be forgiven."

Like Ashe, Scott knew how to hold a grudge. He would hate his father for betraying Ashe with Lola, and Rachel was grateful that he didn't know—that he would never know if she could help it. But that thought was quickly replaced by another.

*Scott will never forgive me for what I did to him.*

Rachel swallowed a sip of tea, which did nothing to ease the lump in her throat. "But what if the other person deserves to be happy? Doesn't that trump everything else?" she asked. Her voice cracked on the last word.

"And what? Consequences be damned?" Scott asked.

"If it's not hurting anyone, I just can't see how it's a bad thing to make something right," Rachel replied.

"Think we'll have to agree to disagree on this one."

Rachel set her fork down, abandoning the rest of her pie. Would she ever be able to tell Scott the truth without having him hate her for it?

# 35

Angry voices carried out the open windows at Catch's house. Rachel slowed her pace, pausing at the base of the back steps. She peered in the window of the back door. In the kitchen, Ashe stood a few feet away from Catch, arms crossed over his chest, glaring down at her. A few strands of hair fell across his eyes when he shook his head. "You knew, didn't you? About Rachel's brother?"

"She told me about him, yes," Catch said.

"You know that's not what I meant. You knew Scott was her brother and you didn't tell me." The accusation was hard and sharp.

Rachel stepped back into the shade of the overhang. She still had a view inside though she was no longer directly in either Catch's or Ashe's line of sight.

"I couldn't."

"What do you mean, you couldn't? This isn't something that's up for discussion. How could you not tell me? How could you not tell her? She's been looking for him for most of her life and you knew all this time where she could find him."

Fisting a hand on her hip, Catch tilted her head up and met his hard eyes. "It's not that simple, Ashe. Your parents had me bind it. But hiding a secret as big as that has consequences, and they forgot the truth right along with everyone else."

"Why?" Ashe's voice lowered so Rachel had to creep closer to the window to hear him. She stepped on one of the basil plants growing under the window, the thick stalk and fragrant leaves crushed under her shoe. He pressed, "Why wouldn't they want anyone to know he wasn't theirs?"

"Who knows why your parents make the decisions they do. Seeing as how that was one of their better ones, I wasn't going to pry."

"Rachel blames herself for him disappearing. Do you have any idea—"

Catch pounded a hand on the counter, cutting off whatever else he had been about to say. "That girl was given something she wasn't ready for and no one to teach her how to control it. It's not her fault what happened."

"Well, she doesn't believe that," Ashe said.

"Rachel's stronger than she thinks. And she knows who he is now, knows that he's had a good life with people who love him. I don't know if that helps or hurts, but she knows. Give her some space, a little time to figure that out on her own. She's almost there. And when she is, I can help her."

"And what about Scott? Does he know?"

Rachel steadied a hand on the side of the house and listened.

"No, your brother doesn't know any better than you did. He won't remember her. All he's ever known is being a Riley. That's who he is."

Ashe dragged his hands through his hair, gripping it in his fists. "I can't believe you did this, Catch."

"Don't you dare put this on me. I only did what I was asked. And I did it for a sweet little boy who desperately needed someone to love him."

"But Scott had a family. Whatever you did with your pie might've kept him from going back to them," he said.

How had Rachel not thought of that? With all of the secrets that had been wished into the open without Rachel even knowing it was happening, it fit that Catch's ability could also counteract hers. Maybe that's why she landed in Nowhere in the first place. Why the town wouldn't let her leave.

"I wasn't talking about Scott," Catch said, pulling Rachel's attention back to Ashe.

Her heart ached for him, and for the girl she had been in the months after her brother disappeared.

She fled around the corner and out of sight seconds before Ashe slammed though the back door. Her chest throbbed from holding her breath, but she waited against the side of the house until her hands stopped shaking.

The sky was a mass of clouds in irritable shades of gray. Dim shadows moved across the lawn as the thinner limbs on the fruit trees flailed in the wind. Rachel sat on the top step of Ashe's back deck, elbows propped on her knees, unable to make it any closer to his door.

Ashe's footsteps, scuffing over the wood, stopped before he reached her. Her heart hammered in her chest. She just barely heard him over the pounding in her ears.

"How did this happen?" he asked.

"I'm sorry." Rachel looked over her shoulder at him. He stood a few feet away with a baseball cap pulled low over his eyes, so she wasn't sure what he was thinking. But his mouth, set in a hard line, gave her some idea.

He sat next to her and pulled her hand onto his knee. She linked her fingers with his. He rubbed his thumb along the back of her hand. Whether it was to comfort her or him, she wasn't sure.

"Me too." He dropped his head and stared at their joined hands. "I used to have dreams of things that happened during my childhood, and everything was the same as what really happened, down to what I was wearing and what the place smelled like or felt like and what I was thinking. Everything was exactly as I remembered, except Scott wasn't there. Not for any of it. I'd wake up and, for just a second, I'd forget I had a brother. But now it seems that those dreams were real, so it's been a little hard to wrap my head around."

"How do you think it's been for me? I finally found my brother, after years of being told he wasn't real, and he doesn't even remember me," Rachel said, struggling to keep the desperation out of her voice. "And I can't tell him because it sounds crazy."

"You'd also be turning his whole life upside down."

"Don't you think I know that?"

Ashe pressed his lips together, taking a moment. "We need to think about all of the consequences before either of us does anything," he said.

Rachel yanked back her hand. "What do you know about consequences?" Her throat ached from the tears she held at bay, but she forced the words out. "You weren't the one who lost him. The one who's had to live with the guilt of ruining everyone's lives."

Ashe leaned toward her, holding her so she couldn't retreat from him again, and cupped her cheeks in his hands. Then he rested his forehead against hers, his breath hot and sweet on her face. "Not everyone's," he said.

"You don't know what I went through. What I put my family through."

"So tell me. Help me understand." He brushed his thumb over her cheek before pulling back and giving her some space.

"I wished Michael would get lost when I was little. I didn't mean it, but that didn't seem to matter. After wishing him away, I spent years in and out of hospitals—in therapy, where they tried to tell me he never existed though everything inside of me screamed that he was real. I'd fall asleep most nights replaying some memory of him and begging the universe to bring him back. When that didn't work, I tried to use the wishing as a bargaining chip. I swore if he didn't come back I'd stop making wishes come true. So I stopped. And after a while, what everyone said about him being my imaginary brother made more sense than what had really happened."

Her confession hung between them, thick and palpable like heavy smoke. She swallowed to ease the pressure that tightened her throat. He shifted next to her and hunched his shoulders. The tension pulsed from him, battering against her already weakened defenses. In that moment, if he had asked her to keep the secret of her brother forever, she would have agreed. Just knowing Michael was okay felt like more than she deserved.

"Have you tried to leave town again? Do you know if you can now that you've found what you were looking for?" he asked.

"Nope."

"Does that mean you're staying?"

"Yeah, I think so. I hope so. But I guess that depends on what happens with Scott."

"Is he the reason you haven't tried to leave?"

"Not the only reason," she said, lifting her eyes to meet his. "Even when I didn't think I should stay because of what I might accidentally do to someone because of a wish, I wanted to. And now that I don't have to go, I'm not as worried about being stuck here."

A faint smile played on Ashe's lips, then disappeared before it could fully form. "What are you gonna do about him?"

"I'm not sure."

"But you want to tell him."

"And you don't want me to," Rachel said.

There was nothing else to say, and they both knew it.

When she stood to leave, Ashe followed her a few steps. His hand grazed her shoulder and trailed down her back as she turned. "I know I keep asking you for time and it's not really fair. But we'll figure it all out, okay?" He caressed her jaw, his touch gentle and warm.

Rachel leaned into him, letting the steady beat of his heart against her cheek convince her everything would be all right. She finally had a place to call home and people she loved like family. That was motivation enough to find a way to make things work.

# 36

"You and I need to have a little chat," Catch said, jabbing her finger into Rachel's shoulder the next day when Rachel walked into the kitchen for dinner.

"About what?" Rachel said, feeling defensive. Her nerves were frayed and she was barely holding it together. She wasn't up for one of Catch's "talks." "I didn't tell Scott, if that's what you want to talk about."

"We'll get to what to do about that in a minute. But first you're gonna sit your meddling butt down and tell me what you did."

"I don't know what you're talking about," Rachel said, but sat after Catch pointed threateningly at the stool with a wooden spoon.

"Don't play dumb with me. You know damn well what you did."

Rachel ran through what she'd said or done in the past few days to piss Catch off this much and came up empty. "Care to give me a hint?"

"I got a call from the doctor today with my latest test results."

"Oh? What did he say?"

"So, you were behind it?" Catch asked.

"Depends on what the results were," Rachel said, suddenly nervous. *Oh, God. What if I made the cancer spread?* She pushed the panic down and tried to slow her breathing.

"The scans came back clean. Not one tiny speck of cancer anywhere in my abdomen. Probably not anywhere else either, but that's the only part they checked." Rachel couldn't help the smile that settled across her face, but she tried to hide it from Catch, who was clearly still pissed off despite the good news. "Now I've gotta go back in for more damn tests since obviously someone screwed up the scan. 'Cause according to my doctor, and all logical schools of thought, there's no possible way I could be cured. Not like that." Catch opened her fisted hand and waved her thin fingers like she'd made something disappear. Her mouth pinched tight as her eyes narrowed on Rachel. "So, now I'm gonna be subjected to more prodding and poking and damn MRIs and questions and days of observations just because you couldn't let an old woman die. And I can't very well go in there telling them you wished me well, now can I? They'd think the cancer had gone to my brain and put me down like a rabid fox."

"I'm not sorry," Rachel said after a moment. She crossed her arms over her chest and met Catch's glare. "You can be mad all you want, but it won't make me regret anything."

"You've got some nerve, girlie."

"So do you, thinking you could keep this from everyone," Rachel said, jumping off the stool and facing Catch. "Did you really think I wasn't going to do something about it? That I'd just sit back and watch you die?"

"It wasn't your choice to make," Catch shouted. "I'd made my peace with the world, with the things I've done and haven't done. I was ready for it."

Ashe shoved through the back door hard enough for it to bang against the side of the house. "What the hell is going on? I could hear y'all halfway to my place."

"We're having an argument," Catch said. "What the hell does it look like?"

"Did you tell him?" he asked, looking first at Rachel, then at Catch.

Rachel's hands ached from fisting them so tightly. She opened them and flexed her fingers. She wanted to scream at both of them. Instead she calmly said, "No. I told you I'd talk to you about it first."

"Then what are y'all fighting about?"

"It's none of your business," Catch said, shaking the spoon at him.

"Too bad," he said. He took the spoon from her and tossed it onto the counter. He stopped halfway between them, hands up like a boxing referee. "Rachel?"

Rachel pulled her shoulders back and fisted her hands on her hips. "I did something that she didn't like. And I'd do it again, no questions asked."

Smacking her hand on the counter, Catch said, "It wasn't your place to do anything."

"So says you. I'd bet Ashe would feel differently," Rachel said.

Ashe crossed his arms over his chest and took a deep breath. "Would one of you just tell me what the hell happened?"

"Since it's no longer an issue, it shouldn't be a problem to tell him, right?" Rachel asked with a sharp look at Catch.

"Fine." Catch pushed away from the counter, then started rolling back the plastic covering on whatever pie she'd made that day. "If you even think about yelling at me about this, you won't get pie for a month."

The corner of his mouth turned up in relief. "That bad, huh?"

Catch made four long cuts through the crust. The knife came out gooey and dark red. "I had cancer. And not the nice kind that goes into remission."

"It was killing her, Ashe," Rachel cut in.

"I'm sorry, what? Cancer? You have cancer?" Ashe asked.

"You shush. You told me to tell him, so let me tell him," Catch said to Rachel with a snarl of her lips. She turned back to Ashe, saying, "Had. Past tense. And Little-Miss-Wish-Everything-Away here made it disappear. Poof. Just like that. It's all gone."

"Oh, my God," Ashe whispered. He braced a hand on the counter beside Catch. He reached for her, but she pulled away before he could touch her. "But you're okay now? You're not dying?"

"No, I'm not dying," Catch said, annoyed despite the reassuring words.

Rachel moved back to the stool so she was in Catch's direct line of sight. But the stubborn woman refused to look at her. "Try not to sound so happy about it."

Catch dumped pie onto plates and shoved one into Ashe's hand. Then she slid a plate to Rachel.

No one ate a bite.

"Okay, so what did Rachel do to piss you off?" Ashe asked after it was clear Catch wasn't going to say more.

"I told you. She made it all go away."

He tapped his fork on the plate. "I'm failing to see how that's a bad thing."

"She made a wish without asking me how I'd feel about it." Catch shook her empty fork at Ashe for emphasis. "I never baked for anyone that didn't want it. That's just not how these kinds of things are done."

Rachel shoved her plate away, not completely trusting that the pie didn't hold a secret Catch wanted kept quiet. "You weren't doing anything about it, so someone had to."

"What about the people on the other end of those secrets? The ones who were kept in the dark? They didn't ask to be lied to, to have their lives manipulated on someone else's whim," Ashe said. His jaw clenched as if he'd stopped himself from saying something more.

"I've always done what was right, Ashe. You know that," Catch said.

"So did Rachel," he said, his tone softer. "She saved your life. I'm not gonna let you be mad at her for that."

Catch jabbed her fork into the top of her pie once, twice. She continued until she had hacked it to pieces. "Do you know how difficult it is to prepare yourself to die and leave everything and everyone you know and love? And now I'm gonna have to go through all that mess again when my time comes back around."

"Maybe if you had told someone, asked for help, it wouldn't have been so hard," Rachel said.

"Maybe," Catch said, her shoulders relaxing as she set down the fork. "Just don't go getting a savior complex, Miss-Likes-to-Stick-Her-Nose-in-Other-People's-Business."

"I make no promises when it comes to those I love." Reaching across the counter, Rachel held Catch's hand. Then she slipped her other hand into Ashe's, telling herself she'd find a way to keep what she had with both of them, no matter what.

Rachel awoke to the scent of cinnamon and baking peaches. She breathed it in deeply, the smell making her hungry. The sky was still the hazy blue that preceded sunrise before the twinkling light of the stars was drowned out by the sun. She made her way downstairs in the dark. It wasn't until she reached the main floor that she remembered Catch was still mad at her. She tiptoed through the foyer and into the dining room. "Have you forgiven me yet?" she asked from the kitchen doorway.

"Enough to let you help me bake," Catch said without bothering to look up. She scraped a ball of dough from the mixing bowl and dropped it on the counter.

"I'll take it."

She settled in next to Catch and smoothed the dough with quick, short strokes of the rolling pin. The wooden shaft rattled with every back and forth. She peeled up the dough, gave it a quarter turn, and rolled some more while Catch created the filling by adding pinches and handfuls of ingredients.

"Catch, do you have any ideas about why none of my wishing to get Michael back ever worked?" she asked, her voice wavering. She pressed the pie crust into the dish, smoothing the sides down with the tips of her fingers. She used her thumb to create a wave around the top edge. "I mean, I've been trying to wish him back since the moment I realized he was gone."

"If I had to guess, I'd say you weren't ready. Like I've said before, you didn't trust yourself or this gift of yours. And if you don't believe in it, it's not gonna work right." Catch put a hand on Rachel's shoulder and squeezed. Then she moved to the microwave to melt the butter. "What if I told you that now that you have him back, you could probably wish for everything to be back the way it was?"

Rachel knocked the handle of the rolling pin. It rolled off the island and dropped to the floor with a thud. She stared at the puff of flour that danced in the air above it. Catch bent down to retrieve it. "Would that work? Is that my loophole?" Rachel asked.

"It's the only thing that I can think of that might do it," Catch said.

"If I did that, he wouldn't know Ashe. Or you."

"That's probably true. I guess he could find his way to us one day, but it would be different. He wouldn't be ours anymore, that's for sure."

Rachel traced her finger through the flour on the counter and swiped her hand across it, erasing all traces of the name she had been writing. "I don't know that I can do that to Ashe."

"Well, he wouldn't know any better, would he? If he never had a brother he wouldn't know that he missed him." Catch removed the cup of bubbling butter from the microwave. She stirred in the white bubbles that floated on top with a fork.

"That feels . . . awful."

"That's life. Either way, somebody loses. Whether they know it or not. Ashe would lose his brother, you'd lose Mary Beth. You would never come to Nowhere to meet me or Ashe. Everything you've been building here would disappear. Now, I'm not trying to tell you what to do. I just want to make sure you don't discount the things you might regret if you reset everything."

Brush in hand, Rachel hesitated. Her fingers ached from gripping the rubber handle so tightly. It shook and dripped butter onto the counter. She wiped at it with her other hand. "Maybe I can word the wish so that we all still find each other?" she asked.

"Maybe you could, but it wouldn't be the same. For any of us. I've been around a while, and I've seen enough of life to know that you can't change one thing without everything else it touched being affected."

"So, I have to choose."

Catch patted her back. "Yes, you have to choose. But nobody said it's got to be right now." She pivoted to grab the bowl of peaches and raspberries she'd set aside to soak in a dry sugar bath and left them on the counter by Rachel's hand.

*Please forgive me.*

Rachel splashed a hasty wish onto the crust. She took the fruit mixture and covered her yellow words before Catch could see what she'd done.

The bottom of the pie dish was still warm when Rachel carried it through the backyard in her bare feet. Her footsteps were light on the grass, which was long enough to tickle her ankles. The dew made it wet, slippery. She concentrated on each step, one in front of the other, until she cleared the shadows of the trees. Streaks of red and pink peeked between the limbs. She kept both hands on the pie to keep them from shaking.

Ashe's lights were on, but she didn't knock. Her hands were sweaty under the pan. She set it on the railing where he'd be sure to see it when he looked out the door. Tucking the folds of the cloth underneath it, she whispered her wish for her brother.

*I wish Scott lives a happy life.*

The air swirled around her in a warm rush. It smelled like fruit and sugar and home.

She glanced back at the house when she heard laughter drift out the open window. Smiling, she tiptoed down the stairs.

A few steps from the trees, Lucy's quick, excited bark stopped her. Rachel turned as Ashe pushed through the door, nudging the dog with his leg to keep her inside the house. His eyes landed on the pie, then swiveled up to find Rachel as he walked farther onto the deck. Any lingering doubts she had about keeping Scott's identity a secret vanished when Ashe smiled at her.

Ashe deserved to be happy too. And she wanted to be the one to make it happen.

"You know," he said, lifting the corner of the cloth and inhaling deeply, "when you bring someone a pie, the polite thing to do is stick around long enough for him to thank you."

She laughed, enjoying the way her skin warmed at the sound of his voice. "I'll see you when you come over for breakfast. You can thank me then." Without waiting for a response, she threw a wave over her shoulder and started back toward Catch's house.

"Yeah, but then I'd have to wait," he said.

"Wait for what?" she called.

His footsteps sounded on the wood deck and then went quiet. A moment later, he wrapped his fingers around hers, spinning her back to face him. Rachel braced her other hand on his chest and pushed up on her toes to meet his lips. The kiss was long and sweet. A promise of everything yet to come.

When they finally released each other, the fruit trees shook in the breeze, their leaves releasing a contented sigh that carried across the yard. Their branches had stretched out to fill in the void from the tree Rachel had removed. She almost couldn't see the dark spot where the dirt had yet to dry from the remnant plum poison. It was the size of a pit now. Soon it would be nothing more than a story she told about how she got lost in Nowhere and found her way home.